THE PRINCE WARRIORS AND THE SWORDS OF RHEMA

The Prince Warriors series

Book 1
The Prince Warriors

Book 2
The Prince Warriors and the Unseen Invasion

Book 3
The Prince Warriors and the Swords of Rhema

Unseen: The Prince Warriors 365 Devotional

PRISCILLA SHIRER
WITH GINA DETWILER

B&H
PUBLISHING GROUP
Nashville,
Tennessee

978-1-4336-9021-1

Published by B&H Publishing Group
Nashville, Tennessee

Dewey Decimal Classification: JF
Subject Heading: COURAGE \ WAR STORIES \ TRUST

1 2 3 4 5 6 7 8 9 • 21 20 19 18 17

For Jude
Our third-born son.
Our Prince Warrior.

Contents

Prologue   ix

Part One: The Mountain   1

Chapter 1: A Hole in the Water   3

Chapter 2: Finn   13

Chapter 3: The Mountain of Rhema   22

Chapter 4: The Black Dragon   34

Chapter 5: Impossibilities   42

Chapter 6: Smoke and Swords   50

Chapter 7: The Descent   61

Chapter 8: The Krÿsen   64

Chapter 9: New Things in Old Places   67

Chapter 10: Training Days   79

Chapter 11: New Developments   89

Chapter 12: Fact or Fiction   99

Chapter 13: Viktor   108

Chapter 14: Beware the Wolf   114

Chapter 15: The Rooms   123

Chapter 16: The Gift   133

Chapter 17: Charming   140

Chapter 18: Prowling   148

Chapter 19: Questions   152

Chapter 20: Devouring   159

Chapter 21: Finding Viktor   168

Chapter 22: Viktory   174

Chapter 23: A New Plan   182

Chapter 24: Lost and Found   186

Chapter 25: Under Foot   195

Chapter 26: Footsteps   205

Chapter 27: Doors   210

Chapter 28: A Narrow Escape   219

Chapter 29: Healing   226

Part Two: The Pods   **231**

Chapter 30: The Unleashing   233

Chapter 31: The Plague   244

Chapter 32: Preparation   253

Chapter 33: Cedar Point   259

Chapter 34: Resistance   265

Chapter 35: Rising and Falling   275

Chapter 36: Ambassadors   286

Epilogue   291

Acknowledgments   297

About the Authors   299

Prologue

Blood dripped from the edge of the blackened shard of metal. One drop, then another, slow and steady, into a large, crudely made iron chalice. The Chief Weaver stood over the chalice, reaching in and pulling out slender threads of bright red. The Weaver's fingers were long and thin, clever fingers, twisting and forming the threads so quickly no human eye could follow.

But there was no human eye in the room.

On his massive throne sat Ponéros, ruler of Skot'os. He watched the shape unfolding before him: a human form. The beginnings of feet, the mere outline of legs. The legs and feet were most important—they needed to be quick and strong. Ponéros had demanded this.

Around the Chief Weaver, dozens of other weavers lurked, fashioning fingers, hands, arms, shoulders. The slaves brought their work to the Chief Weaver, who added the pieces to his creation, entwining them skillfully.

How much longer? Ponéros spoke impatiently.

The process cannot be hurried, Sire, said the Chief Weaver. *Not if you want my best work.*

I don't have time. . . .

Time is not a thing to be feared. The Chief Weaver remained precise and methodical, unruffled by his master's impatience. He carefully pulled some threads of dark gray fabric that stuck to the scrap of metal and handed them off to another of the weaver slaves, who set about making a set of clothes.

The Chief Weaver had once been a servant of the Source, the true ruler of Ahoratos, the Unseen Realm. But like many others, the servant had crossed the chasm in search of fame, of riches, of admiration. Ponéros had promised him all that and more. The Chief Weaver was one of the lucky ones. He was not kept in a cage. He was allowed his freedom, so long as his work pleased his master. The Chief Weaver knew there would come a time when his master would no longer be pleased—that would be the end of him.

The Chief Weaver had made human suits for Ponéros before. But never like this. There was something quite unusual about this blood—it had come from a Prince Warrior. A *young* Prince Warrior. The Chief Weaver did not know where Ponéros had gotten it; he could not remember ever having true Prince Warrior blood to work with before. At least, not from a Prince Warrior that was alive and free in Ahoratos. This would be the Weaver's masterpiece. A perfect specimen. Undetectable.

The Weaver wove together the slim torso, the strong shoulders, muscular arms. He stitched on the hands—large hands with strong, nimble fingers. This was a young human, younger than he had ever made for the Master before. He wondered dimly what the Master was planning.

Then, finally, he placed the head, molding the face. Handsome. Pleasant. A wry smile. Dark hair.

The eyes were most difficult, however. The Chief Weaver could not get them to look quite . . . human. Every other part was perfect. But the eyes had a strange, colorless sheen to them, an emptiness that could not be filled by anything in the Chief Weaver's arsenal of tricks. The hair would help; he made it longer in front, so that it partially covered the eyes.

When the human suit was ready, the weavers added the clothes—skinny jeans, T-shirt, tennis shoes—and placed it before their master. They backed away, bowing low. They waited in fearful anticipation for his approval.

Ponéros rose and stepped down from his throne, his footsteps making a resounding, clanging noise. His huge shadow fell over the weavers as he picked up the human suit and examined every inch. The Chief Weaver became worried that his master would find some small imperfection and rip the suit apart, forcing them to start all over. It had happened before. And the eyes—there was nothing he could do to fix the eyes.

But then a strange sort of smile cracked Ponéros's rigid face.

You have done well, Weaver.

The Chief Weaver bowed again.

Ponéros's massive body began to ripple along the edges, becoming like liquid, melting down to a dark puddle on the floor. Then the puddle snaked toward the human suit, entering through the feet and creeping upward, filling the suit, giving it shape and form. Suddenly the eyes blinked, the head swiveled, the mouth curled. Ponéros turned to the weavers, spreading his new arms, flexing his new muscles, testing his new legs. He took several steps and stopped, turning, walking again. He had to get the feel of it, of being a human boy, a teenager. The slight slouch, the way the hands went into the pockets. The rhythmic walk, cocky and smooth. All the details had to be right.

The eyes are still . . . telling, the Chief Weaver said. *The older ones may suspect something if they look too deeply into the eyes. Perhaps it is best to avoid the old ones completely.*

Ponéros nodded.

What will you call yourself, Sire?

Ponéros raised his two hands in the air, closing his fists. His voice had changed, now smooth and pleasant. Human.

"My name is Viktor."

PART ONE

The Mountain

CHAPTER 1

A Hole in the Water

L et's race. Girls against boys."
Brianna and Ivy stood beside each other, hands on hips, facing Levi and Xavier. It was the day after Thanksgiving, but the weather was strangely warm. The pond sparkled in the sunshine. The kids had spent the afternoon paddling around in the brand-new tandem kayaks that Evan and Xavier's parents had bought as an early Christmas present for the kids.

"You're kidding, right?" asked Levi, trying not to laugh. "You think you two can beat us?" Levi and Xavier looked at each other. Xavier was taller, but Levi had twice as many muscles as both girls put together.

"A sloth could beat you two," said Ivy, flipping her wavy, red hair.

"That's probably not true, technically," said Manuel, who sat at the edge of the dock with Evan, tossing fishing lines into the water. Manuel preferred water activities that didn't require actually getting into the water. "A sloth can only travel at a speed of about .15 miles per hour, while a kayak could reach a speed of—"

"What's a sloth?" asked Evan.

"Okay girls, let's do it," said Xavier, reaching for a paddle. "Last one to the other side of the pond has to buy the winning team a triple-decker sundae at the Snack Shack."

"Each," said Levi.

"Deal," said Brianna. "Prepare to lose your allowance on ice cream."

"We get the yellow one," Ivy added. The two girls jumped onto the dock where the kayaks were tied up and took turns getting in.

"What about us?" said Evan, ditching his fishing pole. "I want to race too!" Evan used to be afraid of going in the pond, which was so big it might as well be a lake. It was quite deep and might (he thought) have been inhabited by a sea monster at one time or another. But since his travels to Ahoratos, which included *riding* a sea monster, those fears had evaporated.

"All that's left is the rowboat," said Levi. He and Xavier pulled the green kayak next to the dock so they could get into it. "It might leak a little."

"I'll row. You bail." Evan grabbed Manuel's arm and dragged him over to the old rowboat on the shore of the pond.

"That doesn't look seaworthy," said Manuel doubtfully.

"That's okay; this isn't the sea anyway."

"Don't forget your life jackets," said Xavier with a grin. "You know Mom is watching from the kitchen window and will be out here in a second if you don't put one on."

"Yeah, I know. She has eyes in the back of her head." Evan grabbed two life jackets from the edge of the dock and tossed one to Manuel, who held it with a puzzled expression, as if he wasn't quite sure how to put it on.

Xavier and Levi used their paddles to push away from the dock.

"I think they've got something up their sleeves," Levi said, watching the two girls, who had their heads together as if forming a plan. "Probably going to capsize us or something."

"Like they could get close enough to try," said Xavier with a smirk. He turned to the girls. "You ready?"

"Just a sec." Brianna rested her paddle on her legs and took a tube of lip gloss out of her pocket. She slathered glitter all over her lips.

"You need to fix your hair too?" asked Levi in a jeering voice.

"You're so funny," said Ivy. "On your mark, get set, GO!"

The two kayaks took off, the kids paddling furiously away from the dock. The girls called out a chant, "Catch us if you can!"

"Push us off!" Evan had already jumped into the rowboat and grabbed the oars. Manuel put on the life jacket and bent down to push against the stern of the boat. It didn't budge. He drove his bony shoulders even harder against the boat, his feet sinking into the soft dirt.

"Come on!" Evan urged.

"It . . . won't . . ." Manuel shoved again, and finally the boat edged away from the shore. Evan stuck the oar into the water and gave it an extra push. The boat started to float free.

"Jump in!" Evan shouted.

"Jump?" asked Manuel, wide-eyed.

"Hurry!"

Manuel took a breath, grabbed hold of the stern, and threw one leg over, his glasses sliding down his nose. The little boat rocked like crazy.

"Whoa, man!" cried Evan. "You almost tipped us over!"

"Sorry!" Manuel pulled in his other foot and reached up to hold onto his glasses as Evan started rowing like mad to make up for lost time. They were already twenty feet behind the two kayaks.

Manuel looked with consternation at the water collecting around his ankles. He shivered a little—the water was cold.

"It's leaking!"

"Grab the bucket! Start bailing!" Evan heaved with the oars. Manuel grasped the little sand bucket that rolled around on the bottom of the boat. It had a big crack in it. He sighed and began dumping small amounts of water overboard, bailing and tossing as fast as he could. He had to stop every once in a while to push his glasses up his nose.

"How far behind are we?" Evan was facing backward as he rowed, so he couldn't see the kayaks ahead of them.

"Um . . . I don't know. . . ." Manuel straightened to see around Evan, squinting into the sun. The pond was lined with large willows and had a bend in the middle, so he couldn't see all the way to the other side. "I don't see them."

"Huh?" Evan twisted his head around to see. "They're probably hiding behind those big trees. They think they're so funny. Just want us to think they won already."

Manuel shivered again. "Perhaps we should go back." The water sloshed up his leg. "I've got some homework. . . ."

"No way. We'll show them we won't quit." Evan rowed with renewed energy.

"Wait—what is *that*?" Manuel nearly stood up, rocking the whole boat.

"You're gonna tip us! What's the matter?"

"Look!" Manuel pointed to something over Evan's head. Evan stopped rowing and turned around. For a moment he didn't see anything. Then he gasped.

Just ahead of them a dark circle had appeared in the water. It was perfectly round, about five feet wide. It looked like a hole.

A hole in the water?

"What is that? A whirlpool?" asked Evan.

"Can't be," Manuel said. "There is not enough current here—"

The boat continued to drift toward the hole. Evan tried to row in the opposite direction, but the boat kept moving toward the hole, as if pulled by an irresistible force.

"Help!" Manuel yelled. "Help!" He started to gasp, his asthma acting up the more scared he got. "I need . . . my . . . inhaler . . ."

"Wait—look!" said Evan. "Do you see what I see?"

Manuel leaned over the edge of the boat to see what Evan was pointing at. There was something shimmering on the surface of the hole. Fuzzy and indistinct at first, it soon took on a definite shape.

"It's the Crest!" Evan cried. The Crest of Ahoratos. "That means this is—"

"The Water!" Manuel paused, realizing the sheer impossibility of what he had just said. "Wait a minute. *The* Water? But what is the Water doing here? In *this* water? On earth?"

"I think we need to go down there and find out."

"What? Down *there*?"

"That must be where the others went. Come on! We don't want to miss out!"

"No, no, no!" Manuel yelped as Evan pulled the oars into the boat, allowing it to steer itself toward the hole. "This is not a good idea!"

"Relax, Manuel! Count!" Evan didn't feel scared at all, even though it was very peculiar that the Water should appear *on earth*. That had never happened before. The Water meant adventure. Something amazing was going to happen. He wasn't about to miss it.

"One . . . two . . . three . . ." Manuel felt his stomach jump up into his throat as the boat edged closer to the hole. He always counted when he was scared out of his wits. "We need to tell your mother . . ."

"Oh, she probably knows!" Evan gripped both sides of the boat as it tipped forward. He let out a cry of utter joy. "Woohoo!"

"We're going to die!" Manuel shouted, the sound lost in the rush of the Water all around them, in their eyes and ears and mouths. "Four . . . five . . . six . . ." The boat went vertical and dropped into the hole.

"Like . . . Space . . . Mountain . . ." Evan choked out. He could see nothing but dark. He couldn't even feel any water—it was like being in a protective tube in the middle of a waterfall. Like the tube rides he'd been on at Splash Zone, although those rides didn't generally go straight down. He realized then that he wasn't even in the boat anymore. The boat had disappeared. He was falling feet first, his arms stretched above his head.

"Not . . . having . . . fun!" Manuel's voice gurgled somewhere nearby.

"I am!" Evan shouted, although the words seemed to go right back down his throat. "BEST . . . RIDE . . . EVER!"

———

The next thing Evan knew, he was in the Cave. Bluish, glowing stalactites dripped from the high ceiling, and rows of stalagmites encircled the floor like tiny mountain ranges. Sparks—little white puffs of light that floated everywhere in the Cave—danced around his head. He reached out to try and grab one, as he always did, but it evaded his grasp.

Manuel arrived a moment later, his eyes squeezed shut, two fingers holding his nose closed. He was no longer wearing his glasses. He didn't need them in Ahoratos.

Evan nudged him. "It's okay, Manuel. We're here. We made it."

"'Bout time you showed up."

Evan whirled to see Xavier and the other kids already there. They were all in their warrior clothes, as he was: dark gray pants and shirts. They also wore their armor, the white triangular breastplate, the wide, plain belt, the tall boots, and the helmet, which looked sort of like a bike helmet except the surface was faceted rather than smooth.

Evan resisted the urge to stick his tongue out at Xavier. He was nearly ten, too old for stuff like that, even if his older brother still got on his case from time to time.

"We thought you ditched us," Evan said.

"Hey, we were as surprised as you were."

"Still, a little warning would have been nice," said Manuel, letting his tense shoulders relax a little.

"Greetings, Warriors." A diminutive figure in a purple robe appeared from nowhere, his face hidden by a draping hood. Ruwach. Their guide in Ahoratos.

"Welcome back." His voice was huge compared to his body, so big it filled the kids' minds as well as the Cave. They had never actually seen Ruwach's face, although they'd had glimpses from time to time of something that might have been a nose or eyes. Ruwach was still very much a mystery to them, and he seemed to like it that way. But he was also their friend; his very presence had become a strange sort of comfort to them.

"Ruwach!" said Ivy, running over to hug the small figure. Brianna did the same. "We're so glad to see you!" The boys looked at each other and rolled their eyes.

"I am glad to see you as well," said Ruwach with a slight chuckle. "I have something special to show you today—"

"I have a question," Manuel said, raising his hand as if he were in school. "Why was the Water on earth? I mean, normally when the Crest brings us to Ahoratos, we have to find the Water ourselves, but this time it found *us*, on earth, which seems out of the ordinary."

"Today is an out-of-the-ordinary day," Ruwach said. "You will understand in a little while. We must go now."

The kids glanced at each other. Ruwach seemed to be in an unusual hurry, which meant they were about to do something exciting and probably dangerous. Which might be fun but then again, might not.

"Where are we going?" Evan asked.

"Someplace you have not yet been. You will see. Follow me."

CHAPTER 2

Finn

Finn ran to the edge of the rocky precipice and skidded to a halt, sending a flurry of pebbles into the deep fog below. His heart beat like crazy in his chest. He couldn't look down without feeling dizzy. He panted hard, struggling for breath.

The narrow rock he stood on shook as the pounding footfalls of the Forgers closed in. Finn had no idea where he was now. But he knew he had nowhere to go.

Finn had been out exploring the land of Ahoratos, learning the ins and outs of being a Prince Warrior. After a life spent in the dark prison of Skot'os, the beauty and splendor offered on this side of Ahoratos nearly overwhelmed his senses. Forests with trees as tall as mountains, rivers and streams with water that sparkled like fine jewels, rolling hills choked with wildflowers of every imaginable color. Color itself was something wholly new to Finn, who had lived in a world of endless gray for as long as he could remember.

He was about to head back to the Cave when he heard a sound—like a cry for help—so pitiful and sad it nearly broke his heart. He'd heard that sound before, coming from his own mouth as he had sat in Ponéros's prison, losing all hope that he would ever get out. He ran toward the pathetic wail, which led him to a bridge that spanned a deep chasm.

He stopped, gazing at the pretty, cobblestoned walkway with the ivy-covered railings. Was this the Bridge of Tears that separated Skot'os from the rest of Ahoratos, the one he had heard about when he was still a prisoner? He wasn't sure.

But then the cry came again. Finn drew nearer. As he did, he noticed that halfway across the bridge, the rustic cobblestones morphed into black steel girders, which disappeared into a thick fog on the other side. He felt a chill run down his spine. *Skot'os must lie beyond that fog,* he thought. But he assumed that as long as he stayed on this side of the bridge, he would be okay.

Again the horrible cry of distress filled the air, and a figure emerged from the fog, limping toward Finn over the metal girders. He gasped—it looked like a prisoner of Skot'os. The figure was dragging one of his metal-encased legs behind him, obviously struggling, desperate to escape from that dark, malevolent place. Finn felt a rush of adrenaline—he had to help rescue this prisoner as he himself had been rescued! He had been hoping for an opportunity like this ever since he'd received his armor from Ruwach and begun learning the ways of the Prince Warriors.

Without thinking further, Finn ran over the bridge toward the prisoner, who looked at him pleadingly, whimpering, unable to speak any words.

"I'll help you!" Finn whispered. "Quickly! Come with me!"

Finn reached out to take hold of the prisoner's arm—but as soon as he did, he knew he'd made a mistake. The prisoner's half-human face darkened and hardened, his body lengthened, straightened, new plates of metal taking over the uneven patches of human flesh. The prisoner's human-looking eyes disappeared behind round, red, glowing discs. This was not a prisoner at all. It was a Forger. One of the freakish, metalized agents of the enemy.

Finn snatched his hand away and turned to run. The Forger grabbed for his shoulder, but Finn managed to evade him. He glanced back and saw that there were several more of them, charging out of the mist on the Skot'os side of the bridge. They'd lain in wait for him. It was a trap.

Finn was naturally pretty fast, and his boots made him feel as though he were flying over the cobblestones. But the Forgers' huge steps covered twice as much ground at the same time. Once off the bridge, Finn tried to run back to the Cave, but he wasn't sure of the way. And he was too busy fleeing Forgers to pay attention to the blinking light of his breastplate.

Now he regretted it. Somehow, he had made a wrong turn and ended up trapped on this narrow ledge that jutted out over a seemingly bottomless pit. He skidded to a halt and heard the sound of pebbles cascading into the deep fog below. There was no escape.

His heart pounded. He struggled to breathe.

"Ruwach! Someone! Help me!" Finn cried aloud.

He got no reply.

The Forgers closed in on him, their metal hands reaching out to grab him. Finn knew he was done for. He would turn back into the half-metal prisoner he'd been before. No. He couldn't let that happen. He wasn't going back there again.

Then he remembered his shield. He pulled the tiny red seed out of his pocket and thrust his arm out before him. The shield burst forth from his tightly closed fist, a spray of brilliant red lights creating a dome of protection around him. The Forgers stopped in their tracks and roared, waving their metal arms around angrily.

Finn let out a breath of relief. He kept his arm straight out and tried to take a step forward, pushing back against the strength of the Forgers with his shield. But they appeared to be immovable. He tried again with no luck. He kept his arm erect but began to feel the pressure of the Forgers mounting as they closed in on him. Pushing. Pressing. He struggled to keep his shield deployed.

As he stood there, protected but still surrounded, he felt the ground under his feet shift. He glanced down and saw a crack forming in the rock of the precipice. In a moment it would break off, and he would fall into the pit.

"Tell me what to do!" he called out, hoping Ruwach, wherever he was, could hear.

The orb of his breastplate began to spin, churning out words that hovered in the air before him.

Resist the enemy, and he will flee.

Finn remembered this instruction from The Book the last time he'd been with Ruwach in the Cave. That word rolled around in his mind.

Resist.

The only other time he'd heard about resistance was from his high-school football coach during weight training. "The heavier the resistance, the more muscle you will build. The stronger you will become!" he had bellowed over the *clank-clank* sound of the heavy metal plates.

Resist the enemy, and he will flee.

Build strength.

Heavier. More muscle.

Finn braced himself, gathering all his strength and focusing it on the arm that held the shield. This was all he could think to do. He opened his mouth and let out a thunderous growl as he pushed his shield into the Forgers with all his might. Then he took one step toward them.

Resist . . . resist . . .

He took another step, gasping for breath, every muscle in his body straining to the breaking point. He could feel the rock he stood on give way; he could hear the ominous cracking, the showering of pebbles as it began to break. He kept his focus on his shield, moving, pushing, resisting.

His renewed resolve seemed to weaken the Forgers, for now they were inching backward, their heavy iron feet kicking up dust and dirt that lodged in their metal joints, causing them to stumble.

Resist!

The faltering of the Forgers gave Finn new energy, and he pushed harder and harder, leaping over the crack just as the rocky precipice broke free. He teetered on the edge of the chasm, throwing all his weight into the force of the shield. He thought his arm might break from the effort, but he kept it out straight, his fist clamped on the seed. He took another step. And another.

Resist.

Soon he was clear of the edge and gaining traction, pushing the now powerless and clumsy Forgers backward. A new plan formed in his mind. He sidestepped in a circle so that the Forgers were forced to swivel with him. Now *they* were the ones with their backs to the chasm.

Finn let out a yell, a brawling victory cry as he thrust the Forgers steadily backward, his resistance as lethal to them as kryptonite to Superman. The Forgers howled as if in pain, waving their arms helplessly.

Finn was practically running now as he steered the Forgers right to the edge. With one last powerful thrust he sent them reeling over the cliff. He watched as all of them cascaded into the mist below, disappearing from view. He stood motionless for several seconds, shocked and paralyzed at the sound of their pitiful cries. As the noise subsided, Finn retracted his shield and stared out into the empty distance.

He closed his eyes and let out a long, long breath. It was over. He'd done it. He'd faced the Forgers and beaten them. But instead of pride, he felt an over-whelming sense of gratitude. Without the guidance of Ruwach, the instruction from the Source, and the power of the armor, he would never have prevailed.

"Well done, Prince Finn."

Finn whirled to see Ruwach standing behind him, his hands folded into the long sleeves of his purple robe, his face still invisible in the deep hood. Finn knelt at once, bowing his head. He always did this when Ruwach appeared to him; Ruwach had taken away his metal parts and made him whole again. Fully human again. His only desire now was to serve Ruwach and the Source with all of his being.

Suddenly Finn noticed that Ruwach was not alone. The other Prince Warriors he'd met in the Cave walked up beside him, looking at Finn quizzically. They seemed surprised to find themselves here. With him.

"What happened?" asked the tallest one, Xavier. "Where'd those Forgers go?"

Finn pointed silently to the edge of the cliff.

"What . . . they just—went over?" said the youngest, Evan. He looked shocked.

"Did you throw them off?" said Levi, the kid with the low-cut afro.

Finn shrugged. "I just . . . resisted."

"You did indeed," said Ruwach. "They didn't anticipate you would."

"Who? The Forgers?"

Ruwach nodded. "They did not expect one so young or newly freed to know the secret power of resistance."

Finn lifted his head a little in a humble sort of pride.

"You were tested," Ruwach continued, "and now you have been strengthened by your resolve. You are ready now." He paused as if in thoughtful reflection. "In fact, you all are." He extended one of his long arms out to encompass the kids.

"Ready? For what?" said the dark-haired girl, Brianna, tilting her head.

Ruwach's arm stretched up; his white glowing hand emerged from his sleeve, one long finger pointing toward something in the distance. Finn and the children all turned to look in that direction.

Ruwach was pointing to the tall mountain that stood at the very center of Ahoratos. Its peak was invisible underneath a veil of clouds, but only for a moment. When Ruwach pointed, the clouds began to separate, pulling back like a curtain to reveal the top of the mountain fully for the first time. It was entirely flat, as if the tip had been cut off.

"Cool," whispered the red-haired girl, Ivy. "A volcano."

"Possibly a fumarole," said Manuel, who seemed to know about such things. "Although I've never seen anything quite like *that*."

A thick white vapor steamed from the flat peak of the mountain. It did look an awful lot like a volcano. Except different. For although the mountain appeared very still and calm, they could sense a movement within it, like the pulse of blood pumping through a vein. Somehow, the entire mountain seemed to rise and fall steadily. And they were certain that they could hear a soft whispy sound ascend from its flattened peak, each hushed exhale in cadence with the steady rhythm.

It was as if the mountain were . . . *breathing*.

"The Mountain of Rhema," Ruwach said. He spoke the words very quietly, as if even he were awed by them. "The mountain awakens when it is time."

"Time for what?" Xavier stepped forward, his eyes glued to Ruwach.

"Time for you to receive your swords."

CHAPTER 3

The Mountain of Rhema

Yes!" Evan jumped in the air, beside himself with joy. "Finally! Swords! Real swords!"

"Chill, Van," said Xavier, using the nickname he'd given his little brother when he was a baby. He put a hand on Evan's shoulder to calm him down, although he was just as excited. It was about time, after all.

"But why are we out here?" Levi said, glancing around. "The swords are in the Cave, right? We saw them in the Hall of Armor the first time we came to Ahoratos."

"You must receive your sword from the mountain," said Ruwach.

"From the volcano?" asked Ivy, tilting her head in confusion.

"It's the Mountain of Rhema," Xavier said, as if he'd been the only one listening. *Rhema*. He wondered what the word meant. He'd have to look it up when he got home.

"You must draw your sword from the breath of the mountain," said Ruwach.

"The mountain can breathe?" Brianna asked, fascinated.

"It is the breath of the Source," said Ruwach.

"Oh, so, the Source is *in* the mountain," Ivy declared.

"No. The Source is not of one place but every place. The Source lends breath to the mountain when it is time for Prince Warriors to receive their swords."

They were all silent, contemplating this.

"So, it's not a fumarole," Manuel said, scratching his chin thoughtfully.

"What's a *femoral*?" asked Evan.

"Fancy word for volcano," said Brianna.

"Not exactly—" Manuel began. But Ruwach cut him off.

"You must leave now. Time is of the essence. Go."

"Go?" asked Xavier, pointing to the tall, distant peak. "You mean . . . up there?"

"Yes. You must reach the top of the mountain before the sun has turned once in the sky."

"But you're coming too, right?" Evan asked. "I mean, that's a really big mountain. We could get lost. . . ."

"Your armor will lead you, as always," Ruwach said. His voice was becoming more distant as his form began to fade. "Keep your eyes open, Warriors. The enemy does not want you to succeed. . . ."

"Wait!" shouted Brianna, but Ruwach was already gone.

––––––––––

The kids stood looking at each other for a long moment, wondering what to do.

"Guess we need to go," said Xavier, glancing up once more at the very tall, smoking mountain. "If we want our swords."

"It's strange we have to go and get them," said Levi. "I mean, all the other pieces of armor Ruwach just gave us."

"Guess the swords are different," said Ivy.

"I'm not sure I actually need a sword," said Manuel, backing up a little. "I mean, I don't think I'd be much good in a sword fight anyway. So why don't you guys go on up, and I'll stay here and keep watch—"

Levi shook his head. "No, Manuel, you've tried staying behind before. Remember how that turned out? You're coming too. And so is Finn, right Finn?"

Everyone turned to look at Finn. He had been so quiet; they had almost forgotten he was there. He was older than the rest of them, high-school age, and a lot bigger too. He seemed a bit out of place, but he met their curious gazes with a shy smile and a shrug.

"Guess so."

"Great," said Levi with a nod. "Let's go."

"How about we get Tannyn to give us a ride?" asked Evan, looking around for the dragon/sea monster who'd helped them out of so many jams. "He's got to be around here somewhere."

"Only Ruwach can send for Tannyn," said Ivy. "And he didn't. So I think he expects us to walk."

"Walk? All the way up there? Before the sun sets? Impossible!" said Brianna.

"If Ruwach says to go," said Xavier, "it means we have everything we need to do it. Right?"

Brianna sighed. "I guess so."

"All right then." Xavier took a step. As soon as he did, his breastplate lit up, a bright steady beam. Xavier let out a breath; he knew he was going in the right direction. He had learned to trust the breastplate, even when it pointed in a direction he didn't really want to go. "This way."

He started walking, with Levi close behind. The girls followed, with Manuel and Evan and Finn bringing up the rear. They walked in silence for a while, Xavier always on alert for anything out of the ordinary. He had learned to be vigilant even on this side of Ahoratos where Ruwach ruled, for the enemy had a way of setting traps in the most unlikely of places.

The trees were thick here, with wide, knotty trunks and heart-shaped leaves. Xavier noticed that the gnarled branches of the trees had fringed tips, which made them look almost like . . . hands.

Hands? Xavier shook away the thought. They were just trees. They rustled slightly in the wind, but that was totally normal.

"What kind of trees are these?" asked Brianna, who had noticed them as well.

"I've never seen this species before," said Manuel, "which is not unusual in Ahoratos."

"The leaves look like hearts," said Ivy, reaching out to touch one. "They feel like velvet." Suddenly the leaf closed up around her hand; she snatched it away with a gasp. "Guess they don't like being touched."

"Like your Venus flytrap, Manuel," said Evan.

"Kind of reminds me of those creepy vines in the Garden of Red," said Brianna with a shiver.

"Yes—too bad I can't take a specimen home." Manuel had a large collection of weird plants in his room. But everyone knew it was forbidden to take anything from Ahoratos back to earth without permission. Breaking that rule had caused the Prince Warriors more than enough trouble already.

As they continued up the mountain, the path steepened. Evan walked beside Finn, who had slowed so he could keep up. The two of them fell a bit behind. Evan glanced up from time to time at the bigger boy, who seemed very shy and yet somehow in need of a friend.

"That was pretty cool, how you took out those Forgers," Evan said finally. "Were you scared?"

Finn shrugged a little. "Sure. But I didn't want to go back there."

"To Skot'os?"

"Right."

"So, you haven't been back to earth since you got out of Skot'os?"

"Nope."

"Do you want to go?"

"Not sure."

Evan couldn't get Finn to say more than a few words at a time. He figured Finn was not used to people asking him questions.

"Well, look, if you need a place to stay when you go back, just come to my house. We have an extra room. And my mom is really nice."

"Thanks." Finn gave him a small grin. Evan smiled back.

Just then Evan saw something bright yellow slinking down the trunk of a tree near Finn's head. It was long and thick and slimy looking, with a cluster of antennae sprouting from one end. Evan stopped to gawk at it.

"Hey, Manuel, you gotta see this worm!"

Manuel turned around to see what he was looking at. "Hmmm. More like a slug than a worm, although some worms do grow to be over five feet long—"

"It looks like a banana!" Evan said.

Brianna and Ivy went back to see. The worm/slug thing hunched its back as if it didn't like being looked at.

Brianna made a face. "Gross."

"Don't touch it," said Ivy. "Probably bites."

The creature lifted its head from the leaf and appeared to look straight at Evan, its antennae twirling. Its head started to swell up like a balloon.

"I think it likes me," Evan said, putting up his hand as if to wave hello. Suddenly the worm's mouth gaped open, and it shot out a sticky glob of yellow goo all over Evan's palm.

"Ahh!" Evan jumped back in shock. "That worm just sneezed on me!"

The girls started to laugh.

"That's what you get," said Brianna.

Evan rubbed his hand against his pant leg, trying to get the slime off. "Stupid worm." He felt his face grow hot at the sound of the girls' laughter. Even Manuel was snickering a little. Evan looked over at Finn, who was clearly trying to hold back from laughing.

"You all right, man?" Finn asked.

"Yeah," Evan said. And then they both broke out laughing. It *was* kind of funny.

"Hey, guys, what's the holdup?" asked Xavier, who had come back to see what was going on. He looked at Evan, who quickly put his hands behind his back. "What happened to you?"

"Nothing," Evan said. He wasn't going to tell his brother that he'd just gotten worm snot all over him. Xavier would just make fun of him, like he usually did. It made Evan mad sometimes. Xavier thought he was so perfect, but he had plenty of faults too. Like he had no idea how gross he smelled when he came home from basketball practice, with big sweat stains under his arms. Xavier called it his "manly musk." To Evan it smelled like fish butt. And there were lots of other things as well: the way he left gobs of toothpaste in the sink, how he took off his sneakers in the car and stunk everything up. . . . Evan could thinks of dozens of things Xavier did that were way worse than worm snot. But he figured no one wanted to hear about that right now.

"Let's go then," said Xavier impatiently. He turned away and started walking again.

After what seemed like hours, they reached the edge of the tree line. Xavier called a halt to assess the situation. Above them the mountain loomed, serene and majestic, whiffs of smoke curling from its peak. The terrain before them changed from packed dirt to rocks and big boulders jumbled on top of each other, as if there had been an avalanche. Xavier looked around for an alternate route, but the armor was still pointing straight up.

"Looks like we're going to have to climb for a while," he told the others. "Anyone ever done any rock climbing before?"

"Just on the fake rock wall at school," said Brianna.

"Well, this is kind of like that. Look for handholds and toeholds. Don't rush. Three points of contact at all times. Be careful. If you have trouble, call out. Okay?"

The kids nodded.

Evan had to work twice as hard as the others just to keep up. Not for the first time he felt aggravated that his legs were still so short. When was he going to grow, already? His mom always told him to be patient, but in times like this he just wished he would sprout some big strong legs and maybe a few extra muscles.

He saw Xavier way up ahead, practically leaping from rock to rock with his long legs. Levi and the girls managed to keep up, although Manuel was having a tougher time. His legs were so gangly; they didn't seem to do what he wanted them to.

Evan reached up toward an edge in the rock above him; he strained his arm and wiggled his fingers but couldn't reach it. Then he felt someone grasp his leg and push him up so he could get a grip on the boulder.

"I got you," said Finn, who was behind him.

"Thanks," said Evan, glancing down at Finn, who waited patiently for him to complete the maneuver. Whenever he had trouble getting a handhold or foothold, Finn was there to help. He didn't rush ahead like the other kids, trying to outdo them, even though he was the biggest and could probably climb these boulders faster than any of them. Evan was grateful for that.

He soon realized that his boots felt different—thicker and spongier, gripping the boulders like glue. He stopped to examine his foot and noticed that the toe of his boot had curved so it hugged the boulders. And the whole bottom of the boot was rubbery, giving it extra gripping power. He remembered how these boots had sprouted sticky tendrils like Spider-Man to help him climb up the side of a building once. They had also helped build the stone steps of a bridge over a steep chasm. They seemed able to transform to any kind of terrain, wherever the Prince Warriors had to go.

Evan was just about to announce his discovery to the rest of the kids when Manuel's squeaky voice pierced the air.

"Help! I'm stuck!"

Evan looked up. The others in front turned around. Manuel's leg was trapped between two big rocks. He pushed up uselessly with his arms to try and free himself. Brianna and Ivy reached out to grab his arms, but they couldn't get a good enough grip to pull him out.

"I wasn't looking—stepped into a crack . . ." Manuel said, panting.

"Oh, man," said Levi, climbing back down toward him. "He's really stuck."

"I'll get him out," said Finn suddenly. He shimmied past Evan to where Manuel was stuck, still struggling to move his leg. "Hold still." Finn waited until Manuel had calmed down a bit. Then he bent to one knee, balancing himself on the rock above Manuel, and slipped his arms under Manuel's arms, clasping his wrists together.

"Just relax. Let your leg go limp. Ready?" Finn asked. Manuel nodded. Finn began to lift Manuel toward him, tugging the stuck leg back and forth in a gentle and steady rhythm. Manuel was soon able to move his leg slightly, working it out of the crack as Finn raised him up.

Once Manuel was free, Finn set him down on the top of the boulder. Manuel sat still for a moment, dusty and shaking but otherwise okay.

"Thank you," he said to Finn in a weak voice. Finn waved him off, as if it was no big deal.

"Good thing we brought Finn along, huh?" asked Evan.

"Yeah, that was stellar," said Brianna.

"You okay, Manuel?" Levi asked.

"I think so, but perhaps we could—rest a bit?"

Evan was glad for the break—he was just as tired as Manuel. His lungs ached, and his arms and legs shook with exhaustion. They still had a long, long way to go. He wondered how they would ever make it to the top at this rate before the sun set, although it was always hard to tell how long a day was in Ahoratos.

He closed his eyes, lifted his chin, and took a deep breath. And that's when he smelled it. And *felt* it. Something cool on his face—it smelled moist and pleasant, like the air after a rainstorm. He opened his eyes, squinting, and looked up to the top of the mountain. The thin streams of mist that had been spewing from the crest were now cascading down the mountain. He wondered if the mountain was about to explode like a volcano. But the mist was not moving in all directions; it came straight for them. Couldn't be an accident. Somehow, he just knew he wasn't in danger. He relaxed and inhaled and felt the mist seep down into his lungs, easing the ache.

"Hey guys," he said. "Do you smell that?"

The others looked up and saw the curling vapors around their heads. They breathed deeply, filling their lungs.

"What is it?" Xavier asked.

"The breath of the Source," said Ivy.

"Stellar," said Brianna.

"I do feel better," said Manuel.

"Can you keep going?" asked Levi.

Manuel tested his foot, rotating the ankle and bending his knee. "I think so."

"Good thing," said Ivy.

"Yeah, good thing," said Evan. "We wouldn't want to have to carry you all the way up—"

"Evan!" said Xavier. "We better get moving. Everyone ready?" The kids nodded and got into position again, no longer as tired as they were a moment ago.

They had barely resumed the climb when Evan felt a shadow overtake him, followed by a noise like the flapping of wings. He instinctively ducked. *Ents?* he wondered, searching the sky for the large, metallic bugs with their jagged wings and poisonous stingers. He saw nothing but the mountain and sky and the drifting skypods.

"What's up?" asked Finn, from behind him.

"Oh, nothing I guess." Evan shrugged and kept climbing.

Then the shadow passed by again. This time, Evan caught sight of huge, spiny wings disappearing over the top of the mountain.

He felt his stomach rise up into his throat. He could think of only one creature that could possibly have wings like that.

CHAPTER 4

The Black Dragon

D ragon!" Evan shouted.

Xavier looked up in time to see a dark shape slipping around the side of the mountain. Perhaps it was Tannyn keeping an eye on them. Or a big bird, like an eagle. Maybe there were eagles in Ahoratos. He couldn't be sure. He just knew he couldn't let the kids get sidetracked. This climb required all their attention.

"Stay focused," he said to the others. "Keep moving."

A few minutes later Levi called out: "There it is again!"

This time Xavier saw it too: a sleek, black dragon circling the top of the mountain, its massive wings spread wide, gliding on updrafts. Its forked tail appeared to be covered in long, sharp spikes.

It was definitely *not* Tannyn.

"What if it attacks us?" asked Manuel. "We can't use our shields and climb at the same time."

"Just keep going," said Xavier. Yet he couldn't help but wonder what that dragon was going to do. If it saw them, why didn't it attack? What was it waiting for?

Xavier felt a sweat breaking out on his brow, despite the fact that it was getting colder the farther up they climbed. He reached into his pocket to make sure his seed was still there. He turned to check on the others behind him and saw the worried expressions on their faces. He smiled to reassure them, even though he felt just as nervous as they did.

Finally, the rocky slope ended at a steep cliff face. There was nowhere to go except for a narrow ledge that appeared to wind around the side of the mountain. Xavier had to jump to get to it, but he was glad to feel a flat surface under his feet after climbing those rocks for so long. Levi jumped after him, then turned to help Ivy, who snatched her hand away.

"I can do it myself," she said with a huffy breath. Levi put his hands up and mouthed "Sorry" as Ivy jumped onto the ledge by herself. Brianna was next; she looked at Levi and put out her hand for him to grab so he could help her, even though she too could have done it all by herself.

Soon all of the kids had made it to the ledge. They took a moment to rest, to fill their lungs with the breath of the Source once more.

Xavier scouted out the path before them. The ledge rose at a gentler grade, traversing the side of the mountain. There was nothing below it but a mist-shrouded abyss. They'd have to be extremely careful, keeping close to the rock wall, and rely on the gripping power of the boots in order to not fall to their deaths. But at least it would be less arduous than climbing boulders.

Xavier went back to tell the others. "Looks like we will need to stay on this ledge for a while. Whatever you do, keep close to the wall. Don't look down. Keep focused ahead."

They all nodded, understanding.

"What about the dragon?" asked Evan.

Xavier glanced up—the dragon continued to circle high in the sky.

"Maybe he's not interested in us. But keep your seeds ready, just in case."

The kids got up and followed Xavier as he made his way across the ledge. They walked in silence, concentrating on the narrow path, on the person in front of them, on anything except the shadow passing above them. Xavier felt very exposed; there was no place to hide here, no cover, and they were too far along to make it back to the boulders if something should happen—if the dragon came for them, or if there was a rock slide or avalanche. But he dared not risk falling by trying to go any faster.

You have everything you need.

Whenever Xavier felt doubts and fears overwhelm him, those words from Ruwach came back to him, calming him. He was thankful he wore the helmet, which blocked any "unuseful" thoughts from taking over his brain.

As time went on, Xavier noticed the dragon was dropping lower, closer. He could see its glittering, armored scales with needlelike spikes, almost like the quills of a porcupine. Longer, sharper spikes ridged its back, wings, and tail. Its neck was layered in thick scales with short, pointed spikes sticking out all over its head. Steam curled from its nostrils. Xavier felt its beady yellow eyes zero in on him and lost his breath completely: the eyes told him it was on the hunt and it had found its prey. He quickened his pace along the ledge, urging the rest to follow.

As if sensing that the Prince Warriors were trying to get away, the dragon suddenly dove straight for them, its skeletal wings spread wide, the spikes on either side of its head fanning out. Xavier froze, throwing out one arm to halt the others. He dug his hand into his pocket, grasping the seed and crying out, "Shields!"

All the kids deployed their seeds as the dragon opened its mouth, revealing several rows of serrated teeth. But no fire came out. Instead, it banked left and whipped its long, forked tail toward them, discharging several razor-sharp spikes, each one a few feet long. The spikes sped like javelins toward the kids and slammed into the side of the mountain, sending up small explosions of pebbles and dust. The black dragon veered away, its tail lashing the air, circling for another strike.

"What was that?" Brianna gasped, gazing up at the spikes that surrounded them, hemming them in.

"Did that thing just shoot spikes? From its *tail?*" asked Ivy, breathless.

"Never saw a dragon do that before," Evan choked out. He glanced at Finn, whose eyes were riveted on the black dragon. "Did you?" Finn just shook his head.

Xavier looked to his right and saw that several of the dragon's spikes now blocked their path forward along the ledge. They would have to climb over them, or under them, somehow. Which would make the trek much more dangerous.

Then from high above, Xavier heard a piercing screech that filtered through his shield like the wail of a distant siren. But within the sound, he thought he heard words too:

You . . . will . . . fail. . . .

His helmet began to glow, pressing down over his ears. The words were instantly replaced by Ruwach's whispering voice: *You have everything you need.*

But what do we need? Xavier thought to himself. Even if they could get rid of the dragon, how would they get rid of these spikes that blocked their path? He grasped a spike and yanked as hard as he could, trying to pull it out. But it wouldn't budge. He put his seed away so he could use both hands. When that failed, he tried to break it off, but it was too thick and strong. Levi reached over to help; the two of them heaved and strained, but the spikes were immovable.

"We could really use those swords right now," murmured Levi.

"We have everything we need," said Xavier doggedly. He kicked and shoved at the spikes in frustration.

"What's happening?" yelled Evan from the other end of the line. Manuel and the girls were silent, watching Xavier and Levi with nervous eyes.

"Can I help?" Finn asked, bending forward so he could see what Xavier and Levi were doing.

"Don't do that!" cried Evan, pushing him back. "You'll fall!"

"Just hang on!" Xavier called back.

"We should go back down!" Manuel yelped. "Look! Here it comes again!"

The dragon came in like a jet, strafing the mountain with more spikes. Bursts of rock and dirt clouded the air and ricocheted off their shields. Xavier's shield was down; his eyes filled with dust so he couldn't see. Then something hit his leg, causing it to collapse under him. He reached out blindly as he fell sideways, somehow managing to grab onto one of the embedded spikes.

"Xavier!" Levi shouted. Xavier swung with one hand like he was on a trapeze. He reached out the other hand and felt Levi grab it. But then Levi's grip slipped, and he was swinging again. He kicked with his legs to try to get back to the ledge, but he was just too far away.

He shook his head, clinging to the spike, trying to get his thoughts in order. All he heard were the screams of the other kids and the distant, braying cry of the dragon. . . .

You . . . will . . . fail. . . . You . . . will . . . fall. . . .

"Xavier!" Levi cried. Xavier glanced over his shoulder to see Levi removing his belt. "Just hold still a second!" He threw one end of the belt like a lasso, encircling Xavier's leg. Brianna grabbed Levi's shirt, holding him steady as Levi hauled the belt toward him, pulling Xavier in.

"Keep going, Levi!" Brianna cried.

Once Xavier's boot touched the ledge, it grabbed on like a suction cup. "Give me your arm!" Levi shouted. Xavier took a breath and let go of the spike, as Levi hoisted him back to the ledge. The two of them collapsed together against the wall, winded and scared. The others gasped.

"Xavier! Are you all right?" asked Brianna.

"Yeah," said Xavier, pulling himself to a sitting position. "Thanks, man."

"No problem," said Levi.

Above them the dragon continued to circle, its shadow like a presence in their souls, inescapable.

"What now?" Brianna asked.

Xavier closed his eyes, resting his head against the wall. He had no idea what to do now.

Manuel sank down against the wall. "We can't get through with that thing up there," he murmured.

"Manuel's right," said Evan, sinking down next to Manuel. "We'll never get those swords."

"We have to," said Ivy. "We have everything we need!"

The black dragon shrieked again.

You . . . will . . . fail. . . .

"No, we won't!" Ivy answered back in a loud voice as her helmet glowed and pressed against her ears, blocking out the words of the dragon.

As if in answer, the dragon swooped in for an attack. The Warriors raised their shields, bracing for another round of deadly spikes.

And then a new sound joined the dragon's piercing wail—an out-of-tune warbling the kids instantly recognized.

CHAPTER 5

Impossibilities

"Tannyn!" Evan shouted, pointing to the sky, where the big green dragon soared into view.

Tannyn gave the kids a wave with one huge wing while breathing a stream of blue fire at the black dragon, which responded with a blast of steam that doused the flames instantly. The two dragons collided in midair, teeth slashing and tails whipping, the sound like crashing trains. Fire and steam exploded around them, teeth flashed in the slanting sun, claws raked against dragon scales. The black dragon appeared invulnerable, its armored hide impervious to Tannyn's fire or his bite. Yet Tannyn had never looked so fierce, so terrible. His nostrils flared; his red eyes glowed with fury. He somehow managed to dodge the black dragon's deadly spikes, dipping and weaving so fast the black dragon couldn't seem to hit him.

Suddenly, as if changing tactics, the black dragon broke away and flew straight toward the kids, its mouth dropping open, spikes springing up on its head. The kids choked back screams as Tannyn shot after it. The black dragon got within striking distance of the kids and began to whip its tail toward them, but before it could release a spike, Tannyn clamped down on its forked tail, trapping it in his teeth. The black dragon screamed as Tannyn flung it around and slammed it against the side of the mountain. The whole mountain seemed to shudder with the impact, an avalanche of rocks raining down on the kids' shields. The black dragon let out one more mangled roar as it began to fall, tumbling down the side of the mountain and disappearing into the deep valley below.

"Go, Tannyn," Brianna whispered, holding tight to Levi's sleeve.

Tannyn swung his head to the kids and let out a big "Gorp!"—a combination greeting and burp. But there was little time for celebration, for in the next instant another black dragon, this one even bigger than the first, flew into view from the side of the mountain.

"Look out!" shouted Ivy.

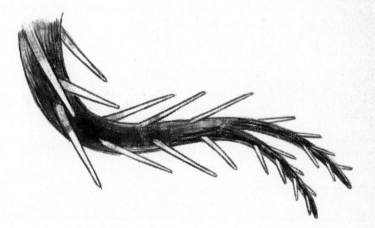

Flicking its forked tail, the new dragon went straight for Tannyn. The kids watched in horror as several spikes sailed through the air at warp speed, straight for their beloved friend. Tannyn twisted around to avoid them, but there were too many; one of them pierced his neck. Tannyn let out a plaintive yelp of pain as he was propelled backward, his wings floundering as he tried to stay in the air. He opened his mouth to throw a flame, but nothing came out. The spike had choked off his fire breath.

The black dragon locked onto Tannyn once more, closing in and launching more spikes. Tannyn was too weakened to get away; several spikes pierced his tail.

"Tannyn!" Brianna whispered, her hand flying to her mouth. "I can't watch." She turned her head away.

Tannyn pumped his wings desperately to stay in the air, despite the spikes embedded in his neck and tail. The black dragon, sensing victory, went in for the kill. Tannyn seemed to have given up. But just as the black dragon was upon him, Tannyn summoned one last trembling bit of strength and whipped his tail around, slamming the embedded spikes into his opponent's wide, open mouth. The black dragon let out a strangled scream. Then both of them fell into a spin, still connected by the spikes, and disappeared into the misty abyss.

"Tannyn!" Brianna screamed this time, the horror in her voice echoing in the now empty air.

The rest of them were very quiet, hoping to hear Tannyn's warbled greeting rise up from the depths below, announcing that he was all right. But there was nothing to hear, except the sound of their own beating hearts.

"Is he . . . dead?" asked Ivy, her voice very small, as if she dreaded saying those words out loud.

"He can't be dead," said Evan, sniffing. "He can't be."

The kids were silent a long moment, gazing into the mist. Tannyn did not return. Nor did the other two dragons. All was very still.

"The sun!" said Manuel. He pointed to the sky, where the sun was sinking fast.

"Tannyn saved us, but we're still stuck here," said Brianna. "The spikes. How are we going to get them out?"

"We can't get them out," said Levi.

"I really wish Ruwach had given us those swords," Evan grumbled. "We need swords to cut through those spikes. How are we gonna get around them?"

Get around them. Xavier got to his feet slowly and examined the spikes that blocked their path. They were densely packed and stuck out well over the ledge. *You have everything you need. Okay,* he thought to himself. *The black dragons are gone, for now at least.* If he and the others couldn't cut through the spikes or pull them out, they had only one option that he could see. They had to get around them. Or—

"We'll need to climb through them," he said finally.

"No way!" said Evan. "You can't climb through those things."

"I know it doesn't look possible," said Xavier. "But we've been in these situations before. What may look impossible isn't always."

"It will take too long," said Manuel. "We'll never make it in time. Look! The breath is already going away!" They all looked up to see that the cascades of mist had receded slightly. "The day is almost over. The breath will be gone by the time we get there."

"We have to try," said Levi. "It's the only thing we can do."

Xavier nodded to Levi and then turned to face the spikes. They *had* to get through them. They had to get to the top of the mountain. That meant there had to be a way.

Xavier noticed that the first few spikes were high enough from the ledge that he could crawl under them, so he did. But then he encountered several spikes much closer together. Somehow he'd have to squeeze between them. He sucked in a breath and felt his belt tighten around his middle. *The belt holds everything together.* That's what Ruwach had told them when they first put it on. The belt had gotten them through river rapids and a waterfall. It would get them through this jumble of spikes too. He stuck his head between two of the spikes and wriggled his shoulders back and forth, pushing one through and then the other. Once his arms were free he grabbed onto another spike and pulled the rest of his body through inch by inch. He realized that although the spikes had looked impossibly dense from his vantage point on the ledge, once he was inside of them there was more space than he had realized.

"You can do it!" he called out to the kids. "Just find a way through!"

"Xavier's big," Evan said. "If he can do it, we can too."

One by one the others followed Xavier into the spikes, searching for an opening, a space big enough to crawl through. Xavier continued to shout at them to keep a good grip and not look down.

"The belt will tighten around you," he said. "It will help you so you won't get stuck."

Keep going, Xavier said to himself. *Find a way.* Sometimes he had to climb up, sometimes he had to crawl under. His body felt more nimble than usual, more flexible, like he could slide through a keyhole if he wanted. Was this because of the belt? He wasn't sure, but he was glad of it.

Once Xavier had made it all the way through the spikes, he helped pull Levi through the remaining tight stretches.

"I feel like a pretzel," Levi gasped as he finally popped out of the last cluster of spikes.

The girls had an easier time since they were much smaller. Manuel got himself tangled up a couple of times, and Evan and Finn had to wait until he untangled himself and kept going.

Finn had the hardest time because he was the biggest. Evan went before him, talking to him the whole time, encouraging him.

"You can do it, Finn! Just one more, see? It's not so bad! Kind of like a jungle gym where the bars are really close together. You can do it!"

A few times Finn was completely stuck, and it didn't look as though he would ever get through. But Evan kept talking to him, and the other kids soon joined in. Finn kept pushing and squeezing until, inch by inch, he was able to get himself through the spikes. When finally he tumbled out of the last tight spot onto the ledge, the others let out huge breaths of relief.

"I knew you could do it!" Evan said, holding out his fist. Finn, tired and sore, did a fist bump with Evan and then dragged himself to his feet.

"What next?" Manuel asked, looking a bit afraid to hear the answer.

"We've got to hurry," Xavier said. The sun had begun to redden. The air felt cooler; a brisk wind kicked up. It felt good at first, after the exertion of climbing through the spikes. Xavier started more quickly up the ledge; the others followed, limping and straining but moving as fast as they could.

But as they continued, the ledge grew narrower and narrower, until they had to sidestep so as not to fall off. The sun dipped below the tip of the mountain; it was soon so dark they were unable to see more than one step on either side of the ledge. The wind turned icy, raising goose pimples on Xavier's skin. Yet despite the wind, he found it was actually getting harder to catch his breath.

Soon the ledge was no wider than Xavier's foot. He suddenly wished he didn't have such big, size-12 feet. His feet had grown so much in the past year that his mom constantly complained about having to buy new sneakers for him all the time. Big feet were great for basketball. Not so great for inching along a ledge a mile in the sky.

He slid along carefully, cautioning the others. He could see almost nothing ahead. He was certain the ledge would eventually disappear altogether. Thankfully, his boots still felt sticky enough to give him a firm footing.

"Everyone okay?" he called out. He leaned forward slightly, although he couldn't really see them at all. He heard grunts and "yups" in response. Satisfied that everyone was with him, he started to move again, side-stepping, pressing his back against the wall.

Until the wall wasn't there anymore.

CHAPTER 6

Smoke and Swords

Xavier didn't realize he was falling until he actually landed. He thought he had just gotten dizzy or stepped into a weird daydream. The back of his legs slammed against a hard edge as he flailed his arms to regain his balance. His head, thankfully cushioned by the helmet, cracked against something sharp. He lay a moment, stunned, trying to get his bearings.

"Xavier!"

Xavier heard Levi's and Brianna's voices calling to him, wondering where he went. But they seemed far away. He sat up and looked around, rubbing the back of his leg, which stung badly. He'd have a bruise for sure. His breastplate dimly lit the space—he'd apparently fallen into a narrow crevice in the rock wall. His back rested against a hard edge. He felt around to see what it was. A flat, smooth top, a shelf or ledge of some sort. He reached higher, and there was another one. Steps.

He turned slightly and saw the faint outline of a narrow staircase nestled in the crevice, so perfectly fitted that it seemed to be a part of the rock itself.

"Xavier! What happened?" Brianna's voice called more sharply this time.

"I'm okay!" Xavier shouted. "There's a crack in the wall, and I fell in. But I found something—steps. Like a—staircase." Xavier pulled himself to his feet and went up a couple of the steps. "I think this is the way to the top. Come on!"

He moved up a few more steps, anxious to see where they led but also concerned that his friends found their way without falling in as he did. So he waited until the glowing breastplates began to appear, one at a time, in the narrow fissure. The kids were all talking at once.

"Found it!"

"Okay."

"Cool."

"It's dark."

"Ouch!"

"That was my foot."

"Sorry."

Finally he heard Finn's voice: "We're all here."

Xavier was thankful Finn had chosen to stay in the back to make sure the others—especially Evan—made it through safely. Hearing his calm assurance gave Xavier a sense of peace in moving forward.

"Cool. Watch your step going up."

Xavier glanced behind once more to confirm that all six breastplates were in place before continuing up the staircase. It twisted and turned in the rock, changing directions unexpectedly; he was almost glad he couldn't see how far up it went. *One step at a time,* he said to himself over and over. He looked back often to be sure the others were still following, although he was certain if someone began to lag or got into trouble, Finn would let him know.

As time went on the air became murkier, until Xavier realized that they were walking, literally, into a cloud. The texture of the air grew thick and heavy, settling on him like a blanket, making it harder to breathe. The dense mist reflected the light of his breastplate so he could no longer see the step in front of him. He warned the others about this, cautioning them to be careful and feel for each step. He could not see the sun at all. He just hoped it was still there.

Finally, just when he was certain this climb would never end, Xavier's head poked out of the cloud. He stopped short, staring in awe at the view that greeted his tired, mist-filled eyes. He felt a lump rise in his throat. The Mountain of Rhema. It looked much different from this vantage point than it had from below. Instead of seeming remote and forbidding, it was a vibrant, pristine landscape of brilliant color and absolute serenity.

"Hey man, why'd you stop?"

Xavier heard Levi's voice but didn't respond. He couldn't find words in his throat. He took a few more steps until he was completely out of the cloud. It was like stepping onto a new planet. Once his feet had reached the top stair, he stepped out onto a wide ledge that encircled a huge crater.

The crater seemed almost as big as the Grand Canyon, which he had visited a few years back with his family. A thick bed of clouds surrounded the crater, so it seemed to be floating. The inside of the crater sloped steeply from where he stood to a small hole in the center that glowed red as if there was fire deep within. It mirrored the color of the huge and swollen sun, already sinking beyond the edge of the world, setting cloud and sky aflame.

Xavier felt light-headed, like he was getting dizzy. Maybe it was the altitude—he knew they must be up pretty high. He'd heard about people getting sick and disoriented at the tops of big mountains. How high were they? How long had they climbed? He couldn't sort out what had happened before this moment. Dragons and spikes and . . . suddenly Xavier wasn't sure how he'd gotten to the top of the mountain at all.

But he did notice one thing that made his heart plummet.

There was no longer any smoke coming from the crater. Not even the smallest whiff.

"We're too late," he murmured as Levi broke through the cloud and stepped up to join him. "The breath is gone." Xavier felt a weakness in his legs. They had traveled a very long way. And all for nothing.

"So this is . . . the mountain? Of Rhema?" Levi murmured. He sounded uncertain, as if he, too, were confused by the altitude or the otherworldliness of the view.

Xavier took several deep breaths, feeling as though there was not enough air to fill his lungs. He heard Levi breathing hard too.

One by one the others came up out of the cloud and took their places on the edge of the crater. They were all quiet, each of them as breathless as Xavier and Levi because of the beauty of the scene and the scarcity of the air.

And yet Xavier knew they all felt as he did when they saw that the breath of the Source had stopped flowing—discouraged and crestfallen. They had failed.

"The breath," Brianna whispered. "Where is it?"

"We need it," said Ivy, her voice weak. "I don't feel well."

"Altitude," said Manuel, breathing in short gasps. "I could use my inhaler. . . ."

"But the sun has . . . not set . . . all the way," said Levi, straining for air. "Maybe there's a chance—"

Xavier gazed at the last bit of sun that rested on the horizon. He shook his head. No, it was too late. No breath. Gone. He wanted so badly to lie down and rest. Close his eyes for a moment. He struggled to resist this feeling, to stay alert, but it was getting more difficult.

Then something stirred from the hole in the center of the crater, which had been so perfectly still since they'd arrived. Xavier strained his eyes, struggling to focus. Had he only imagined it? A deep purple shadow appeared, slowly emerging from the depths of the red hole. Xavier blinked, thinking he was seeing things. Hallucinations, brought on by light-headedness, he was sure. But the shadow continued to rise until it spanned the whole crater, turning everything red to purple.

The shadow had a form that seemed familiar, a flowing cape, wide sleeves, a pointed hood. It was Ruwach. But he was huge, his robe not solid but transparent, rippling as if he were in the center of a storm. And his face, normally dark inside the hood, was now a brilliant shaft of light that nearly blinded the Prince Warriors.

"Prince Xavier."

A voice rose up from the depth of that incandescent light—Xavier thought he could actually *feel* it against his skin. He swallowed. The voice was similar to Ruwach's but different too.

"I'm here," Xavier said aloud. To his surprise, all the other kids said exactly the same thing. It was like each of them had heard the voice say their own names.

"Prince Xavier, receive your sword."

The fire of the inner crater suddenly burst into seven separate flames, each one extending toward one of the Warriors. Xavier drew back, sensing danger in the fire, yet feeling irresistibly drawn to it. Smoke encircled the flame, spinning around it, stripping it to a white-hot core, straight and true. Xavier could make out the beginnings of a blade.

The curls of smoke continued to spin, forming the hilt of a sword. Xavier sucked in a breath. There it was, hovering in front of him—his sword. The smoke dissipated as the core slowly cooled, the fire dying away. All that was left of the fire was the outline of the Crest of Ahoratos emblazoned on the hilt.

"Take it."

Xavier glanced at the others, saw them reaching for their swords. Their eyes looked as though they were locked in a dream. Xavier still was not sure the sword was real. But the voice—Ruwach—had commanded him. He stuck out his hand toward the hilt, fearing it might be too hot to touch. But the hilt was cool, cold even. He wrapped his fingers around it, drawing the sword toward him. It felt real. Heavy, like a real sword. He wrapped his other hand around the hilt, staring up at the gleaming blade, reflecting the brightness of the sun—

The sun?

Xavier looked into the sky, realizing that the sun was no longer setting. It had reversed course, rising in the sky, creating a nimbus of golden light around Ruwach's shadow.

The voice spoke again.

"Your armor is complete now. You were guided by the breastplate and given sure-footedness by the boots. You were held together by the belt, protected from the enemy's lies by the helmet, and shielded from danger by the shield. But the sword is different. The other pieces of armor are used for your defense, but the sword is for offense, attack. Therefore, you must learn to wield it with wisdom. Only then will it be useful."

The shadow of Ruwach began to recede, as if drawn back into the glowing red hole in the crater.

Wait, Xavier wanted to shout. *Come back. Show us how to use them.* But the shadow soon disappeared.

For a long time no one said anything, afraid to disturb the sacred stillness of the moment.

But then Evan began to shout. "This is so cool! We got the swords! Look at us!" He struck a heroic pose, sword pointed in the air.

The silence broken, the others began to laugh along with him, also striking cool poses for each other.

"Wish I had my phone," said Ivy. "This would make a great picture."

Xavier felt unsettled by their sudden playfulness. He wanted to remind them that the sword was not a toy, that they had to learn to use it correctly, to wield it with wisdom. And yet as he looked at his beautiful sword he couldn't help but break into a wide grin. It hadn't been a dream or a hallucination. They really did get their swords.

"It's heavy," said Manuel, holding his with both hands.

"Duh," said Evan, rolling his eyes. "It's a sword! A *real* sword!" Evan swung his sword in a circle; Manuel had to jump backward to avoid being hit.

"Please be careful!" Manuel cried.

"Sorry."

"Let's wait until we are not standing on the edge of a crater, okay?"

"There's something engraved in the blade," said Brianna. "But I can't read it. The letters are kind of funny."

"That weird Ahoratos language," said Ivy. She tried to pronounce a few of the letters but gave up quickly. "Maybe Ruwach will explain it sometime."

"We should go back down," said Xavier. "We've been here long enough."

Suddenly Ruwach's voice rose up from the crater like a holy whisper, although his shadow was long gone. "Be alert and courageous. Descending with the sword can sometimes be more difficult than ascending without it."

"What did it say?" asked Evan, too busy with his new sword to pay attention.

"He said going down might be more difficult than going up," said Xavier.

"More difficult?" asked Evan with a huff. "Why couldn't Ruwach just whisk us back to the Cave or at least take us to the castle for some ice cream? We completed the mission, didn't we? We got the swords before the sun set. That should be enough. Shouldn't it?"

"Don't you think it's strange that it was Ruwach we saw, coming out of the mountain? Where the breath was coming from before?" asked Brianna, her voice lilting as if she'd just thought of something she hadn't considered before. "What if Ruwach . . . *is* the Source?"

"Huh?" said Ivy. Then she, too, appeared to be thinking about the connection.

"Nah," said Evan, shaking his head. "Not possible."

"Maybe . . . he *is* the breath," said Finn in a low voice. The others looked at him.

"What do you mean?" asked Evan.

"He came up out of the crater . . . like the breath."

"You're saying Ruwach is the breath of the Source?" Evan said, his voice rising in disbelief.

"I *can* breathe a lot better now after he showed up," said Manuel, inhaling deeply.

"So can I," said Brianna. "I don't feel dizzy or light-headed anymore."

They looked from one to the other, amazed at this possibility.

"You mean he's not just a little purple dude who runs around sending us on wild goose chases? Why didn't he just say so?" asked Evan, throwing up his hands.

"He likes it better when we figure stuff out ourselves," said Brianna.

"Tell me about it," said Evan with a deep sigh.

"Well, whatever he is," Xavier said, "he told us to go down, so we better get moving." He glanced around, wondering which way to go.

"I hope we don't have to go back down the way we came up," said Manuel, glancing at the cushion of cloud that surrounded them.

"This way," said Finn. He was pointing to where the staircase had been. Only it wasn't there anymore. Instead, the clouds had parted to reveal a wide rocky slope covered in green moss.

"Where'd that come from?" asked Evan.

"No ledge! Awesome," said Ivy.

"Are you sure it's real?" asked Xavier. He was breathing easier, and his head felt clearer. But he wasn't a hundred percent sure that he could trust his own senses.

"Let's go!" shouted Evan, who didn't seem to be having the same trouble. He dashed past Finn and ran down the hill, swinging his sword around as he went. The others followed, laughing and shouting with joy.

"Wait!" Xavier ran after them, calling out the words Ruwach had spoken: "The descent is harder . . ."

But no one was listening.

CHAPTER 7

The Descent

The kids ran down the mossy slope to the tree line, relaxed and carefree, happy to be away from boulders and ledges and spikes and black dragons. The sun had risen higher, warming the air, which filled their lungs so they felt as though they had energy to spare.

Evan couldn't wait to get back home with his beautiful sword. He couldn't wait to show all the kids at school! It was going to be so much fun to see the looks on their faces.

"Evan, wait up!" Xavier shouted to his brother from farther up the slope. Evan ignored him. He turned on Finn and playfully brandished his sword, as if challenging him to a fight.

"En garde!" Evan shouted.

Finn didn't seem to want to fight. He held the sword at his side, as if it made him nervous. "Nah."

"I'll fight you!" said Ivy with a daring grin, stretching out her sword to challenge him. Evan turned to face her, setting his legs into a lunge like he'd seen sword fighters do in the movies.

He heard a loud rustle and looked behind him, thinking someone or something was coming out of the trees. But there wasn't anything. Must have been the wind. He turned his attention back to Ivy, brandishing his sword once again.

"Careful, Evan, that's dangerous," said Brianna.

"Danger is my middle name!" said Evan proudly. He raised the sword over his head and twirled the blade in a circle, accidentally slicing off a small branch of a nearby tree. The tree began to shake, its branches creaking and flexing in a way trees didn't normally act.

Ivy saw it first. But before she had time to warn Evan, the tree had scooped him up and twirled him like a top, binding him up in its branches from shoulder to ankle, like a spider would a fly.

"Help!" Evan screamed. "It's got me! Help me!" He started to cough. "I . . . can't . . . breathe . . ."

Finn rushed forward and smashed his sword against the limb that held Evan. But the tree reached out more fingerlike branches and grabbed Finn's sword arm. Soon he, too, was dangling helplessly, kicking and bucking as more branches closed over his legs and other arm, holding him fast. He grunted, struggling to get away, but he could barely move at all.

Around them more trees were coming to life, reaching out toward the other Warriors with long, bony branches, the thin, fingerlike tips curling into claws. Ivy screamed, dropped her sword, and turned to run, but a branch caught her around the waist, trapping her in mid-motion. Brianna grabbed hold of Ivy's arm, desperately trying to pull her away as the tree slowly reeled her in. Manuel fell to his knees, put his hands over his head, and started counting.

Xavier and Levi rushed in and swung their swords at the branches holding their friends. They too became entangled as more and more trees came to life, their branches lashing out to form a kind of cocoon around the Prince Warriors, closing them in.

"Evan! What did you do?" Xavier yelled as he struggled to free himself from the branch that had him in a vise grip.

Evan squeaked in reply.

"We're . . . doomed. . . ." Manuel croaked out.

Xavier closed his eyes, his breath almost gone. He had to agree.

CHAPTER 8

The Krÿsen

T hat's enough."
The voice rumbled through the trees, making the leaves shiver. The branches relaxed suddenly, dropping their quarries, who collapsed on the ground with gasps and grunts. The Warriors struggled to rise, weak and sore, gazing around in confusion. The trees looked like trees again, standing straight and still.

And Ruwach hovered before them, his arms folded in his draping sleeves.

"Ru!" said Evan, his voice still squeaky from his ordeal. "Boy, are we glad to see you!"

"Now do you understand?" asked Ruwach in the same, deep, rumbling voice.

"Understand what?" asked Brianna. Then she looked down at the sword in her hand and gasped in horror. The sword was not a sword anymore. It was a small thin piece of dull metal with a rounded top and a rather plain handle.

The same thing happened to all of them—beautiful swords becoming tiny, very dull little utensils.

"Hey!" said Evan in protest. "This isn't a sword. It looks like . . . a butter knife!"

The others nodded in horrified agreement.

"What have you learned?" asked Ruwach.

The kids looked from one to the other, unable to figure out what he meant. Then Xavier spoke up.

"Wielding the sword with wisdom," he said. "That's what you told us. That the swords would be useless otherwise."

Ruwach turned to Xavier and nodded his hood. "The sword has great power in the kind of warfare you will be facing, but it requires great care. It is not like the other pieces of armor. You have seen this already. The trees tested you and found you wanting."

"So it was a test?" asked Levi. "That whole tree-grabbing thing?"

"And we failed," said Ivy, her voice low.

"It was not a test for my sake," said Ruwach. "But for yours. So that you would understand the importance of this lesson."

"But our swords are like—*gone*," said Evan, holding up the little knife glumly.

"Your swords are not gone. What you hold in your hand is the Krÿs," said Ruwach.

"The rice?" asked Evan. "It doesn't look like rice."

"Not rice, *KR-ICE*," said Brianna, sounding it out.

"How do you spell that?" asked Manuel.

"So it's not a sword," said Evan, confused.

"The Krÿs *is* the sword," said Ruwach, ever patient. "It will rise to its full potential, in the right circumstances."

"How does it do that?" asked Evan.

"You will learn the secret of the Krÿs if you seek it."

"Oh, I get it, this is like *The Karate Kid* movie, right?" said Evan, growing excited. "And you're like Mr. Miyagi, and we're like the karate kids. And you're going to make us go through all sorts of weird training so we can get our 'black belt' in sword fighting—"

"Evan!" moaned Xavier, rolling his eyes. "Will you stop?"

"Go now," said Ruwach, unfolding one long arm as if pointing the way. Before Evan could ask another question, Ruwach—and the mountain—were gone.

CHAPTER 9

New Things in Old Places

Levi was getting ready for bed when he glanced out the window of his room and noticed the tree house.

He hadn't been out to the tree house in quite a while. His dad had built it when he was six so that whenever Levi wanted to run away (which was pretty often in those days) he would have a place to go. Sometimes he went out to read his favorite adventure books by flashlight or practice sketching in a drawing pad he preferred to keep secret. Often he stayed out so long he fell asleep, and when he woke up he would find a plate of cookies and a thermos of milk sitting on the windowsill—a gift from his mother.

Lately though, he'd been too busy to go to the tree house. He thought maybe he was outgrowing it. He'd outgrown a lot of things, like wearing the same shirt every day and not brushing his teeth. He did that for a full week once—not brushed his teeth, that is. He came home from camp one summer and his mom had been horrified that he hadn't even opened the brand-new travel toothbrush she'd packed. There were a lot of things he used to think were cool that weren't anymore. The tree house was one of them.

He picked up his phone and looked at the screen: 10:00 p.m. Same day as the kayak race. Yet it felt as though a year had passed.

He grabbed the Krÿs and threw a jacket over his pajamas. Climbing out the window onto a thick tree limb, he crawled a short distance then shimmied through the narrow doorway. The neighbor's dog started barking, which it always did at even the slightest movement in the yard. That dog never missed anything.

Levi turned on the small battery-powered lantern and looked around. Large, complicated spiderwebs inhabited every corner. The floor was very dusty. Levi cleaned off the top of the short three-legged stool he kept there and held the Krÿs to the light, wondering what sort of secrets it held.

The lantern dimmed and went out. Dead battery. Levi frowned, then went to find a flashlight in the wooden box where he kept his special tree house supplies. But something was lying on top of the box—a large rectangular object Levi had never seen there before. He reached over to pick it up. It was heavy.

It was a book.

Levi grabbed the flashlight from inside the box and shone it on the book. He recognized it then, the heavily embossed cover with the familiar symbol, the odd-shaped letter *A* for Ahoratos. This was the same book about the Prince Warrior that Brianna had, and Evan and Manuel too. He wondered if Brianna had brought it over and left it there for some reason. But even Brianna, his best friend for ages, had never been in the tree house. This was a place Levi kept all to himself.

He opened the cover and began leafing through the pages. The illustrations were pretty intense, very colorful and dramatic. The writing was in a fancy type that was hard to read, about a Prince Warrior who went on all sorts of perilous adventures. Each chapter highlighted a different piece of the Warrior's armor, all of which Levi now had, although the armor in the book was much fancier and more elaborate than Levi's was. More like the kind of armor people wore in gladiator movies that he and his dad liked to watch.

He went right to the chapter about the sword, curious to see what the book said about it. On the title page there was a large illustration of a beautiful, gleaming sword. It looked so real he had to touch it. But when he did, his finger went right through, as if there were a hole in the page.

Curious, Levi shined the flashlight directly onto the page. The light revealed a strange outline in the blade of the sword—a shape that looked an awful lot like his Krÿs. He picked up the Krÿs and pressed it to the page to see if the outline was really the same. To his surprise, the Krÿs slipped right into the picture, as if the hole he had discovered was perfectly conformed to the knife's shape and size. The Krÿs blended into the illustration of the sword so that it became almost invisible.

The page began to flicker, like static on an old television set. Then a word flared across the top of the page.

Implanted.

This writing was not in that strange, other-worldly language. It was in plain English. Levi's eyebrows lifted in surprise.

Fearing he'd lost the Krÿs, Levi reached into the page again and pulled the small knife back out. It came out easily, and the word disappeared from the top. The page went black. Amazed, Levi put the Krÿs back in and took it out several times. Each time the page seemed to come alive.

He didn't know for sure whether or not he was imagining this. His experience on the Mountain of Rhema was already pretty fuzzy. Reality blurred with his own imagination. But he had definitely gotten the sword, even if it had turned into this funny, useless little knife-like thing.

But the Krÿs definitely seemed to belong in this book, as if it was a storage place. So was that the secret? Or was there something more to it? And what did it mean by "implanted"?

Levi felt there had to be something else, something more significant than just a hiding place for the Krÿs. He re-inserted the Krÿs, but this time he didn't take it out quickly. He waited. He wasn't sure what he was waiting for exactly. The page flickered on like it had before, and as the static cleared away, the word *Implanted* appeared once again across the top of the page. For a moment nothing else happened. He was just about to take the Krÿs out again when he noticed that the blade in the illustration began to glow softly. And then Levi saw more writing beginning to take shape below it. The letters appeared slowly, forming into a single word:

Received.

Levi stared at both words which now sandwiched his Krÿs—one on the top of the page and the other on the bottom:

Implanted. Received.

What on earth did that mean?

"I see you figured it out."

He jumped. His dad was leaning against his bedroom window, looking into the tree house, a big grin on his face. The bedroom light reflected off his bald head. Levi wondered how long his dad had been watching him.

Levi's dad, James Arthur, was known as Mr. J. Ar to his friends and all the kids at the Cedar Creek Rec Center, where he acted as basketball coach and part-time manager. He volunteered nearly every day, because he said he grew up without knowing his own father and didn't want that to happen with his son. Mr. J. Ar was really tall and broad-shouldered, with massive hands that could palm a basketball with ease.

Everyone looked up to him, but Levi especially, even though he wasn't all that fond of basketball.

And Levi's dad also happened to be a Prince Warrior.

"Figured out what?" Levi asked.

"How to implant the sword."

Implant. There was that word again.

"What do you mean?"

"You *implant* the Krÿs in the book, and the book *receives* it. Then it *infuses* the Krÿs with the power of the Source. It's sort of like when you charge your phone. Except different."

"This book does that?"

Mr. J. Ar nodded. "Cool, huh?"

"I guess so. Ruwach didn't tell us very much about it. I mean, we climbed this huge mountain and almost didn't make it. Then we got the swords and had a little trouble with trees—but then the swords turned into these things."

"Well, that climb is no picnic, I know," Mr. J. Ar said with a laugh. "I still remember my trek up that mountain. It can't be done without courage and perseverance. And going back down can be even worse."

"You can say that again. There was this huge black dragon—"

"Ah. So you saw Antannyn."

"Who's that?"

"The biggest and baddest of the black dragons. A particular favorite of the enemy."

"Well, it got into a fight with Tannyn and—killed him." Levi's head dropped at the memory.

Mr. J. Ar raised an eyebrow at his downcast expression. "I'm sorry to hear that," he said.

"I never saw a dragon shoot spikes from its tail. . . ."

"Thorns."

"What?"

"The black dragons shoot thorns. Thorns are a big problem for true Prince Warriors. You always have to be on guard against them."

Levi sighed, looking down at the book in his hands. "Where did this book come from? I mean, I never saw it here before."

"I left it up here awhile ago, but you haven't been here in a long time."

"No, I got really busy, and I'm getting too big, I guess." Levi laughed.

Mr. J. Ar nodded. "Oh, son, some places you should never get too busy or too big for. It's good to visit the old places. You never know what you're going to find. Aren't you glad you came today?"

"Yeah. This is pretty cool."

"Better come inside and get some sleep. Big day tomorrow."

"What's tomorrow?"

"You and the other kids need to learn how to use your swords."

———

Levi went to bed and dreamt of dragons and swords and steaming mountains. He dreamt of fire and smoke and thorns—thorns on trees and dogs and houses, thorns everywhere. The dream was so real and so frightening that he woke up several times, sweat pouring down the side of his face. He had to get up and get a drink of water before going back to sleep again.

"Time to get up, kiddo." His father's voice boomed into his latest dream—jolting him out of a fantastical ride on Tannyn's back, gliding over the world. It had been so vivid that he could actually feel the wind pressing his face, his stomach going up and down with Tannyn's dips and dives. He felt sad all over again about Tannyn, grateful that he could ride that goofy, wonderful dragon one more time, even if it was only a dream.

"What time is it?" he asked in a groggy voice. He ran a hand over his tapered afro. He liked to keep his hair cut low in the summer and then let it grow out in the fall when the weather was cooler. It wasn't long enough yet that his mom had started complaining about it.

"Seven," said his dad, throwing open the curtains, although it was barely even light out.

"In the morning? Why do I have to get up so early?"

"Need to get to the Rec before it opens. I already talked to the other kids. They'll meet us there. We need a couple hours to get started. Don't forget your Krÿs— and your book."

"But Finn—how are you going to call him? We don't know where he lives or his last name or even if he has a phone. I mean, he might not even be back on earth yet."

"If he is, I'm sure Rook will find him," said Mr. J. Ar.

"So Rook's coming too?"

"Sure. Rook is helping me with the training. Grandpa Tony too. Both are very good swordsmen."

"Brianna's grandfather? Isn't he kind of old?"

Mr. J. Ar laughed. "Some skills just get better with age."

————————

When they got to the rec center, Mr. J. Ar unlocked the front door and then turned on the lights. A short time later, Mr. Blake dropped off Xavier and Evan with a big box of donuts. He'd given Manuel a ride too, since Manuel lived across the street from the Blakes. The boys sat down at one of the tables and ate donuts while they waited for the rest to get there.

"Your dad told us to bring our Prince Warrior book," Evan said to Levi. "But he didn't say why."

"You'll find out," Levi said with a secret grin. It was cool knowing something no one else knew.

Brianna and Ivy came in with Grandpa Tony, who greeted the boys with hand-clasps and fist bumps and then went to talk to Mr. J. Ar. Brianna and Ivy sat down at the table. Levi saw that Brianna had a new backpack; instead of the old pink, bedazzled backpack she'd had for years, she was carrying one of those new hipster styles made of a woven fabric in a bright pattern.

"Where'd you get that?" Levi asked her.

"Oh, Ivy gave it to me," Brianna said. She whipped out her favorite glitter lip gloss and slathered her lips.

"It was a birthday present," said Ivy.

"It's cool," Levi said, impressed, although he felt weirdly sad too. Ever since they became friends, Brianna spent most of her time with Ivy now. She didn't come over to Levi's house nearly as often, and she didn't hang out with him at the Rec like she used to. Levi didn't mind so much; it was just that sometimes he actually missed her. He didn't tell her that though.

"Donuts!" said Brianna, reaching across Levi for the box of donuts. She took a sugarcoated donut and passed the box to Ivy, who helped herself.

The front door opened, and Rook (a former prisoner of Skot'os) came in with a satchel slung over his shoulder. He turned and motioned to someone outside the door. Finn appeared, glancing around cautiously before entering. His formerly round, thick afro had been tapered down on the sides like Levi's, except with a thicker tuft on the top. He was dressed in jeans and a Cedar Creek High School football T-shirt.

"It's Finn," whispered Evan. "I think it's his first time back here. He told me he hadn't been back since he was freed."

"He cut his hair," said Brianna.

"Hey man," said Levi, rising to greet him. They clasped hands. "How's it feel to be back?"

"Okay, so far," Finn murmured. His eyes darted about nervously.

"You play football?" said Levi, noticing the shirt.

"Used to."

"Finn!" Evan ran over and gave him a fist bump like he did with his very best friends. "Wanna stay at our house?"

Finn's eyes flicked to Rook, who gave him a nod and a smile. "Finn's hanging with me for a while," said Rook. "Until he gets everything figured out."

"Everyone bring your books? And your Krÿsen?" said Mr. J. Ar, coming to the table. Xavier, Manuel, and the girls took their books out of their backpacks. Levi, Evan, and Finn sat down at the table; Levi already had his book out.

"I don't have one of those," said Finn, pointing to Levi's book.

"I've got one for you." Rook produced a Prince Warrior book from his satchel and set it in front of Finn. Finn glanced up at him, questioning. "It's cool," Rook said.

"Levi is going to show you what he has discovered about the book," said Mr. J. Ar. Levi looked up at his father, surprised. "Go ahead, son. You show them."

Levi felt everyone staring at him; he cleared his throat. "Well, I was just looking at this page with the sword last night. And I noticed there was a hole here. . . ." Levi opened his book to the sword page and stuck his finger into it, as he had done in the tree house. The kids made noises of surprise. "I figured out that the Krÿs actually fits in here." He pressed his Krÿs into the page. The kids gasped when they saw it sink right in and virtually disappear. After a moment they saw the words appear on the page.

"Implanted?" said Brianna. "What does that mean?"

"Implant means to insert securely," said Manuel.

"Yeah," said Levi. "So when you implant the Krÿs in the book like this, it gets filled up with power."

"Wow," said Evan. "I've looked at that book a million times and never noticed that page before."

"The book reveals different things, in different ways, at different times," said Grandpa Tony. "It's a special book."

"How did you figure it out, Levi?" asked Brianna.

Levi shrugged. "I don't know. I just did."

"I don't have a book," said Xavier. "Only Evan does."

"The book can handle more than one sword at a time," said Mr. J. Ar. "You and Evan can both use the same book."

"Like we have to share a phone," said Xavier with a sigh.

"You'll know the sword is powered up when the crest appears in the hilt," said Grandpa Tony. "If the crest fades, it means the sword is losing power. It only takes a few minutes to charge, so you shouldn't have a problem as long as you keep the book handy."

"We keep an extra book in the trunk in the closet," said Mr. J. Ar. "You can use that anytime. Especially in emergencies."

The kids practiced implanting their Krÿsen into the books and taking them out again. Once the swords were fully infused and ready to use, Mr. J. Ar told them to go to the supply closet where the trunk of armor was kept and put their armor on. "Let's meet in the gym. Rook will work with Finn and Xavier. Tony, you take the girls, and I will work with Levi, Evan, and Manuel. Let's do this, people."

CHAPTER 10

Training Days

The kids and adults put on their armor and carried their Krÿsen into the gym, breaking into groups that Mr. J. Ar had assigned. Evan stood between Levi and Manuel and waved his little knife around, as if trying to make it bigger.

"Careful, Evan, you're going to hurt somebody," said Levi.

"With this little thing, the worst I could do is butter them," said Evan, sarcastically. "How do you make it bigger, Mr. J. Ar?"

"If you'd listen, I would tell you," said Mr. J. Ar somewhat impatiently.

Evan stopped waving his knife and stood quietly.

"That's better. First, set your feet one in front of the other and bend your knees. Make sure you have a strong stance. To activate the sword, you need to raise the handle and press it to your breastplate, blade up. Point it slightly away from your chin, so you don't slice yourself up. Like this." Mr. J. Ar demonstrated by pressing the handle of his Krÿs to his breastplate. As soon as it made contact, the sword grew to its full length, nearly half as tall as Mr. J. Ar himself.

"Whoa!" said Evan. "Awesome!"

Levi followed the instructions, touching the handle of his knife to his breastplate. He felt a slight buzz in his palm, and the knife jolted out of his hands as the small blade grew to its full length. Evan burst out laughing.

"Gotta hang on tight," said Mr. J. Ar, picking up the sword and handing it back to Levi.

"Your turn, Evan."

Evan braced himself and pulled the small knife to his chest. Instantly the huge blade popped up, narrowly missing his chin. He threw his head back in surprise and fell over backward, landing on his butt. He glowered at Levi, who was now snickering at him.

"Not so easy, huh?" said Levi.

Mr. J. Ar gave Evan a hand back to his feet. "There's a reason you get in your stance first. One foot in front, one in back. To keep your balance. And remember not to point the blade directly under your chin."

"Got it," said Evan.

Then it was Manuel's turn. He set his legs apart as he'd seen the other two boys do, gripped the handle of the Krÿs extra tight, and touched it to his chest. Nothing happened. He tried again and again. Still nothing.

"Mine's broken," he said finally.

"Blade up," said Mr. J. Ar. He reached out and adjusted Manuel's grip; the blade extended so fast that Manuel jumped, although because he had his feet properly set, he didn't fall over.

"Good job," said Mr. J. Ar, giving him a pat on the shoulder. "You're a good listener, Manuel. Now that the sword is activated, it can be wielded. Remember what Ruwach has probably already told you: the sword is an offensive weapon. But it should only be used against the enemy or a servant of the enemy. And it can only kill the inhuman kind of enemy. The unseen kind. Do you understand this?"

The boys nodded eagerly.

"Okay. Lesson one," said Mr. J. Ar. "Stay calm. Stay focused. Never rush in. Take time to breathe. To think. Plan your first move with care. Your first move will probably decide how the whole fight will go. You want to end the fight as soon as you can. And you want to win. Got it?"

The boys nodded.

"Good. Lesson two. Your stance. This is how you stand when ready for battle. Like we already learned, keep your knees slightly bent, one foot forward, one foot back. Never side by side. Your sword should be pointed at your opponent's head or chest at all times. Let me see you try it."

The boys raised their swords, pointing the tips at Mr. J. Ar's chest.

"Good. Keep your tip up at all times. Keep your elbows close to your body. Don't overextend your arm. Don't go swinging wildly. You are looking for quick, targeted thrusts and cuts.

"Now I know you've all watched a lot of sword-fighting movies, but those are mostly not very true to life. The actors are usually aiming for each other's swords. But in real life, you don't aim for your opponent's sword, you aim for your opponent. Every move you make is designed to kill. If you parry, which means block your opponent's attack, you should always turn it into a counterstrike."

"But Forgers don't fight with swords," said Evan.

"That's right," said Mr. J. Ar. "But there are other servants of Ponéros that do. We're going to cover the basics first. Then we will talk about Forgers."

Mr. J. Ar began with parries, showing the boys how to block a sword attack. Then he had the boys practice for a while, attacking them in slow motion until they learned to react correctly and have their swords in the proper position.

"Above your head, Manuel. If you hold your blade in front of your face, you are going to get it right up your nose."

Evan snickered at this.

The instruction went on for more than an hour. Brianna and Ivy practiced their new moves against Grandpa Tony, taking turns attacking him until he begged for mercy. Rook had Xavier and Finn spar with each other, stopping them often to correct their positions. Then Mr. J. Ar had all the kids sit on the bleachers while he and Rook did a demonstration of sword-fighting techniques, both in slow motion and real time. Levi was amazed at how fast they were and how quickly they were able to react to the other person's attacks. He vowed to practice every day so one day he could be as good a swordsman as his dad.

Once the demonstration was over, Mr. J. Ar called for a break. The kids filed tiredly into the main room and took turns at the water fountain. Then they sat around a table and ate cookies provided by Brianna's grandmother while Mr. J. Ar, Grandpa Tony, and Rook went into the office for a discussion.

"At this rate, it'll take months before we get good at this," said Ivy. "There's so much to learn. More than I thought."

"It's kind of fun," Brianna added. "Although I never thought I would be able to use a real sword. Or be in a real battle."

"I'm not very good," Manuel said. "No hand-eye coordination. And my depth perception is very poor."

"I'll help you out if you need it, don't worry," said Evan, not knowing for certain what *depth perception* really was. He patted Manuel on the shoulder as Mr. J. Ar had done.

"Sure you will, Squirt," said Xavier with a laugh. Evan made a face at him.

"Hey, Manuel," Evan said, ignoring his brother, "how come your dad isn't here helping?"

"What do you mean?" said Manuel.

"Well, he's a Prince Warrior, isn't he? I mean, he has a book."

"He does?" Manuel looked mystified.

"Sure. I saw it on his desk that time we went to your house to see the shield you made."

"He was snooping," said Xavier.

"Was not! The door was open, and I saw the book. But it looked kind of different. The crest was all changed. I didn't get a chance to look at the rest of the pages—"

"I didn't know my father had a book," said Manuel, thoughtfully. "He never mentioned it. I got my book from my mom before she died."

"Maybe we can go over to your house after this and look at it," said Evan.

"Evan!" said Xavier. "It's none of your business."

"I just want to see," Evan said.

"My father doesn't like anyone going into his study," said Manuel. "Including me. He's been rather reclusive lately."

"Is that a sickness?"

"No—it means withdrawn, secretive. He keeps to himself."

"Oh, right, since your mom—"

"Evan!" Xavier hissed.

"Sorry," Evan said, tucking his head into his shoulders.

"It's okay. It's true, though," said Manuel with a sigh. "He doesn't like to talk about it."

Mr. J. Ar emerged from the office with Rook and Grandpa Tony.

"All right, kids, break is over! Back to work!"

———

Mr. Blake picked up Xavier, Evan, and Manuel after practice was over, just as the Rec was opening for the day. Mr. J. Ar had given them each a wooden sword to practice with at home. The boys talked excitedly about what they had learned, recounting their favorite moments.

"I liked when Mr. J. Ar almost lopped Manuel's ear off," said Evan, laughing.

"I kept closing my eyes," said Manuel. "Probably not the best thing to do in a sword fight."

"No matter what I did, Rook always managed to knock the sword out of my hands," said Xavier. "He was so fast. I couldn't keep up."

"Hey, Manuel, you want to come over to our house and practice?" asked Evan.

"No thanks," said Manuel, shaking his head. "I have homework."

"Homework? It's Thanksgiving vacation!"

Manuel tried to think of some other, more plausible excuse but then just shrugged. "My father wants me home."

Mr. Blake pulled into Manuel's driveway.

"Thanks for the ride," Manuel said as he got out of the car.

"No problem. Say hi to your father for us," said Mr. Blake. "He's home, right?"

"Yes, that's his car," Manuel said, indicating the car in the driveway. "I appreciate the ride home. Tell Mrs. Blake I said hello."

"Will do, Manuel," said Mr. Blake with a smile. "You sure you're okay?"

"I'm fine, thank you."

Manuel waited until the Blakes' car had backed out of the driveway and turned down their own driveway before going into the house. He opened the door, listening for sounds of his father. The door to the study was closed.

"Papá?" He waited, but there was no immediate answer. He started to go up the stairs to his room but then changed his mind. He walked over to the study door and knocked softly. "Papá? Are you in there?"

No answer. He knocked harder, but still nothing. Manuel paused. He knew he shouldn't go in, but he had to see for sure. He took a deep breath and turned the knob of the door.

He opened it slowly, peeking in, wondering if his dad had fallen asleep in his wingback chair. But he wasn't in the room at all. Maybe he had gone to fill the bird feeders. Mr. Santos loved to watch the birds and document any new bird he saw. It was practically the only activity he enjoyed anymore; he was always working.

Manuel slid into the room and looked around. There it was, sitting on his father's desk, just as Evan had said. A Prince Warrior book. Evan was right. Manuel crept over to the desk and peered at the book, pushing his glasses up his nose. It *did* look different. The symbol of Ahoratos appeared to be upside down. Manuel opened the book and looked through the pages. The changes were small: a chapter heading rearranged, a sentence crossed out or rewritten, a note scribbled in the margin. The pictures were missing small details. The shield illustration contained no red seed in the center of the brass boss. And the picture of the sword did not have the Crest of Ahoratos in the hilt, nor were there any letters engraved in the blade. When Manuel touched the blade, his finger did not go through the page as it did with his own book. He realized that the Krÿs could not be implanted in this book. It was powerless.

Manuel heard the back door slam and darted out of the study in time to see his father tramping through the kitchen, pulling off his thick cardigan.

"Oh, hi, Papá," Manuel said brightly, hoping his nervous state wasn't too noticeable.

"Manuel? Did you just get home?"

"Yes. Mr. Blake dropped me off."

"Oh—I did not hear a car pull away." Mr. Santos dropped his sweater on the back of a chair and passed by Manuel, giving him a rub on the head as he headed to his study. Manuel touched his head absently, feeling warmed by his father's unexpected show of affection.

"Did you go to fill the bird feeders?" Manuel asked, following him down the hallway. He wondered to himself: *did I shut the book or leave it open?* He couldn't remember.

"Yes."

"Any new birds today?"

"No. But the hummingbirds are returning." Hummingbirds were Mr. Santos's favorite. "Where did you go this morning?"

"Just with my friends, over to the Rec."

"It is open so early?"

"Well, no. We were . . . helping Mr. J. Ar with a project." Manuel didn't want to lie, but he didn't want to tell his father what they were actually doing either.

"You are going to your cousins' for dinner," Mr. Santos said. "Be ready to leave at five." He turned the knob of his study door and opened it.

"Papá—" Manuel said. "Can I ask you something?"

Mr. Santos stopped in the doorway, gazing at his son abstractedly. "Yes?"

Manuel bit his lower lip. He wasn't sure how to ask. "You know the book Mamá gave me? The one about the Prince Warrior?"

Mr. Santos stiffened. "Yes, I know this book."

"I was just wondering if you had ever read it."

There was a long pause. Mr. Santos shook his head. "It is a nonsensical book. For children. You are too old for such things, Manuel. It was a nice memento from your mother. A way to remember her. She was—special. But do not take such things so seriously." With that, Mr. Santos disappeared through the door and shut it with a click.

CHAPTER 11

New Developments

As soon as Xavier and Evan walked through the door of the house, Evan zoomed past his mom who was sitting in the living room watching TV and went straight to the kitchen.

"Mom! Is there any food?" he yelled, hoping his mom could hear him. His morning of sword fighting had made him really hungry.

There was no answer. Evan opened the refrigerator door. Nothing looked instantly edible. Lots of Thanksgiving leftovers in little plastic containers.

"Lunch isn't for another hour," said Xavier, coming into the kitchen. "You ate four donuts this morning. How can you still be hungry?"

"I'm starving now!"

"Have some cereal."

Evan headed for the pantry. Xavier decided to go up to his room to look up some stuff on his computer. He liked to look up stuff he didn't understand. His dad had taught him to do that whenever he was stuck on something, and it had just become a habit. As soon as they had gotten back from the Mountain of Rhema, Xavier had looked up the word *Rhema*. It was the Greek word for "breath." That had made sense, since the mist that came from the mountain was the breath of the Source. He had wanted to look up *Krÿs,* but he had no idea how to spell it. With a *C* or *K*? With an *I* or a *Y*? Ruwach hadn't told them that. He had tried all different ways but hadn't found anything that seemed right. Maybe Krÿs was something that only existed in Ahoratos.

Right now, he was interested in finding out more information about sword fighting. Rook was an amazing fighter; he showed Xavier and Finn a lot of cool moves. But Rook told them he had never fought a black dragon himself, although he'd seen them plenty of times. Rook had told him that the black dragon's armor was so thick that a single sword blow wouldn't kill it. Rook thought it would take a least a dozen swords to bring down one dragon, but even he wasn't totally sure. Xavier knew there were a lot of online sites devoted to dragon slaying, and even though they were all made up, he wondered if there might be some useful information he could take into a real battle—if he ever had to face one of those monsters himself.

On his way up the stairs, Xavier passed by the living room and saw his mom still sitting in front of the television, staring intently at the screen. He thought it was strange she hadn't answered Evan when he called.

"Hey, Mom," said Xavier. No response. He spoke louder. "Mom! We're home."

She glanced over at him. "Oh, hey, baby," she said, returning to the screen. "Have you seen this?"

"What is it?" Xavier sat down beside her on the couch.

It was a news program. The video footage was an aerial view from a helicopter, showing a gigantic boulder sitting in the middle of a runway at the airport.

There was a passenger plane parked at an odd angle beside it, as if it had nearly crashed into it. The boulder looked to be at least as long as the plane and twice as tall. The area around it was taped off with yellow police tape, and people in hazmat suits aimed strange-looking instruments at it. Much farther away, news vans and police cars were parked with lights flashing. The caption on the screen read: "Giant boulder appears on airport runway. Flights delayed for hours." The TV reporter was talking excitedly, waving one arm in the direction of the humongous rock.

"Officials are stumped as to what sort of rock this is. There is some speculation that it might be of alien origin, although there is no evidence that the object fell to earth from outer space."

"It's so strange, isn't it?" said Mrs. Blake. "Right in the middle of the airport! Thank goodness it didn't fall on any planes."

Xavier swallowed hard. He knew what that rock was. He'd seen more than one of them before.

A skypod. One of the large floating objects that dotted the skies of Ahoratos. He also knew what it contained: Ents. Thousands of Ents, trapped by the Prince Warriors.

The news reporter was still talking when the camera switched to a shot inside the airport showing people being loaded onto busses, looking extremely unhappy. "Dozens of flights have been delayed, as the airport had to be completely shut down until it can be confirmed that this object is not a threat. Hundreds of people have been evacuated to local hotels, where they will have to stay until they get word that the airport has reopened. Even if it does, there is likely no chance that this huge rock can be moved off the runway quickly. . . ."

Xavier excused himself and went into the kitchen, where Evan was wolfing down a bowl of cereal.

"You need to see this," he said, grabbing Evan by the arm and dragging him into the living room. Evan, still complaining about being separated from his food, went quiet as he watched the news show. Finally, Mrs. Blake turned off the TV.

"Well, I guess the experts will figure it out," she said, seeing the worried expressions on the boys' faces. "I didn't mean to scare you—Evan, are you all right?"

Evan nodded mutely.

"Well, you boys need to clean up your rooms and take showers. I'll get some lunch together. How about hot turkey sandwiches?" She went into the kitchen.

Evan and Xavier sat on the couch, staring at the blank TV screen.

"A skypod," Evan whispered. "Full of Ents."

"Yeah," Xavier said. "But it's impossible. A skypod couldn't come to earth."

"Maybe it could."

Xavier looked at his little brother. "How?"

"Ru said there would be . . . consequences."

"Consequences? What are you talking about?"

Evan took a deep breath, summoning the courage to tell his brother the truth. "Xavi, I really wanted to open my locked room, you know, the rooms in the Cave that we saw when we first got our armor. I didn't understand why it was taking so long for Ru to let us open it. And, I found the key . . . and . . . umm . . . I took it."

Xavier's mouth dropped open. "You *took* it?"

Evan nodded. "I was just going to open the door and take a peek inside, just to see what was in there. And then put the key right back. But somehow or other I didn't get a chance and then . . ."

"Then what?"

"Then we came back to earth."

Xavier's gaping mouth closed. "You brought the key to *earth*?"

"Yeah. I knew it was against the rules Ru gave us. We aren't supposed to bring anything back from Ahoratos to earth. But it was sort of an accident."

"But you fixed it all, right? I mean, you're the one who opened the quaritan and stopped the unseen invasion of the rec center. So—everything was fixed, right?"

"Not exactly. Ru said there are always consequences for every action, sometimes even after we make things right." Evan pointed to the blank TV screen. "I'm wondering if this is it. That skypod probably came through the portal I opened." Evan's head dropped, tears forming in his eyes. "It's all my fault."

Xavier wanted to be mad. Evan was always getting them into trouble. His goofing off on the Mountain of Rhema had awakened those angry trees. Now this. A portal opened. Skypods falling to earth. Xavier liked rules, and he was good at following them. But Evan never thought things through. Now he was making them all suffer. It was just too much.

But seeing Evan's tears, knowing how badly he felt about all that had happened, Xavier couldn't be angry with him. He sighed, putting an arm around his brother.

"Look, Van, it's okay. I mean, it *will* be okay. Ruwach will fix this. And as long as no one messes with the skypod, the Ents won't be able to get out."

"Are you sure?"

"Pretty sure, I guess. Don't worry; everything's going to be fine."

Evan wiped his tear-streaked face. "I hope so."

"Let's go get some lunch," said Xavier, coaxing him up.

"No thanks," said Evan. "I'm not hungry anymore."

The kids returned to the Rec early the next morning for more sword-fighting lessons. Mr. J. Ar, Rook, and Grandpa Tony focused on Forger fighting this time.

"As Evan pointed out yesterday," Mr. J. Ar began, "Forgers don't fight with swords. Their mission is to grab and hold and turn you into metal. In order to kill a Forger, you have to go straight through its chest or cut off its head. This is easier said than done, since the Forgers are a whole lot bigger than you are, and they have massive arms. If you go for the legs, you might be able to knock them over, so you can thrust the sword through. Remember: Forgers are not flesh and blood. They are not human. Only metal."

"Flesh and blood?" asked Brianna. "I got an instruction on my phone about that this morning when I woke up." She fished out her phone and opened the page. "Here it is: *Do not fight flesh and blood. Fight the darkness in the unseen world.*"

"Exactly. Remember that. Stand your ground. Be brave."

Mr. J. Ar and Rook demonstrated a Forger attack, with Mr. J. Ar pretending to be the Forger. The kids thought it was hilarious, even though Mr. J. Ar was trying to be really scary. Then they broke up into groups again and practiced Forger-fighting techniques.

During their break in the main room of the Rec, Brianna brought up the subject of the skypods.

"They found two more," she said. "One at the high school football field and one in the grocery store parking lot right in town!"

"Oh, no!" said Ivy. "More of them? It's an epidemic!"

"They've figured out the skypods aren't bombs," said Xavier, who had been watching the news nonstop since the story broke. "Something about the size and weight of them. And they are organic, even though no one can figure out where they came from."

"My dad is really excited," Manuel said. "He got a phone call yesterday from the agency that is handling the skypods. They want him to come and examine them personally. Because he's a geologist, I guess. And a professor at the college." Manuel sighed. "He's going over to the high school this afternoon. I haven't seen him this energized in a long time."

"You should go with him," Xavier said. "Will he let you?"

"Maybe. He usually likes to work alone, but I'll ask," Manuel said.

"Great. Let us know what he says about it."

Manuel nodded. "I will."

———————

Evan tried to concentrate on the sword fighting when they started practicing again, but his mind kept returning to the skypods. He felt responsible. He had to undo what he did, somehow. But he had no idea how. He wished Ru would call them back to Ahoratos, so he could ask him.

He knew there was a way to get to Ahoratos without being called by the Crest, but he didn't know what it was. Mr. J. Ar knew, and Rook knew, because they both went to Ahoratos whenever they wanted to. But they hadn't told the kids yet. It seemed to be some deep secret that "they had to figure out for themselves." As usual.

"Time for some practice bouts," Mr. J. Ar announced suddenly, calling all the kids together. "Pair up: Finn and Xavier, Manuel and Ivy, Brianna and Levi." Mr. J. Ar paused, realizing Evan was left out. "Evan, how about you spar with Rook?"

Evan nodded without energy. He followed Rook to a corner of the gym so they would have some room to work. Rook got into his sparring stance, but Evan just stood there, looking at the floor. Rook relaxed and bent down to see Evan's face.

"You okay, kid? You look worried about something."

"Uh, it's nothing."

"And by *nothing*, do you mean the pods coming through a portal you might have opened?"

Evan stared at Rook. "How did you—?" Then he shook his head. Of course Rook knew. Evan had almost forgotten how Rook had been there the whole time; he'd protected Evan from the Ents in the Quaritan Field. He'd probably known all along that Evan had that key in his pocket, which had made him a prime target for the enemy.

Evan sighed. "It's my fault that those pods are here. I need to get back to the Cave and talk to Ru. I need to find out how to get rid of them. Before something terrible happens." He raised pleading eyes to Rook. "Can't you show me how to get there? Please?"

Rook took a breath, thinking it over. "It's really not up to me to tell you that. If Ruwach hasn't told you yet, it's because you don't need to know yet. And anyway, the best thing for you to do right now is the assignment that Ruwach has given you: learn to use your sword."

Evan nodded. "I guess so."

"So," Rook said, raising his sword again. "Let's practice."

CHAPTER 12

Fact or Fiction

Manuel rode with his father to the high school, where the latest skypod had been found. He was relieved his father had allowed him to come along. "They will think you are too young, so I will tell them you are my assistant," said Mr. Santos. He seemed more like his old self, laughing and even joking with Manuel. For the first time in a long time he was really excited about something.

Manuel held half a dozen field manuals in his lap that his father had insisted he bring along. Mr. Santos did not care much for computers or other "newfangled" gadgets, as he referred to them. He loved his dusty old books.

Manuel opened the top book and glanced through it. His father's writing was everywhere—notes in the margins, cross outs where he had rewritten a sentence or a description under a picture. Obviously Mr. Santos didn't agree with the author of the book on a few things.

Manuel noticed the book in question dealt with meteorites and other "space rocks."

"Do you think it's a meteorite?" he asked his father.

"It does not look like any I have seen," Mr. Santos said as he drove. "A meteorite of that size would have created a huge crater in the earth upon landing, but this rock is just resting on the ground. The largest meteorite ever found on earth was nine feet long and weighed sixty-six tons. This one is twenty times that size at least. How could it just have fallen to the ground without creating a crater? I do not understand."

"Maybe it's a porous rock," Manuel suggested. "That would be much lighter."

"Impossible," said Mr. Santos. "Unless it came from a volcano. And the nearest volcano is two hundred miles away."

"You're right," said Manuel. It had been a long time since he and his father had had a conversation like this. Manuel missed that. They used to talk about rocks all the time. From the time Manuel could walk, his father took him on mineral and geode hunts all over the country. They even went gold prospecting once. Mr. Santos taught Manuel how to spot veins of gold and silver in granite. How to tell different types of quartz. If his mother was with them, she would talk about the plants they saw along the way and how some plants could actually grow inside the tiniest cracks in rocks. Sometimes they stayed out for so long that Manuel would complain that he was hot or tired and wanted to leave. Now he wished he could go back, just once more.

Mr. Santos had to park pretty far away, because the whole block was jammed with government vehicles, news vans, and police cars. The police had set up a cordon to keep curious onlookers away from the mysterious rock. A very tall fence made of plastic had been erected around the whole site, although the pod was so huge that most of it was still plainly visible.

Mr. Santos pulled into a convenience store parking lot and grabbed his bag of tools—hammers, chisels, and a Geiger counter. He exited the car and hurried over to the high school. Manuel, carrying the books, struggled to keep up. A policeman stopped them at the yellow tape line.

"I'm sorry, sir, this site is off-limits."

"My name is Aarón Santos. I am a geologist. I was called here to examine the specimen."

"Okay, just a minute, I'll check," said the cop. He turned away and clicked on his shoulder radio, talking for a minute and listening to the response. Finally, he turned back. "Someone is coming to get you," he said.

A minute later, an older man in an official looking jacket came running over to the taped line. "Ah, Mr. Santos!" he said, waving a clipboard around like it was a conductor's baton. "Thank you for coming! Come through, please! Let him through!"

Mr. Santos and Manuel ducked under the yellow tape and entered the enclosure. Manuel suddenly felt very important to be "inside" where the action was.

"I am Joseph Von," said the man with much excitement. "We spoke on the phone." He shook Mr. Santos's hand vigorously. He was much shorter than Manuel's father, with a thick mustache and bushy eyebrows that wiggled about like frantic caterpillars.

"This is my son, Manuel," said Mr. Santos. "He's quite a good scientist himself."

Manuel beamed up at the man, pleased his father had complimented him. He didn't do that very often. "How do you do?"

"Nice to meet you, Manuel. That is a lot of books you are carrying."

"Yes, sir."

Mr. Von gave him an indulgent smile and turned back to his father. "Mr. Santos, we have determined that the specimen is not radioactive. We've had zero readings on our Geiger counters. Nor can we find any evidence of a biohazard threat. But we still know nothing of its composition. We need you to tell us if it is indeed extra-terrestrial. As a precaution, we will have you put on a hazmat suit. Perhaps your son should wait here. . . ."

"Please let me come," said Manuel, fearful that he would be left behind. "I can wear a suit too. Please, Papá."

"Fine, fine," said Mr. Santos. "It will be a good experience."

Another official brought hazmat suits for Manuel and his father. Manuel set the books down so he could put on the suit. He decided to leave the books behind as they proceeded inside the plastic fencing. They were getting a little too heavy anyway.

There was the rock, the skypod, standing before them. Manuel had never seen one up close before. It was so much bigger than it looked when it was actually in the sky over Ahoratos.

Mr. Santos approached the rock with caution and ran his hand over the surface. It was lumpy but over-lain with a smooth coating. It reminded Manuel of a peanut butter ball dipped in chocolate, like the ones his mamá used to make. Mr. Santos opened his bag of tools and took out a chisel and hammer. He set the chisel against the rock and hit it with his hammer several times, but he could not even make a dent in it.

"Hmmm. Extremely dense. Which is consistent with a meteorite," he said, talking mostly to himself. "The surface is smooth, almost shiny—caused by the outer layer melting when it comes through the atmosphere."

"So it is a space rock?" said Mr. Von hopefully.

"I can't say for sure yet. We must discern the composition. All meteorites contain massive amounts of iron." Mr. Santos pulled a large magnet from his bag and held it to the rock. But the magnet was not attracted at all.

"No attraction, therefore no iron," said Mr. Santos, his eyebrows knitted together. "Very strange. I would suggest taking a core sample."

"You mean—drill into it?"

Manuel whirled around to his father. "No, don't do that!"

"Manuel, do not interfere."

"No, Papá, seriously, don't drill into that rock."

Mr. Santos looked at his son curiously. "Why not?"

"Because—it might be dangerous. There might be something dangerous inside." Manuel felt the panic rise up to his throat, remembering what he knew about the skypods being filled with Ents.

"Nothing organic could possibly survive inside a solid rock," said Mr. Santos. "You should know that, Manuel."

"What if it isn't solid? What if it is hollow? Like a geode. That would explain its apparent lightness—"

"You know as well as I do, Manuel, that meteorites are far denser than earth rocks," said Mr. Santos with a growing edge in his voice. "This rock definitely came through an atmospheric barrier. It is not of this earth."

Manuel struggled for some other excuse to delay this operation. "But you would need a very powerful drill—this rock is too hard for an ordinary drill."

"Yes, we will need some very heavy-duty drilling equipment. But there are companies that specialize in such things. Like the drill that was used to free those men trapped in the collapsed mine a few years ago."

"Oh, yes, I remember that story!" said Mr. Von. "Quite remarkable. I will make inquiries."

"I doubt there are any in this area," Manuel said.

Mr. Santos ignored him. "Check with the local quarries. They may have a truck-mounted drill available. They would need at least a five-inch drill bit. Bigger, if you can find one."

Mr. Von pulled out his cell phone and began talking into it. "We need to get a drill, as big as you can find. . . ."

Mr. Santos left the area and returned to the place where they had put on the hazmat suits. After they had taken them off, Manuel picked up the pile of books and followed his father back to the car, all the while wondering what to do now.

Ruwach, please, help me! He knew that somehow Ruwach could hear his unspoken plea.

"Papá, can I talk to you about something?" he said finally. Mr. Santos turned to look at him, a trace of annoyance on his face.

"What now?"

"That rock—haven't you seen it somewhere before?"

"Seen it somewhere? In one of my books, you mean?" He pointed to the pile of books Manuel held.

"No, not these. In—the Prince Warrior book."

Mr. Santos said nothing, a strange look spreading across his face.

"Papá, it's a skypod! From Ahoratos!"

Manuel could not tell exactly what his father was thinking. But he knew his father understood what he was talking about.

"Nonsense," Mr. Santos said, turning away. "All that is nonsense. Fairy tales. Your mother—"

"What about Mamá?" Manuel said. "She told you, didn't she?"

Mr. Santos paused, at a loss for words. Then he quickly walked to the car without answering.

———

As soon as he got home, Manuel texted Evan and Xavier to tell them what his father was planning to do with the skypod. Xavier, who must have had the phone that the two brothers shared, replied back immediately: *We can't let that happen.*

Manuel knew this. But how could he stop it from happening? Could he go up against his own father, let alone a government agency?

Manuel thought about his father's reaction at the mention of the name *Ahoratos*. There had been disgust in his eyes. But fear as well. His father was a good man. He was very smart. Yet he had changed the Prince Warrior book. Made corrections to it. Mr. Santos didn't believe in the Prince Warrior book. He thought it was a fairy tale. He didn't believe in Ahoratos either, even though he knew all about it. How could he know and not believe?

Manuel loved science more than anything. He loved forming a hypothesis and working toward proving it by the scientific method. He loved rational explanations for things that made sense according to the laws of nature.

And yet, he had been to Ahoratos; he had seen things he could never explain with science alone. A tiny seed that stopped the destruction of the terrible flaming Olethron. Water that led to a dry, mysterious cave. Boots that sprouted spikes. A mountain that breathed. Ruwach himself, a smallish, otherworldly being who had given Manuel and his friends purpose and courage and power. Ahoratos was a real place. And the enemy was real too.

But Manuel's father dismissed this power as a fantasy. Perhaps because it had failed to save his mother.

Manuel pulled his Prince Warrior book from the shelf and opened it. He looked through the gilded pages, marveling at the beautiful illustrations. He wondered why his mamá had died. She'd been sick for a long time. But couldn't the power of the Source—the power that had stopped the Olethron and the Ents—and the wisdom of Ruwach have stopped her sickness too?

Suddenly his phone buzzed in his pocket. He took it out, surprised to see the UNSEEN app already opened, with a message on the screen:

Lean not on your own understanding.

It was as if Ruwach had heard his question, even though Manuel hadn't spoken out loud. He felt a certain peace in the words, despite the fact that his heart still ached for his mamá—and for his papá too.

"If only I could help my papá," Manuel whispered aloud.

A voice in his head whispered back to him:

You will.

CHAPTER 13

Viktor

Xavier's lunch table buzzed with the latest theories about the origins of the mysterious rocks. Xavier listening quietly, eating his fried bologna sandwich layered with cheese, lettuce, and tomato—the same sandwich his father always ate when he was growing up. At least, that's what his father always told him.

"I think they're spaceships," said Eddie, the kid with the freckles. "Disguised as rocks. So they can observe us without us knowing about it."

"Spaceships don't look like huge rocks," said Carleen, twirling one of her braids between two fingers.

"How do you know? You ever seen an alien spaceship before?"

"My dad says it's a government cover-up," said Kevin, the class know-it-all. "Like Roswell. Pretending there are aliens to hide what they're really up to."

Xavier didn't say a word. He couldn't tell these kids that he knew what the rocks were. And that he knew how dangerous they were. They wouldn't believe him anyway.

He wished Ruwach would call them back to Ahoratos so they could figure out a plan for getting rid of the pods before Mr. Santos started drilling. He didn't understand why Ruwach hadn't done that yet. This seemed like a bigger crisis than all the previous ones put together.

"You trying out today?" asked Eddie. Xavier realized he was talking to him. "For the basketball team?"

"Yeah. You?"

Eddie shrugged. "Yeah. Probably won't make it though."

"Why? Is the team that good?"

"Yeah, pretty good. We went all the way to the finals last year. Didn't win though. Coach really wants a championship."

Xavier felt a knot of anxiety form in his stomach. He was the best player at the Rec, but here at this new school it might be a totally different story. What if he wasn't good enough? What if he messed up the try-outs? What if he didn't make the team? His brother would probably never stop making fun of him.

His sandwich suddenly tasted like cement in his mouth. He picked up a carton of milk and drained it.

The day dragged on, each minute like a wrecking ball on Xavier's nerves. When the last bell rang, he hurried to the locker room to put on his gym clothes. Then he followed the other kids to the gym and started doing warm-ups on the court. The coach came in, a tall guy with a slight potbelly, carrying a clipboard. When he blew his whistle all the kids stopped what they were doing and went to sit on the bleachers. Xavier followed along, trying to laugh and joke with the other kids so they wouldn't know how nervous he was.

"I'm Coach Thompson," said the man once all the boys were settled. "My assistant, Ms. Field, and I will be running tryouts today." He pointed to a younger, very fit woman holding a pile of numbered stickers. "We don't have many open spots this year, so if you don't make the team make sure to try again next year."

Coach Thompson quickly took attendance. Then Ms. Field began handing out the large numbers, instructing the kids to stick them on their shirts.

"These are your numbers during tryouts. Makes it easier for me to call on you, since I don't know all your names yet. Put them on and line up for layup drills. Let's roll, people!"

Just then another kid came out of the locker room, bouncing a basketball slowly. Xavier stared at the kid—he'd never seen him before. He was taller than even Xavier, with a darker complexion. He looked a little bit like Manuel. But unlike Manuel, this kid was very athletic looking. He had a muscular physique and a lean, hungry walk. He also looked a bit older than the other eighth graders. Maybe he'd started school later. His dark hair was shaved in the back but long in the front, falling into his eyes. Xavier wondered how he could even see where he was going.

"Sorry I'm late," he said, as if he owned the place. Coach Thompson blew his whistle again and walked over to the kid.

"Who are you?"

"Viktor. Viktor . . . Daimon."

"You're not on my sheet, Viktor."

"Oh, yeah, sorry. Today was my first day of school."

"Oh, you just moved to town?"

"You could say that." Viktor smirked.

"Where from?"

"Oh . . . up north."

"Really? No one told me about you. Typical. Welcome to Cedar Creek Middle School, Viktor. Okay, grab a number from Ms. Field and line up with the others. Let's get started!"

The tryouts began with layup drills. Xavier kept an eye on Viktor. He was good. *Really* good. Xavier felt that knot in his stomach grow to the size of a basketball. From the layups they went on to shooting drills, passing drills, rebounding drills, and weave pattern drills. Viktor did every drill perfectly, and every time he shot a basket, he made it. Xavier, trying his best, made quite a few baskets but not all of them. *I'm just too nervous*, he thought to himself. The anxiety of trying out, coupled with this new kid's amazing skills, had started to rattle him.

After each drill, some players were eliminated until there were only six left, including Xavier and Viktor. They stood together in a line, waiting for their next instructions.

Viktor leaned over to whisper to Xavier. "When's the last time that coach ran a mile?"

Xavier snickered but didn't answer.

The coach walked over to them, holding his whistle as if ready to blow it any second. "Okay, we're gonna do a scrimmage now, 3-on-3. You, you, and you"—he pointed to Xavier and two other boys—"you're blue. You three are red." He pointed to Viktor and the two other kids.

Viktor leaned over to whisper to Xavier again. "Never put the best on the same team, right?" Then he went to join the two other kids, attaching red markers to their chests to designate their team.

Xavier felt a surge of pride. Obviously, Viktor thought he was good, or he wouldn't have said it. He felt his confidence return.

But it was dashed as soon as the scrimmage began. Viktor ran rings around him, literally. The kid seemed to be able to move forward and sideways at the same time, dribbling the ball like it was magnetized to his arm. On defense he was equally ferocious, batting away Xavier's jump shot right at the rim. It was clear Viktor didn't even need his two teammates. He could do it all himself.

It wasn't the way basketball should be played, Xavier thought. Basketball is a team sport. But Viktor just wanted to play Hero-Ball—all by himself. The coach should have blown his whistle and called him on it. But the coach and his assistant were both too stunned by Viktor's performance to interfere.

Viktor's "team" won 20-8. Xavier felt utterly humiliated. But then Viktor came over to him and gave him a good-natured slap on the back.

"Nice moves, man," he said. "Not too many guys get any shots on me. Wanna hang out later?"

Xavier felt flattered to be asked by this cool kid who was practically a professional. He needed to take his mind off the tryouts anyway.

"Sure. I'm going to the Rec after this. Want to come?"

"The Rec? What's that?"

"Sorry, I mean the recreation center."

"Oh, right. No thanks. Sounds like something for little kids."

Xavier blushed. Maybe he was getting too old for the Rec. "It's pretty cool," he said. "We've got a great coach there, Mr. J. Ar—"

Viktor suddenly put up his hand. "Nah, I'll take a pass. Maybe next time. See you tomorrow, Xavier." He started to walk away.

"How'd you know my name?"

Viktor looked startled by the question. He glanced back at the coach and shrugged casually. "He said it." Viktor kept on walking.

Xavier watched him go, feeling a bit of confusion inside. He was pretty sure that Coach Thompson had never said their names during the tryout. He'd called them all by their numbers only.

After a moment, Xavier shrugged, shaking off the concern, and followed the others to the locker room.

CHAPTER 14

Beware the Wolf

When Xavier got to the Rec, Landon and some of his friends were playing basketball on the outside court. Xavier thought about joining them but changed his mind and went to the skatepark instead. It wasn't that he minded playing basketball with Landon, who used to be the biggest bully at the Rec. Ever since Levi had offered him his own shoes to wear, Landon had changed a lot. He didn't pick on other kids anymore. He didn't try to stir up trouble. But Landon was also a really good player, and Xavier didn't want to deal with more competition.

As Xavier approached the skatepark, Levi waved to him and did a backward nosegrind off the rails. Xavier grabbed a spare board and tried to do the same move

Levi had done. Levi made it look so easy; Xavier couldn't get the hang of it. Finally, he just gave up. After his experience on the basketball court that day, he didn't want to feel like a failure at anything else.

"How were tryouts?" Levi asked when they sat down on the bench for a rest.

"Okay, I guess," said Xavier.

"C'mon, you rocked it, right? You're the best."

"Not anymore." Xavier told Levi about Viktor, the new kid who had walked into the tryouts and blown everyone else out of the water, including him. "It would be my luck that this superstar kid shows up on the very day tryouts start, just to ruin my life."

"Hey, they need more than one player, right? I'm sure you'll still make it. What's this guy like anyway?"

"He's cool. He was actually pretty friendly. I invited him to the Rec, but he said it wasn't his thing."

"I'd like to meet him," Levi said.

"Come to tryouts tomorrow. I'm sure he'll be there."

"To try out?" Levi said with a laugh. "Basketball is not my game. But maybe I'll stop by and check it out."

"Hey, where's your dad today? I thought there was going to be a game on."

"Some big project at work, I guess. But he promised he'd be in later."

———

Levi went to the school gym to watch the tryouts the next day so he could see Viktor in action. He wasn't the only one. Several other kids, as well as other assistant coaches, had heard about Viktor and had come to see for themselves. Like Xavier, Levi was slightly amazed that this kid was really in middle school. He seemed so much older—maybe he'd flunked a grade or two. It was possible.

The coach skipped a lot of the drills that they'd done the day before and started doing 3-on-3s with Viktor on one team and Xavier on the other. Levi never saw Xavier work so hard at a game before, with so little result. Viktor never seemed to get tired. He never passed the ball to his teammates either. He could do right- and left-handed layups equally well, and his jump shot was truly unbelievable. At one point, when Xavier and both his teammates had succeeded in blocking Viktor at the edge of the court, he leapt up for a three-pointer and swished the net. It was an incredible shot.

Xavier did his best to slow Viktor down, and he did get some baskets, but he was clearly outmatched. The scrimmage ended 20-10.

"Hey, your team scored ten points," Levi said as Xavier slumped next to him on the bench. "That guy was working hard to block your shots, more than any of the others. So I'd say ten points is pretty good."

"Not really," said Xavier. Viktor came over and gave Xavier a high five, like they were best friends.

"Good job, buddy," he said. Levi was annoyed that Viktor called Xavier "buddy." It was a weird thing to say. He made it sound as if they were old friends, when they barely knew each other.

"This is Levi," Xavier said. "A friend of mine."

Viktor smiled, flipping out one hand in greeting. "What's up?" He tossed his hair off his forehead briefly, and Levi saw that his eyes were very light, which seemed strange for a guy with his dark coloring. They reminded him of those creepy dolls in horror movies that stare and stare without expression.

"Hey," said Levi. "Nice shooting."

"Just getting warmed up," said Viktor with a laugh. "You play?"

"Levi's more of a skateboarder," Xavier said.

"Oh, hey, can you show me some moves?" Viktor asked.

"Sure," Levi said, shrugging off the uneasy feeling that gnawed at him about this guy. He was really very friendly and likable. "Why don't you come to the Rec? There's a bus that goes from here right after school. It's got a sick skatepark."

"The Rec?" Viktor's eyes flickered a little, like he was wary of something. Levi found his hesitation curious. But before he had time to wonder about it, Viktor smiled, and the concerned expression vanished. "Why not? Sure. I'll be there tomorrow."

"Listen up, boys," the coach called out, making all the players look at him. "The team roster will be posted tomorrow morning on the bulletin board outside the gym. Practice starts Monday. Thank you all for trying out. Hit the showers."

The next day, the three boys rode the bus to the rec center after school. Viktor and Xavier sat together, talking about basketball. They had both made the team, along with three other boys who had tried out. Levi knew Xavier had been really nervous, but now he was just excited about playing on the team, especially with Viktor. Xavier seemed to have forgotten Levi even existed; he was so absorbed with everything Viktor said and did.

Levi sat by himself, looking out the window. Brianna and Ivy were on the bus as well, but they sat together talking about stuff girls talk about, and Levi didn't want to get involved in that. He would have even looked forward to talking to Manuel, even though he usually didn't understand half the stuff Manuel said. But Manuel wasn't on the bus that day.

The sun was out, although it was getting colder by the day. The leaves were almost gone from the trees now. Levi thought about the big pile of leaves that had turned into a portal and taken the Prince Warriors to Ahoratos only a few weeks ago. Had it only been a few weeks? Seemed like much longer.

He took out his phone and checked his messages. There was one from his dad: "Have to work late. Won't be at the Rec until later."

And then, without warning, the UNSEEN app on his phone opened and displayed a message:

Beware the wolf.

Levi stared at the message, wondering what it meant. Sometimes he got instructions on his phone that had to do with stuff he was going through at the time. But this message seemed really out of place. Beware? The wolf? What was that all about?

When Levi looked up again, he saw that Viktor was showing Xavier something on his phone. Levi leaned over the seat to see that Viktor was playing *Kingdom Quest*, Xavier and Evan's favorite game. And he was *killing* it. Xavier just stared at the phone, amazed at Viktor's skills. The kids sitting in front of them had turned around to see what they were doing. Even the kid sitting across from Viktor had leaned over to watch. By the time Viktor defeated level 9, which Levi had never seen anyone do before, the whole bus was cheering wildly. Viktor had not only conquered *Kingdom Quest*, he'd conquered the whole bus.

When they got to the Rec, the boys headed to the skate park, followed by a whole gaggle of bus kids who wanted to see what Viktor would do next. Brianna and Ivy went too, curious about the new kid.

"What's he like?" Brianna asked Levi.

"He's cool. Kind of—"

"Kind of what?"

"I don't know. There's something about him that seems . . . weird."

"He's cute," Brianna said; she and Ivy giggled. Levi gazed at her in surprise. Then he sighed, shaking his head. He'd never heard Brianna say anything like that about a boy before. Including him. Levi had always been pretty confident about himself, but all of the sudden this new guy was making him insecure. He didn't like the feeling.

Levi found a spare board for Viktor and started showing him how to skate. Brianna and Ivy stayed to watch, clearly interested in everything Viktor did. Levi felt like he wanted to show off a little, show those girls who the real skateboarder was.

But Viktor did every trick Levi taught him with ease. Within the hour he was doing ollies and kick flips like he had been skating all his life. Many of the other skateboarders had stopped to watch. Even Landon and his friends had come off the basketball court to see what was going on. Viktor was certainly good at attracting a crowd.

"That was awesome," said Brianna, going up to them when they stopped for a break. Viktor turned to her and flashed a smile.

"Thanks," he said. "Levi's a great teacher."

"I guess so. I'm Brianna, this is Ivy."

"Nice to meet you."

Levi did not like the way the girls were looking at Viktor. He tried to draw Viktor's attention away from them.

"Must have been hard to leave your old school," he said. "In the middle of the year."

"What?" Viktor looked perplexed, as if he wasn't sure what Levi was talking about. Then he nodded. "Oh, right. Yeah. I'm used to it though."

"You move a lot?"

"Oh, yeah. A lot. Never stay in one place very long." Viktor's smile gleamed.

Levi's phone beeped. He pulled it out and saw a text from his mom. He typed a quick reply and hit SEND. When he looked up again, he saw Viktor studying him intently.

"What happened to your finger?"

Levi glanced down at the hand that held the phone; the tip of his index finger was still scarred—marked with metal from his encounter with a Forger in Ahoratos. It resembled a burn against his brown skin, except that the mark was a dark gray and kind of shiny. He quickly shoved the phone back in his pocket, hiding his hand. "Nothing. Just an old scar." He saw the back door of the center open and Mr. J. Ar emerge, a whistle around his neck, ready to start a basketball game.

"There's my dad!" Levi said. "I'll go get him so you can meet him."

Levi trotted over to his dad, who was bouncing a ball as he headed for the outdoor court.

"Dad! Wait up!"

Mr. J. Ar turned. "Oh, there you are. What's up?"

"There's this kid—he's new, and he's really—interesting. I want you to meet him."

"Sure—where is he?"

Levi led his dad back to the skate park. But Viktor was nowhere to be seen. Xavier was trying to do the grinding trick Levi had taught him. Brianna and Ivy were sitting on the bench talking and checking their phones.

"Where is this new kid?" Mr. J. Ar asked.

"Uh—I don't know. He was here a minute ago," Levi said. He went over to the girls. "Where did Viktor go?"

Brianna looked around, perplexed. "He was just here. I don't know where he went."

Xavier skated up to them. "Hey, Mr. J. Ar, is there a game going?"

"Yep," said Mr. J. Ar. "You coming?"

"Yeah." Xavier jumped off the board and followed after him.

"You gonna play, Levi?" asked Mr. J. Ar.

"Uh . . ." There was something he wanted to tell his dad, something about Viktor that made him uneasy. But he thought it would just sound stupid, so he waved it off. "Maybe later."

CHAPTER 15

The Rooms

L evi woke up suddenly, sweat pouring down his neck.

Only a dream, he told himself. *It was only a dream.*

But his dreams were getting more intense and real. Forgers and dragons and . . . wolves. Wolves surrounding him, their teeth bared, saliva dripping from their mouths.

He got out of bed and went to the bathroom to get a glass of water. His mom always told him to do this when he woke up from a bad dream, ever since he was a little kid. It usually helped. But tonight it didn't. He still felt scared.

Beware the wolf.

That instruction still bothered him. Maybe that was why he was dreaming about wolves all of the sudden.

He drank the tepid water from the sink and went back to his bedroom. He didn't feel like going back to bed. He was wide awake. He glanced out the window and decided to go out to his tree house for a bit. Maybe being in a smaller space would make him feel safer.

He put on a sweatshirt and crawled out to the tree house. He turned on the battery-powered lantern (he'd remembered to change the batteries) and pulled out his Prince Warrior book, turning to the sword page. He took out the Krÿs, just to make sure it was still there.

He held it a moment, gazing at the small dull blade. It sure didn't look like much. No one who wasn't a Prince Warrior would think anything of it. He thought that was kind of funny—how a thing that seemed useless and boring could have more power than anyone could imagine. Forger-killing power.

He heard a low growling from somewhere outside the tree house. Probably the neighbor's dog again. Levi looked out the window. He couldn't see the dog anywhere. He turned back inside and froze. A huge creature hunched in his bedroom window, staring at him with glowing, yellow eyes, foam dripping from long, sharp yellow teeth.

A wolf.

Levi froze, the breath locked in his throat. The wolf jumped out of the window and onto the tree branch. It lowered its head as it slunk along the branch toward the tree house, growling in low, uneven rasps.

Levi scooted against the back wall of the tree house, still holding the Krÿs in one fist. Sweat poured down his face, dripping into his eyes. No place to run—he was trapped. The wolf paused at the edge of the tree house door and gathered itself, preparing to pounce.

Levi raised the Krÿs, his arm shaking. He could hear his father's voice in his head: *Be strong, be brave, hold steady.* He pressed the Krÿs to his chest just as the wolf lunged with a savage growl. But nothing happened. His heart dropped into his stomach like a ten-pound weight as he remembered that it wouldn't work. It couldn't. He wasn't wearing his breastplate. He saw the wolf's eyes gleam, its teeth bared, the savage growling filling Levi's ears. He huddled against the wall, still holding the small knife, and shut his eyes just as the wolf leapt—

Nothing happened.

Levi opened his eyes, one at a time. The wolf was gone. Vanished. Levi shook his head, trying to clear his vision. There was something else in the space where the wolf had been. The Crest. Rotating slowly, glowing as yellow as the wolf's eyes. Levi reached forward and grabbed hold of it. He felt himself melting, as if his body were turning to vapor, sucked into a tiny gap between the wooden planks of the tree house. Then the tree house disappeared. Levi was spinning, formless, and then sensing all his separate parts knitting together as the spinning lessened.

When it finally stopped, he was standing on the edge of a crater. It looked a great deal like the top of the Mountain of Rhema, except there was no fire or smoke inside the hole at the center of the crater. There was only water. Above him the sky was yellow, smeared with red-black clouds and dotted with skypods. He knew for certain that he was back in Ahoratos.

He felt a sudden wind at his back and turned to see Xavier standing beside him. Then Evan. Manuel, Brianna, and Ivy appeared a half second later, materializing like ghosts blown in by the wind. Each of them was holding a sword.

"I dreamed I saw—a wolf," said Brianna in a breathless voice.

"Me too," said Levi.

"Me too," said Ivy. The others only nodded, as if they too had seen a wolf but were too shocked to speak of it. "Then I saw the Crest. . . ."

Levi felt another sharp wind at his back, and then Finn appeared, also with his sword.

"Wolf?" asked Levi. Finn nodded.

"How did we get on the top of the mountain?" Evan whispered.

"I don't think this is the mountain," said Xavier. "At least not the same one. There's just water down there."

"It's *the* Water," said Manuel. "Look."

They could see then the Crest shimmering on the surface of the Water, reflecting the yellow-red of the sky.

"What are we waiting for? Let's go!" Evan shouted as he jumped off the ledge and slid down the sloping crater toward the Water. The others quickly followed.

Ruwach spread his long arms in welcome to the kids when they arrived in the Cave after going through the Water. As usual, they were completely dry and dressed in their warrior clothes and armor. "You stood up to the enemy and did not let your fear overcome you. You are doing well in your training."

"You mean the wolf—that wasn't real? It was just a test?" asked Ivy, her voice tinged with relief.

"I'm not too crazy about all these tests," Evan grumbled. Xavier nudged him.

"The wolf is very real," said Ruwach with an ominous note in his voice. "All trials are real and necessary. Now has come the time—"

"Ru, we want to know about the pods," Manuel said, interrupting. "My father wants to drill into one—I don't know how to stop him—"

"How did the pods get through the portal anyway?" asked Brianna. "Was it because of the Sypher I brought back?" Everyone looked at her; she shifted her gaze to the floor.

Evan stepped forward. "No, Brianna. It was my fault," he said glumly. "I did it, didn't I?"

"Not you alone, Prince Evan," Ruwach said. Everyone was silent for a moment, looking from one to the other as if wondering which one of them was to blame. "Something else was brought into this world and left behind." Ruwach's whole body turned toward Manuel.

"Me?" said Manuel, brows furrowed in confusion. Then his eyes widened, his mouth dropped open, the realization settling on him like an itchy woolen blanket. "My shield!" he said. "The one I made. But it was destroyed in the Olethron attack."

"Not completely." Ruwach raised his long arms in the air. Immediately the ceiling of the Cave disappeared, revealing a scene like a movie but with no sound. It was Manuel, on his knees on the hilltop, moments after the Olethron attack had ended. He was reaching to pick up a blackened shard of metal from the charred ground when it caught on his sleeve and cut his arm. Manuel saw himself grabbing his arm in pain and throwing back his head, mouthing the words "it's destroyed" and tossing the fragment away. Then the scene faded, the ceiling turning back to solid stone.

Manuel shook his head sadly. "I forgot about that. I didn't realize. . . . But what harm could one little piece of metal do?"

"The enemy will create chaos from any small thing. Even a scrap. It is not the object that causes the problem so much as—the choice. Do you understand?"

"The choice I made," said Manuel, his voice trembling with regret. "I'm so sorry. I wish I'd never made that stupid shield."

"It's okay, Manuel," said Ivy. "We've all made mistakes."

"Yeah," said Finn. "Definitely."

"You can say that again," mumbled Evan.

"So what can we do? About the pods?" Xavier asked.

"And when are we going to be in a battle?" Evan asked. He figured they'd had enough of practicing and tests; it was time for the real thing.

Ruwach raised his arms to quiet them. "Your questions will be answered in a little while. But first, you have a choice to make. Follow me." Ruwach turned swiftly, heading for one of the tunnels that ringed the Cave.

The kids, baffled by his abrupt departure, hurried to follow. Ruwach picked up speed as he led them down the winding tunnel, which lit up purple as he went. They turned one corner after another, their footsteps echoing down the long corridor. Soon the kids found themselves racing down a hallway that looked familiar.

"The Hall of Armor!" Evan said breathlessly.

They passed hundreds of sets of armor arrayed on the walls, each one different, some familiar and some very strange, although they were going too fast to read the placards accompanying each one.

Suddenly Ruwach stopped, and the kids skidded to a halt behind him. They recognized their own armor displayed on the walls, a placard under each one inscribed with their names and birthdates. It was funny to see the armor there on the wall, when they were actually wearing it at the same time.

Beside each suit of armor there was a padlocked door. After all this time, the kids still had no idea what was behind those doors, for Ruwach had refused to tell them or let them see. The doors had haunted them ever since they'd first seen them—taunting them with the promise of hidden treasure. Even though Ruwach had told them repeatedly that they had everything they needed to wage war against the enemy, it was each Prince Warrior's dream to finally open his or her door.

Ruwach reached into his sleeve and removed a key. It was a strange-looking key with four twisted cross-pieces on the stem. None of the kids had ever seen it—except for Evan. He recognized it immediately: this was the key he had "borrowed" and accidentally taken to earth. He shrank back a little at the sight of it.

Ruwach held the key in his illuminated hand. "Now you may choose to open your rooms."

"Choose?" asked Evan.

"Remember what you have learned." Ruwach said nothing more than that.

The kids were silent a moment, not believing the day had come. If they wanted, they could see what was behind those mysterious doors. More weapons or armor? There had to be a reason why the enemy had wanted that key so badly in the first place when he'd tricked Rook into stealing it for him.

Now, finally, they were being given the chance. The kids gathered around the key, each waiting for the other to grab it first. No one moved for a long time.

Then Xavier stepped forward. He reached out and took the key from Ruwach's hand. He held it up, surprised that when he looked at Ruwach's hand again, the key was still there.

"There are two keys?"

"There are as many as are required," said Ruwach.

Xavier shrugged—this was Ahoratos, after all; anything could happen. One by one the other kids stepped forward to take a key: Ivy, Brianna, Manuel, and Finn. Then Evan took his turn, reaching out for the key. There was still a key left in Ruwach's hand when they were done.

Levi's key.

Levi started to reach for the key when Ruwach's often-repeated words echoed in his ears: *You already have everything you need.*

If that were true, if he truly believed it, then why did he need whatever was behind that door? Perhaps this was a chance to prove to Ruwach, to prove to all of them, that he was willing to live by those words.

He took a step backward. "No," he said.

The others looked at him curiously. "What's the matter, Levi?" asked Brianna. "Don't you want to see what's in your room?"

"Yeah, I do. But—I have everything I need."

Ruwach nodded and withdrew his hand. Levi watched the key disappear back into Ruwach's robe. He expected to feel disappointed; instead he felt relieved. And a little encouraged: Ruwach's quick retraction of his key gave him the feeling that he had made the right choice.

Xavier went to his door, staring at it a long moment. He took a breath and slid the key into the lock. He held it there a few seconds. There was still time to take it out, to give it back to Ruwach. To do what Levi had done.

But then, for some reason, he thought of Viktor. Viktor had made him feel that he didn't have everything he needed after all. For the first time in a long time, Xavier had felt inadequate and insecure. Like what he had and who he was wasn't quite enough. He had to be better somehow. Faster, smarter, more skilled. He had to know for sure that he could really make it in the world—in either world, earth or Ahoratos.

He turned the key slowly until he heard a click. Unlocked. Xavier felt his heart beating heavily in his chest; he wondered if the other kids felt the same, but he didn't look around to see. Instead, he took hold of the handle and pushed open the door.

When he did, there was a brilliant flash, like the burst of a camera bulb, inches from his face. Only Xavier didn't see it.

In fact, he didn't see anything.

Because the room . . . was empty.

CHAPTER 16

The Gift

Xavier thought he must be mistaken. He took a few steps inside the long, narrow room, looking around in speechless disbelief. How could this be? Four bare walls. Nothing on the floor. Nothing hanging from the low ceiling. Empty.

"Hey!" Xavier heard Evan's indignant cry and went over to see what was in his room. He hoped that Evan would have gotten *something*, maybe even enough that he'd be willing to share some of it with his older brother. But as soon as Xavier looked inside, his face and his heart fell. Evan's room was exactly the same.

"There's nothing here!" Evan blurted.

"Mine's empty too," said Brianna.

"Mine too," said Ivy, disappointed.

"Perhaps there is a secret compartment—" Manuel began knocking on the walls and floor of his empty room, checking for a trap door or a hidden alcove.

"I don't get it," said Ivy. "Why was Ponéros so interested in the key if the rooms were empty?"

"That's a good question, Princess Ivy," said Ruwach.

"This stinks!" moaned Evan.

Brianna shook her head. "This just doesn't make sense. All this time we've been wanting to open these rooms, for no reason at all."

"There is always a reason for everything," Ruwach responded. He raised one of his draped arms. A bright light shone from the far end of the long tunnel, and suddenly The Book was speeding toward them. It stopped in front of Ruwach, hovering on its glowing pedestal. Ruwach raised his arms and waved them over The Book like a conductor of an orchestra. The Book produced a series of musical notes as the pages flipped open. Ornate letters lifted from the page and hovered in the air.

eB trlae

enmye dsreouv nda heT spowrl

Ruwach made another gesture and the letters rearranged to form words:

Be alert.

The enemy prowls and devours.

"Prowls?" asked Evan with a small shiver.
"Devours?" asked Brianna.
"Like—a wolf," murmured Levi.
"Or like the Ents," said Manuel. "If the pods open, the Ents inside will devour the whole town. There's no way we can protect everyone just by ourselves. Even with our swords."
"You have everything you need," Ruwach said, as serenely as ever. "Always remember that. Go now. Back to the Centrum. Wait for me there."
"The Centrum?" asked Evan. "What's that?"

"The main room of the Cave," said Ruwach. "Where we began. The Sparks will show you the way."

"You aren't coming?" asked Brianna, frowning a little.

"I will be there in a little while."

The kids started slowly down the tunnel, back the way they had come. As Levi followed, Ruwach put an arm out, blocking his path.

"Stay," Ruwach said.

Levi stood waiting. Ruwach did not move until the others had completely disappeared around a bend in the tunnel. Then he turned to Levi.

"You did not open your room."

Levi shrugged. "You said we had everything we needed."

Ruwach's hood nodded. Then he held out his glowing hand with the key. "Take it. Open your door."

"But I thought—"

"Open it."

Levi sighed and took the key from Ruwach's hand. And when he did, Ruwach's hand lay empty. There was no new key to replace it. Ruwach withdrew his hand into his sleeve.

Levi held the key a long time before going to his door. He'd seen the others' rooms. They had been completely and utterly empty. He wondered if his room could possibly have something in it that the others didn't.

Finally, he put the key in the lock and turned it. *Click.* The door creaked when he pushed it open. A blinding flash met his eyes, but unlike the others, he could see it. His eyes slammed shut. Slowly, he blinked back into focus, wiping away the tears that formed in response to the light. When he was finally able to open his eyes fully, he looked around the room—and sighed. It was empty.

Except for one thing.

A red object hovered in the center of the room, rotating slowly. It looked like a large gemstone, about the size of a softball. At first Levi thought it was *hanging* from the ceiling, but then he realized there was no string attached to it.

"That wasn't in the others' rooms," Levi said in a hushed tone.

"It was. Only they couldn't see it," said Ruwach.

"So why can I see it?"

"Go in."

Levi didn't hesitate. At Ruwach's command, he took a few steps inside, looking around at the blank walls. Suddenly the door closed behind him, making it completely dark in the room. He held his breath, unsure of what would happen next. The darkness around him felt very close, as if he could touch it. He had an urge to turn and run to the door and throw it open, to let in light, to get out. But he quelled the urge, breathing through his fear. His hand went to the hilt of the sword in his belt, the feel of it reassuring.

And then out of the dark the red gem began to glow, the light inside it pulsing like a heartbeat. Levi thought he could even hear it, feel it beating inside his own chest. The light soon became very bright, a steady beam shining in his eyes. But the beam did not blind him as the earlier flash had done; it made his eyes open even wider than before, melting away the darkness.

The light began to take on more colors, shapes, like the flickering images of an old movie. Soon he could make out familiar things. The gigantic beech tree at the rec center with its wide canopy. Brianna, huddled against the trunk of the tree, crying. He could see himself holding the helmet out to her, trying to make her put it on. This had happened not too long ago, yet now it was like he was standing on the outside looking in.

And then he saw something else. Something he had not seen that day when he and Brianna were underneath the tree: bright white light all around the two of them, like a halo. Before he could figure out where that light had come from, the vision faded.

It was replaced by a much darker scene: the black steel girders of the Fortress of Chaós. He saw himself and his friends creeping through the fortress, trying to find their way in the maze of girders while dozens of red eyes watched them. Forgers, all around them. Levi remembered how terrifying that was. But there was that strange white light again, surrounding him and his friends. He hadn't seen it then, but he could see it now.

The vision then changed to the chasm, when he and the other Prince Warriors had stepped out onto what looked like nothing at all, and stone steps had appeared under their feet. He saw them stepping, stone to stone, but the stones were not just hovering in midair—each stone had that same circle of light around it, as if this is what held it aloft.

Levi's eyes snapped shut, wearied from the vision, from the brightness of the light. His eyes started to water. He rubbed them in hopes they would recover from the strain of these visions.

But the next time he opened them, he saw himself, all alone, held in the grasp of the huge metal Forger while slowly sinking into the ground. He saw himself crying out for help. But no help came. He remembered how alone and powerless he felt, sinking slowly, turning to metal. He wanted more than anything to forget that it ever happened. He wanted to turn away, to avoid being reminded of that day, the choice he had made to take the wide road, the path to destruction.

Before he could turn away, however, he was captivated once more—by light. There it was again. This time it was a beam of light that rose from his mouth as he yelled to the top of the dome and beyond it, as if it were carrying his cries. He hadn't seen the light that day either. But he was seeing it now.

The beam of red suddenly retreated from Levi's eyes. He was unclear of what was really happening. He felt confused and unsure. Darkness fell around him again, replaced by the image of Ruwach fading into view. It took Levi a moment to realize that Ruwach was actually standing before him now, even though the door had remained closed.

"This is a gift given only to you, Prince Levi. Do not speak of it to the other children just yet."

"Gift?"

"Because you believed even though you did not see, you will now have the ability to see things that the others did not believe."

CHAPTER 17

Charming

Viktor stood on the sidewalk outside the rec center, surveying the parking lot. He could see that Mr. J. Ar's SUV was not there. And Rook wasn't working today, because the Cedar Creek Landscaping truck was not there either. All clear. No older Prince Warriors to hinder his plans. He'd been avoiding them at all costs. Although he was sure that the adults wouldn't know his true identity, if they got a good look at him they might suspect he was not "one of them." He wasn't about to take that chance.

He opened the front door and went into the building. A group of younger girls were sitting at one table, making Christmas ornaments with paper and glue and lots of glitter. A young woman with a blond ponytail was helping them, looking slightly harassed. Other kids sat together playing board games. A few were playing games on their phones. Viktor scanned the faces, searching for one of the Prince Warriors. Then he saw Manuel, the one with the buzz cut and the glasses, sitting all alone, reading a thick book. This was the one who had so conveniently left his DNA and clothing threads on the shard of metal in Ahoratos. Viktor smiled to himself. *Perfect.* He started to move toward Manuel.

"Can I help you?"

Viktor turned to see the young woman looking at him rather sternly, glitter sprinkled over her face and hair. She had a Starbucks cup in one hand and a phone in the other. He gave her his most charming smile.

"Hi. I'm Viktor. Pleased to meet you." He stuck out his hand. She looked at it, unable to take it because her hands were full. But her stern expression melted, and she smiled back.

"Oh, Viktor! I've heard a lot about you! A friend of Xavier's?"

"That's right. We're teammates at school. Basketball."

"Oh, right! I haven't seen Xavier today—maybe he's out back playing ball. I'm Mary, by the way. Miss Stanton."

"Are you the manager here?"

"Yes, well, only weekends now. I have school during the week."

"Are you in college?" Viktor widened his eyes to make Miss Stanton think he was really impressed. "I hope I can go to college one day."

"Oh, I'm sure you will," she said. "Anything I can help you with, just let me know!"

"That's awesome, Mary. I mean, Miss Stanton. Thanks."

She smiled and went back to deal with the girls, who were now fighting over the glitter and getting it everywhere. Viktor made his way to Manuel.

"Hi," he said.

Manuel looked up, focusing. "Hello?"

"I'm Viktor. Friend of Xavier's. We're on the basketball team. You're Manuel, right?"

"Uh . . . yes . . ."

Viktor sat down beside him. "Maybe you can help me out."

"What do you mean?"

"I hear you're really good at science? Well, I'm sort of failing science. And if I fail, I'll get kicked off the basketball team. So I need a tutor. Someone to help me pass the midterms."

"Aren't you in eighth grade? I'm only in seventh."

"Yeah, but you're really smart. People tell me you're the smartest kid in the whole school. I'm sure even the eighth-grade curriculum is way below your abilities."

An eager smile crossed Manuel's face. "Well, that may be true—"

"The test is on Monday," Viktor said. "So I was hoping we could get together this weekend sometime. I could come to your house?"

"I . . . suppose so."

"Great. How about later today?"

"I have to check with my dad—"

"Okay, super. Let me know when you find out." Viktor glanced up and saw Brianna and Ivy through the window. Brianna had a puppy on a leash. *Perfect timing,* he thought. "See you later." He got up to go to the back door.

"But wait . . . you don't even know where I live!"

———

The back doors of the Rec flew open just as Brianna and Ivy walked by. Viktor was in the doorway. He smiled when he saw them.

"Hey," he said. "Brianna, right? And Ivy?"

"Oh, hey Viktor," said Brianna with a shy smile.

"Hey," said Ivy, blushing.

Star, Brianna's puppy, wasn't as pleased to see Viktor. She barked and growled, straining against the leash.

"Star, stop that!" Brianna said, pulling the dog back. She glanced up at Viktor and smiled apologetically. "I'm sorry. She's not usually like that. But she's never been to the Rec before, so she's just nervous."

"No problem," Viktor said. He bent down, putting a hand out to the dog. "Hey, pup. What's the matter? Don't be afraid. I'm not going to hurt you." Star hesitated, then stuck her nose out and sniffed at Viktor's hand. "That's a good girl." Viktor rubbed her behind the ears. "She's really cute. I had a dog too—but it died. Hit by a car."

"What? That's terrible!" said Ivy.

"Oh, you must be so sad," said Brianna.

Viktor sighed, his eyes misting up. "Yeah. I miss him."

"Congratulations on making the basketball team," Ivy said.

"Oh, yeah," said Brianna. "Stellar."

"Thanks. Xavier is an awesome player. Where is he, anyway?"

"He's usually out on the court," said Ivy. She glanced over to the basketball court, but it was empty.

"Sometimes he has chores on Saturdays," said Brianna. "But he'll probably be here later."

"Oh." Viktor tried to look disappointed. "Is Levi doing chores too?"

"He's on his way," Brianna said. "He texted me and said his dad had to stop at work for something."

"Oh, right, well, maybe you two can help me. I found this yesterday, and I thought it must belong to one of them." Viktor pulled out a piece of rolled-up paper from his pocket. The paper looked yellowed and very delicate, like parchment. He unrolled it and showed it to them.

Brianna gasped. The words *Take Captives* were written on the paper in large, ornate lettering.

"Where did you find that?"

"Near that tree over there," Viktor said, pointing to the beech tree—the same tree where Levi and Ivy had saved her from Sypher.

Brianna took the scroll, puzzled. She tried to remember back: she had been under the beech tree with that Sypher on her neck, and Levi had been trying to make her put on the helmet to get rid of it. But she didn't remember the scroll being there too. He had tried to give her that scroll before, for her birthday. It was a message from Ruwach. But she had thrown it away. Had Levi picked it up? And did he have it with him that day under the beech tree?

"So, you've seen it before?" Viktor said, a slow smile spreading across his face.

"Uh—no, not really." Brianna stole a glance at Ivy, who just shook her head very slightly. "Nope. Never saw it before."

"Oh—so you don't know anything about Ahoratos, I guess, huh?"

Both girls stared at him. Then looked at each other, their mouths falling open in unison. Then Ivy turned back to Viktor.

"How do you know about Ahoratos?" she asked in a whisper.

Viktor shrugged. "Because I've been there."

"You have?"

Viktor looked from one to the other. "You have too, right?"

The girls slowly nodded. Viktor smiled.

"You're Princess Warriors? Seriously? Wow, what a coincidence." Viktor shook his head, laughing. The girls started laughing as well.

"Xavier and his brother, Evan, are Prince Warriors too," said Brianna. "Did you know about that?"

"No way!" said Viktor. "And Levi too?"

"Yep. And Manuel."

"Wow. Crazy. So this must be one of yours then." He pointed to the scroll. "Better hang on to that. Wouldn't want it falling into the wrong hands, know what I mean? Glad I found it for you."

"Yeah, thanks," said Brianna, stuffing the scroll into her coat pocket.

"Anytime. We should get together and talk about our trips to Ahoratos sometime, right?"

"Yeah, that would be cool," said Ivy.

"Yeah, stellar," said Brianna.

Viktor smiled again and sauntered away. The two girls watched him go.

"Pretty amazing," said Ivy. "I think he likes you a little."

Brianna nearly blushed. "I don't know about that. He was just trying to be nice. Can you believe he's a Prince Warrior?"

"Yeah. What a coincidence. Good thing he was the one who found that scroll."

"Yeah." Brianna gazed again at the beech tree. "I don't remember Levi having the scroll that day."

"I didn't see it either. But there was a whole lot going on that day. It probably was in the helmet and fell out when Levi dropped it."

"Yeah," Brianna murmured. "That's what I was thinking."

The back door opened, and Manuel stepped out. "Did you two talk to that kid Viktor?"

"Yeah, just now," said Brianna.

"He just asked me to help him study for his science test."

"He's a Prince Warrior," said Ivy. "He knows all about Ahoratos."

"Really? He didn't mention that to me."

"Well, it's not something a person just blurts out, you know."

"True, I suppose." Manuel pushed his glasses up his nose. "He's coming over to my house later."

"Oh, cool," said Ivy. "He kind of looks like you, Manuel. Hey, maybe we should go over too, huh Bri? We could use extra help with science." The two girls giggled. Then Ivy turned to Manuel, her face suddenly serious again. "How are things going with your dad? Is he still going to drill into one of the pods?"

Manuel nodded, frowning. "He's just waiting for them to find a drill big enough. But he goes every day to study them. He's becoming obsessed."

"They found another one—near the drive-in," said Brianna. "That makes four now."

Manuel nodded. "That's where he was going when he dropped me off here. He won't let me come with him anymore because . . ." he broke off.

"Because why?"

"Because he knows I know about Ahoratos. But he denies it. Says it's all made-up. I told him what the pods were, but he refuses to listen."

"What about the book? His Prince Warrior book? Have you had a chance to look at it again?"

Manuel shook his head. "He must have put it away somewhere. Because it's not on his desk anymore."

"Oh, well, don't worry, Manuel," said Brianna. "We'll figure this out. Together. Everything's going to be fine."

CHAPTER 18

Prowling

L evi jumped out of the car and raced into the rec center, bursting through the doors. Miss Stanton was so startled she dropped her Starbucks cup, not for the first time.

"Levi! What's the matter?" asked Miss Stanton, annoyed.

"Has Viktor been here?" Levi asked, searching the room.

"Yes, he's here. He went out back, I think." Miss Stanton bent down to clean up her spilled latte.

Levi dashed through the building and out the back doors. Brianna and Ivy were trying to teach the puppy how to sit, although Star was only interested in chasing dandelion puffs and stalking ladybugs.

"Bean! Have you seen Viktor?" Levi asked, running up to her.

"Yeah, he was here a little while ago," said Brianna. "I don't see him now. But he gave me this." Brianna showed Levi the scroll. "He said he found it by the beech tree. Levi, Viktor is a Prince Warrior! Just like us!"

"He is?" Levi took the scroll and stared at it, wrinkling his forehead. "How did he find this?"

"We think it must have gotten stuck in Brianna's helmet that day of the invasion, and you didn't realize it," said Ivy. "Good thing Viktor found it."

"Yeah . . . ummm . . . I guess so." Levi handed the scroll back to Brianna. "Did he say where he was going?"

"No . . . wait, yes! Manuel told us Viktor was going to his house later, for some tutoring in science. Looks like Manuel went home, so maybe he's there."

"Tutoring? But he's not even in Manuel's grade."

"I know. But Manuel is pretty smart about science stuff."

Levi thought about it. It was possible, of course. But something didn't feel quite right about it.

The back door of the center opened, and Xavier came out, bouncing a basketball.

"You guys seen Viktor?" he asked when he saw Levi and the girls. "He said he was coming to play."

"I've been looking for him too," said Levi.

"He was here, but I guess he left," said Brianna. "Went to Manuel's for tutoring."

"Oh." Xavier looked disappointed.

"There's something bothering me about that kid," Levi said. "I think we all should just steer clear of him."

Brianna and Ivy laughed. "Levi, what's gotten into you?" asked Brianna. "He's super nice. He just wants to make friends. And he's a Prince Warrior, so he's got to be on our side, doesn't he?"

"You just have a crush on him," said Levi, turning on her. He started imitating her voice. "Oh, he's so cute!"

Brianna scowled at him. "Stop it. I do not."

"He's a Prince Warrior?" asked Xavier, surprised and pleased. "He never told me that."

"Did he actually *say* he was a Prince Warrior?" asked Levi.

"Of course he did! Well, I don't know—but he said he had been to Ahoratos and he wanted to talk about our adventures and stuff."

"Levi, what's wrong?" asked Xavier. "Viktor's cool. And if he's a Prince Warrior, that's even better. Plus, he's helping me improve my game a ton—"

"Not everything is about basketball, Xavier," Levi said with a caustic edge in his voice.

Xavier opened his mouth, surprised. "Hey, man, just sayin'," he said. "Whatever. Later, dude." He turned away and headed for the basketball court.

"Levi, what's the matter with you today?" Brianna said. "You're acting really weird."

"Doesn't that kid strike you as a little bit—off? Like he shows up out of nowhere—"

"He moved here," Ivy said. "People do move, you know."

"He's way too good at everything. He's got these weird eyes—"

"Levi, are you *jealous* of Viktor?" Ivy asked, her eyes widening. She glanced at Brianna, and they both started giggling.

"No!" he barked. The girls stopped laughing.

"I've gotta go," said Brianna, giving him a cool look. "Grandpa Tony's coming to pick us up. See you later." She turned to Ivy. "You want to come over?"

"Sure."

The girls sauntered away. Neither of them invited Levi to come along.

Levi watched them walk off, anger churning in his stomach. Why wouldn't anyone listen to him? He needed more to go on. Proof that Viktor was no good.

Mr. J. Ar emerged from the center, a basketball under his arm and his whistle around his neck. Levi ran over to him.

"Dad, can you give me a ride to Manuel's house?"

"Not right now, I've got a game going," said Mr. J. Ar. "Maybe in an hour, okay?"

Levi's shoulders slumped. "Okay."

Mr. J. Ar headed off to the basketball court.

Levi took out his phone and texted Manuel.

Watch out for Viktor. He may be a prowling wolf.

And he hit SEND.

CHAPTER 19

Questions

Manuel opened his front door to find Viktor standing there, a backpack slung over one shoulder.

"Hey! Thanks for letting me come over."

"I wasn't sure you were coming. How did you know where I lived?"

"Oh, I asked Miss Stanton." He brushed past Manuel and went into the house. "I like your house. Your parents home?"

"My dad is in his study. He doesn't like to be disturbed." Manuel shut the door quickly, startled that Viktor would just walk into the house uninvited. He caught up and waved an arm toward the kitchen. "This way." He noticed that Viktor was staring at the study door very intently. *As if he could see right through it.* Manuel shook the thought away. That was ridiculous. "Are you coming?"

Viktor suddenly turned to him, like he'd been in a trance. "Oh, sure—aren't we going to your room?"

"I thought there'd be more room in the kitchen."

"Well, we might disturb your dad if we're right down the hall. Wouldn't want to do that."

"You're right, I suppose," Manuel said. "Okay, we can go upstairs." Viktor turned on his heels and sped up the stairs, taking them two at a time. Manuel hurried to follow him.

They spent the next hour in Manuel's room, discussing the parts of the atom. Manuel explained about protons and neutrons and electrons and their various functions in the atom, although he sensed Viktor was not really listening. He looked around the room a lot, interrupting Manuel to ask about all the stuff he saw on the shelves. When he came across the Prince Warrior book, he pulled it down from the shelf and opened it.

"I've got one of these," he said, flipping through the pages. "So you've been there, right? To Ahoratos. Don't worry. The girls told me you were a Prince Warrior."

"Er . . . ummm . . . yes." Perhaps we should get back to studying—"

"Oh, man," Viktor said, staring at a page in the book. "This is bad."

"What's bad?"

"This chapter," Viktor said, pushing the science textbook aside to show Manuel a page of the book, where a Prince Warrior had pierced a black dragon with his sword. The dragon lay on its side, the sword embedded in its belly, behind its front leg. "This can't happen. The Prince Warrior can't pierce the black dragon's armored hide with the sword. At least not enough to kill it."

"Really? So you're saying this chapter is wrong?"

"Well, not totally. Just exaggerated, I guess. Kind of like a . . . fairy tale."

Fairy tale. The same words his father had used to describe the book.

"So how does one defeat the black dragon then?" Manuel asked, leaning in.

"Oh, it's actually impossible."

Manuel thought about this. He remembered how Tannyn had been pierced and fallen to his death—perhaps it was true. The black dragon could not be defeated. Manuel felt a shiver run down his spine.

"Here, if you want I can take this book home and fix it for you," said Viktor. "I can compare it to my copy and make the changes. There's not that many. Want me to?"

Manuel looked at the book and then back at Viktor. He was about to say yes when he thought of his father's book, all the changes his father had made. And how those changes might have rendered the book powerless to charge the Krÿs. It could be that Viktor was right about the dragons, but Manuel would have to investigate for himself first. He gently pulled the book out of Viktor's grasp.

"I'll think about it," he said.

"Okay, sure, no problem," said Viktor. He glanced at the clock by Manuel's bed. "Oh, look at the time, gotta go!" Viktor grabbed his backpack and headed for the door. "See you in school, Manuel! Thanks a lot for your help!"

After Viktor left, Manuel sat alone in his room, pouring over the Prince Warrior book. He had always thought this book was just a storybook, until he learned that it was how the swords were empowered. That had made it seem more significant. After all, so much of what happened to the Prince Warrior in the book had actually happened to him, in Ahoratos. But now Viktor was saying it was full of mistakes. And he seemed to know about these things.

He closed the book, feeling disturbed by this thought. Then he saw that Viktor's science textbook was still on the desk. Viktor had left it behind.

Great, Manuel thought. *Now I'll have to lug that to school with me on Monday, along with my own books. . . .*

"Manuel!" Mr. Santos's sharp voice from downstairs interrupted his thoughts. Manuel jumped up and rushed to the top of the stairs.

"What is it, Papá?"

"I must go! Will you be okay by yourself for a short time?"

"Yes, but—what's the matter?"

"A drill has been found! They want me to go and look at it, to make sure it is suitable. I will be back soon!" Mr. Santos flew out the door, slamming it behind him.

Manuel walked slowly down the stairs. He looked out the window beside the door, watching his father pull out of the driveway. Then he turned to the study door, which hung open. He took a breath and went in.

His father's study was even more cluttered than Manuel's room. Open books lay on top of each other in big piles on the desk and the floor. Manuel sorted through the room, searching for his father's Prince Warrior book. It had to be here somewhere.

Finally, under the desk he found an old briefcase. It was dusty, except for fingerprints on the clasp, indicating it had been recently opened. But the briefcase was locked with a four number combination lock.

Manuel thought about what the combination might be. He tried his birthday and his father's birthday. Didn't work. Then he tried his mother's birthday: 0-4-2-1. The case clicked open.

Inside was the book. The cover seemed to have faded, so that the Crest was hardly visible at all. He opened it and went to the page with the sword and the black dragon. He gasped.

On the last page of that chapter a Prince Warrior lay on the ground dead, a large dragon thorn piercing his chest, right through his armor.

Manuel shut the book quickly, sweat breaking out on his forehead. Could it be true? Was it possible that the armor wasn't as strong a protection as he thought?

Suddenly the window of the study blew open, letting in a blast of wind that sent the books and papers flying in all directions, crashing against walls, knocking down pictures. A storm? A tornado? *There haven't been any reports about tornadoes,* Manuel thought, covering his head as books and rocks from his father's collection hurtled toward him like missiles. He lay flat on the floor and tried to crawl toward the window, but the force of the wind was so great and the flying debris so dense he couldn't get anywhere near. So he lay still, keeping his arms over his head to protect himself. *Wish I had my helmet,* he thought.

And then it stopped. As quickly as it had started. All was quiet.

Manuel raised his head then got to his feet. He stepped over the piles of debris to look out the window. Everything seemed calm, bathed in a late afternoon sun.

But the study was in shambles. Manuel closed the window, wondering how he was ever going to set it all back where it was. It had been messy before, but he was certain his father knew exactly where everything was. Now even Mr. Santos would have trouble finding what he was looking for in this chaos.

Manuel sighed, put the Prince Warrior book back in the briefcase, and tucked it under the desk. He tried picking up rocks and papers and books, but gave up, knowing it was hopeless. He'd just have to explain to his father that the storm or whatever it was had blown open the window.

He left the study and saw that all the doors and windows of the house were also open. He searched the whole downstairs, shutting windows and doors and checking to make sure there was no damage. Everything looked fine. Nothing out of place. The only room that seemed to have been disturbed was his father's study. Manuel frowned at this. It was very odd.

He went back up to his room and stood in the door-way, his mouth dropping open. The window was open, all his favorite weird plants smashed on the floor. The desk had been completely cleared of everything. His books, his geodes, all of his favorite stuff had been knocked off the shelves and strewn all over the floor.

How was it that only his room and his father's study had been disturbed by the wind? Manuel bent down to pick up his plants, to salvage what he could. His poor Venus flytrap lay in a splatter of dirt and broken glass. It would be okay, but he'd need to find it a new pot. He picked up his books and started putting them back on their shelves.

That's when he realized: his Prince Warrior book wasn't there at all. It was gone.

"My sword!" Manuel said aloud. For his sword, which had been implanted in the back of the book on the sword page, was now gone too.

CHAPTER 20

Devouring

B rianna and Ivy sat on the front porch of Brianna's house, watching Star play on the front lawn. Brianna threw a tennis ball, and Star raced after it as fast as her little legs could go. She grabbed the ball before it even stopped moving but then refused to bring it back to the girls. She stood, holding it in her mouth, wagging her tail, expecting one of them to come and get it.

"She doesn't play this game very well, does she?" Ivy observed.

"Definitely not a retriever," Brianna sighed.

The girls looked up when they heard the hum of bicycle wheels. Brianna saw that it was Viktor riding a bike down the street.

"Viktor!" she called out, jumping up and waving. "Hey!"

Viktor stopped his bike and looked up, an expression of surprise on his face.

"Oh, hey," he said, smiling.

"Do you live in this neighborhood?" The two girls got up and crossed the lawn to the sidewalk. Viktor put one foot up on the curb to keep his balance. He leaned back, one hand on the handlebars.

"Uh . . . no . . . I was just passing through. Funny I should run into you."

Star began barking and growling, tearing around in circles.

"Star! Stop that!" Brianna looked sheepishly at Viktor. "She's just a puppy. Still in training. Would you—like some hot chocolate? Nana Lily's hot chocolate is famous around here."

"Uh . . ." Viktor glanced up at the house. "Sure . . . but are your parents home? I mean, I wouldn't want to intrude if they were."

"I live with my grandparents. And my three annoying sisters. Grandpa Tony's not home—he's at the hardware store. Nana Lily told him to fix the faucet or there would be no dinner." Brianna laughed. "So he's going to fix the faucet."

"Oh, well, hot chocolate sounds great," Viktor said, getting off his bike and laying it down on the lawn. He followed the girls up to the porch, while Star continued to prance around him, growling and barking. "I'll just wait out here." He sat down on the top step, ignoring the dog. Brianna went in to get him a cup. Ivy sat down next to him. He rubbed his hands together, as if he were cold.

"It's getting chilly," he said.

"Yep. Winter's coming. Although it never gets really cold here. Where are you from?"

"Up north."

"Then winter will be a piece of cake for you." Ivy smiled. "You like it here?"

"Haven't been here long enough to say. But everyone's been real nice."

"That was cool watching you skateboard with Levi the other day. Pretty smooth for your first try."

"Yeah. I pick things up fast."

Brianna returned with a cup of hot chocolate and sat down on the other side of Viktor. "So," she said, "when's the last time you were there?"

"There?"

"You know. Ahoratos."

"Oh. Not long ago." Viktor sipped the chocolate.

"Did you get the sword?" Ivy asked.

"I got that a long time ago."

"Really?" Brianna was impressed. "So did you open your locked room too?"

"Sure. Wasn't that awesome?"

"No, it definitely was not awesome," said Ivy. "It was empty."

"Oh, right—it is, the first time."

Brianna straightened. "The first time?"

"Yeah, Ruwach loves to test his Warriors. The first time the rooms look empty. But the second time, you'll see, the rooms are really full of incredible stuff—all sorts of new weapons and cool treasures and fancy armor. Wait till you see the *new* breastplate. So much better than that white triangle thing you have to wear." He paused, glancing at their awed expressions. "Oops. Maybe I'm not supposed to tell you that."

"How long do we have to wait?" Ivy asked, eager to hear more.

"Oh, I don't know, could be awhile. But . . ." He paused, glancing at Ivy with narrowed eyes. "If you really wanted to see, I could probably get you there."

"You mean, go to Ahoratos? Without being called?" asked Brianna.

Viktor nodded. "I do it all the time."

"Can you show us?" asked Ivy. "Please?"

"Sure," Viktor said. "It's the least I can do for this awesome hot chocolate."

"No, wait," said Brianna. "Mr. J. Ar said we needed to figure it out for ourselves. If you tell us, it would be like cheating."

"Oh, don't worry. Ruwach told me it was okay."

"He did?"

"Yeah. He told me I should tell anyone who asked. Look, Ruwach knows things are pretty crazy here, with these pods and all, and you need extra help. And you are *definitely* going to need the stuff in those rooms to deal with the pods, once they get opened."

"Oh, so Manuel must have told you about the drill," said Ivy.

"What? Oh, yeah, sure," said Viktor. He stood up. "If we're going to do this, we need to go somewhere we won't be seen. Could freak people out, if they saw us disappear."

"Right. How about the side of the house?" Brianna said. "There aren't any windows."

"Perfect."

Brianna led Viktor and Ivy around to the side of the house, where Nana Lily had her vegetable garden. A white fence separated the property from the house next door. A large chestnut tree blocked the view from the street. Viktor looked up at the houses on both sides to make sure they weren't being watched. When he was satisfied, he turned to the girls.

"Watch this." Viktor stood legs apart and raised his arms in a V shape, his fingers splayed. He took a deep breath and brought his hands together in front of him, his fingers closing tightly. From between his closed fingers there came something like an electric spark that made the girls jump and Star bark madly. The spark became a bolt that shot out and hit an invisible wall in front of him, spreading up and down, like a gash in the middle of the air. The girls gasped as they saw the gash begin to widen into a dark doorway rimmed in brilliant light.

"There!" Viktor said with a gasping breath. "Run through! Now!"

"Where's the Crest?" asked Brianna. "There should be a Crest—"

"Better hurry! Can't hold it long!" Viktor said, straining with all his might—or so it seemed.

"Let's go, Bri!" Ivy jumped into the portal and disappeared. Brianna still looked uncertain.

"It's going to close in a second!" Viktor said. "Don't leave your friend all alone!"

"Are you coming too?"

"Right behind you!"

Brianna bit her lip and ran through the portal. Star barked crazily as Viktor spread his arms apart, sealing the portal, with the two girls inside. He glanced down at the barking dog and smiled. He picked her up, holding her so he was looking right into her little face. She growled menacingly.

"Sorry, Star," he said. "Your owner won't be back for a while. Maybe forever."

Brianna and Ivy looked around. They were in the Centrum, the main room of the Cave. Ruwach wasn't anywhere around, but since he wasn't expecting them, they didn't think much of that. Nor did they take note that they were still wearing their earth clothes, and they did not have on their armor.

"We made it!" said Brianna. "We're really here. Viktor wasn't kidding."

"Where is he? I thought he was coming too," Ivy said.

"He said he was. Maybe he's already in the Hall of Armor, waiting for us."

"Oh, yeah, maybe." Ivy glanced around at all the tunnels. "Which way is the Hall of Armor?"

"I have no idea," said Brianna.

Just then one of the tunnels lit up purple.

"There!" said Ivy, pointing. "There it is! All lit up for us. Let's go."

The two girls dashed into the purple tunnel and followed it through many twists and turns until they came to the Hall of Armor. Their own armor was there on the wall, next to their doors. But Viktor was not there.

"Maybe he couldn't come," said Ivy. "Maybe someone saw him and he had to close the portal."

"Yeah, maybe," Brianna murmured. "Look, the doors are already open. That's weird."

"Viktor said they would be," Ivy said. "Didn't he? Let's look inside!"

"I'm not sure—"

Ivy ignored Brianna's hesitation and pushed her door all the way open. "Whoa!" The room was huge, much bigger than she expected. And it was filled with everything she had imagined: rows and rows of golden bows, sheaves of arrows, and bright, gleaming swords. There were shields too, huge shields taller than she was. And armor like she'd only seen in fairy tales— gorgeous, engraved breastplates of brilliant gold and silver. Giant chandeliers hung from the ceiling, casting everything in a magical glow. "It's amazing!"

Ivy took a step inside. Immediately the door behind her slammed shut. She turned, puzzled.

"Bri? Did you shut my door?" she called. No answer. She tried to open the door, but it was locked.

Suddenly the room darkened, the beautiful weapons and armor fading from her view. She reached out to grab one of the golden bows, but her fingers slid right through it, as if it wasn't really there at all. Even the walls began to fade, replaced with rows and rows of glowing green bars.

"No!" Ivy yelled. She whirled for the door again, but the door had become bars as well, glowing a sickly green. *Like the door of a prison cell.* She grabbed hold of the bars and shook them, trying to peer through in hopes she could still see Brianna on the other side. But all she saw was utter darkness.

"Bri! Can you hear me? Bri!" She rattled the bars as hard as she could, yelling over and over. "Bri! Open the door! Let me out! Bri! Can you hear?"

But Brianna didn't answer.

She can't hear me, Ivy thought. *Or I can't hear her.* She was cut off. Locked in a prison. Viktor had lured them both into a trap.

"Bri!" she yelled. "If you can hear me, don't open your door! Don't go in your room! It's a trap! Viktor— he did this! Please, please—get me out of here!"

Ivy could feel the bars of the prison cell closing in on her. She closed her eyes, fighting panic. She whispered, hoping Ruwach could hear her: "Please, get me out of here."

"Ivy?" Brianna pounded on the door and called to her friend. She could hear Ivy yelling, calling for her to open the door. She pulled and pulled but the door wouldn't open. She cried out, "I can't open the door! It's locked!" But Ivy kept on yelling, as if she couldn't hear Brianna at all. Ivy was warning her not to open her door. It was a trap.

Viktor.

Brianna felt panic rise in her throat. She glanced at her own door across the passageway—it was still ajar, a golden light emanating from within. It looked so inviting.

It was only then that she realized that she was not wearing her Warrior clothes or her armor. She thought back to when she and Ivy had come through the portal. There had been no Water either.

It was a trap. Viktor had led them into a trap. Now Ivy was locked up and might soon be turning to metal. And Brianna was . . . where was she? How would she ever find her way out, let alone rescue Ivy?

Before she had time to figure it out, the floor under her feet began to tremble.

Footsteps. Big, heavy footsteps. In the distance she saw a pair of round, red glowing eyes.

Forger.

"I'll come back for you!" she whispered to Ivy's door. And she ran down the tunnel, searching for a place to hide.

CHAPTER 21

Finding Viktor

Viktor carried the growling, squirming dog to the front door of the house and knocked. A moment later a teenage girl opened the door. She looked bored but then brightened when she saw Viktor's face.

"Hey," she said.

"Hey," said Viktor. "I just found this dog down the street. Is it yours?"

"My sister's," said the girl, her smile turning to a frown. "Wasn't she there too?"

"Uh, no. The dog was all alone. I saw that it had a tag on with this address."

The girl's eyes widened. "Where'd she go?"

"Well, I'm not sure. . . . I did see a big van driving in the other direction, so maybe she got a ride somewhere?"

"Who's at the door, Crystal?" called a thin female voice from within.

"Oh, just a boy," said the girl. "He brought Star home."

"Star? But where's Brianna?"

"Don't know."

Viktor looked past Crystal to see a woman in a wheelchair come into view with a lined face and soft graying hair. *Nana Lily*, he thought. He knew she'd had a stroke recently and was still recovering. But her gaze was very sharp and bright despite the fact that she was still pretty far away. So he kept his own eyes averted, just as he'd been trying to do with all the older Warriors, in case she might recognize him.

Nana Lily was shaking her head. "Brianna would never leave Star somewhere by herself. That silly dog must have escaped on her own. Call Brianna on the phone."

Crystal pulled out a phone and called, but there was no answer. "She's not picking up."

"Not picking up? Perhaps she went to Ivy's house and the dog tried to follow. You'd better go and get her. Tell your sisters to help you."

"Okay, okay." The girl yelled the names of her sisters, who came tramping down the stairs looking annoyed.

When they were all gone, Viktor stepped inside, went up to Brianna's grandmother, and set the dog in her lap.

"Here you go. She seems scared," Viktor said. The dog was, indeed, shaking.

Nana Lily glanced up at him, squinting slightly. "Do I know you?"

"No, ma'am. Just passing by." Viktor turned away quickly. "I'll just be on my way."

"Thank you for your help—what is your name?"

Viktor pretended he didn't hear. "My pleasure, ma'am." He headed toward the door, but instead of going out, he made sure the old lady wasn't looking before he sprinted up the stairs.

There were only two bedrooms. A small neat one and a larger messy one. He went in the messy room and saw four single beds with piles of blankets and pillows scattered about. He quickly looked under all the beds until he found what he wanted: the Prince Warrior book. He shoved it into his backpack and went to the window. A large tree stood near the house. He stepped out onto the windowsill and jumped, grabbing a branch and monkey-swinging to the ground. He looked both ways, went to the front of the house, and retrieved the bicycle he'd stolen from another house earlier.

He knew Ivy lived a few streets over, so he rode quickly to her house. It was a much bigger home, with double entry doors and a neat front lawn. He saw one of the sisters knocking on the door and ringing the doorbell, but it was clear that no one was home. The other two sisters were in the driveway—they talked together for a bit, looking annoyed that they still hadn't found Brianna.

As soon as they headed back to their own house, Viktor found an unlocked window by the garage and slipped inside. He found the book easily—it was sitting right on the desk in Ivy's room. He shoved it into his backpack and slipped out of the house.

It was getting late. Xavier and Evan should be back from the rec center by now. He jumped on the bicycle and headed to their house.

———

Levi knocked several times on Manuel's door before he answered.

"Hey! Did you get my message?" Levi said.

"What message? I haven't checked my phone lately."

"Is Viktor here?"

"No . . . well, he was, but he left."

"Do you know where he went?"

"No. I've been sorting through the mess from the tornado—"

"What tornado?"

Manuel pushed up his glasses. "Didn't you see it? A tornado. Or maybe a very sudden storm. My room is a disaster. And my Prince Warrior book is missing. My sword was in it!"

"There wasn't any tornado. . . . Wait, was Viktor here when that happened?"

"No. He was gone already. I was looking at my father's book when the windows blew open, and then my book was gone."

Levi thought about this. It was too much to be a coincidence.

"Levi!" his dad called from the car. He had a phone to his ear. "Tony is on the phone. He says that Brianna and Ivy are missing."

"Missing?"

"A boy came to the door with Star, said she was left alone in the street. No one can find the girls, and they aren't answering their phones."

"Did they know who the boy was?"

"No, but both Crystal and Nana Lily said he was tall and dark-haired."

Levi felt a knot forming in his stomach. *Viktor*. Had to be. But where had Brianna and Ivy gone? And what had caused Manuel's book to disappear?

Levi couldn't make sense of it all. He just knew he had to find Viktor before something else happened. He pulled out his phone and called Xavier.

"Hey," he said when Xavier picked up. "It's Levi. Have you seen Viktor?"

"Yeah, he's here now," said Xavier.

"At your house? Can I come over? I just need to talk to him."

There was a pause on the line. "I don't think so, Levi."

"What?"

"I'm kinda busy. I'll see you in school on Monday."

"But Brianna is—" It was too late. Xavier had already hung up.

Levi put the phone down. He looked shell-shocked.

"You okay, Levi?" said Manuel.

"Yeah. I gotta go. See you later."

"Okay." Manuel shut the door.

Levi got into the car, sagging in the passenger seat. Mr. J. Ar looked him over.

"You want to talk to me about this, son?" he said after a moment. "Why all this concern about Viktor? Everyone seems to like him except for you."

"I don't know. Maybe I'm just going nuts. But something is not right about that dude. He's way too slick. And weird things are happening."

"Do you want to go to Brianna's house? See if we can find her?"

"Yeah, but—we need to go to Xavier's first."

"Why?"

"'Cause he said Viktor was there."

CHAPTER 22

Viktory

Levi rang the bell at the Blakes' house. Mrs. Blake came to the door. When she saw Levi and his dad she smiled warmly.

"Levi! James! What are you two doing here?"

"I need to speak to Xavier," said Levi. "I need to—apologize—for something I said earlier."

"I see." She gave Mr. J. Ar a knowing glance. "Xavier and Evan are out by the pond with some friend of theirs named Viktor. You can go around the house if you want."

Levi stiffened, glancing at his dad. "Okay, thanks."

Levi and his dad walked around to the backyard. They saw Evan and Xavier sitting on the dock. Viktor was standing, talking and moving his hands around, as if he was telling them some fantastic story. The two brothers seemed mesmerized.

Levi stopped in his tracks, looking at Viktor. It was the first time he'd seen him since coming back from Ahoratos, since receiving his gift. His eyes widened, responding to the sight of something strange. In the bright sunlight, Levi could see the shadows of Evan and Xavier clearly outlined on the ground. Normal. But Viktor's shadow *wasn't* on the ground—it was still attached to him, outlining his body, shifting with his every move. On the ground where his shadow should have been, there was nothing. No indication at all that a person was standing in the light. Levi knew for sure then that something was terribly wrong. Maybe even Viktor himself was wrong. Levi retreated a few steps, out of their line of sight.

"Son?" Mr. J. Ar said, following him.

"Dad, I don't think we should meet him without the armor."

"What's—"

"Trust me, Dad."

Mr. J. Ar nodded. They walked back to the SUV. Mr. J. Ar lifted up the tailgate. The trunk was in there.

"How did that get here?" Levi asked.

"The armor is wherever we need it to be," said Mr. J. Ar. "Especially in a crisis. So you just might be right about Viktor." He opened the trunk, and they quickly dressed in their armor and took the Krÿsen from the book, stowing the diminutive blades easily in their belts. Levi checked to make sure he had his seed in his pocket.

When they went back to the Blakes' backyard, Viktor was standing with his hands over his head, spread in a gesture of victory. Evan and Xavier were watching him intently, as he closed his hands together in front of him. From out of his fingers came a bolt of lightning, splitting the air open. The bolt became a widening gap, a doorway. Levi felt suddenly dizzy, everything spinning in circles around him, blurring together. His eyes stung so that he had to close them. Tears welled up in the corners.

"Levi? You okay?"

Levi heard his father's voice like it came through a long tunnel, far away. He raised his hands to his face and rubbed his eyes. It took a moment for the stinging to subside and the dizziness to ease so he could see clearly again. He saw Viktor with the weird shadow hovering near him. He saw Evan and Xavier. He saw the doorway that Viktor had created. But he could see something else, something more—something beyond the veil that separated this world from the other.

He could see into Ahoratos.

He blinked, desperately trying to make sense of his vision. On the other side of Viktor's portal was a rounded, wooden door, like the door to the rooms the kids had opened in the Cave. But then it changed, the solid part of it melting away to reveal green metal bars. And someone—a girl—inside the bars. She was crying, though Levi heard no sound. He saw a flash of red hair. It looked like . . . Ivy!

"Stop!" Levi yelled, running toward the boys. Xavier and Evan turned to see who had shouted. Viktor immediately dropped his hands, although the portal remained, shimmering beside him. He smiled and waved at Levi.

"Hi Levi! Nice armor. I was just showing these guys—" Viktor stopped talking, paling a little when he saw Mr. J. Ar moving toward him, looking like the mightiest of Warriors in his stately armor. Levi glanced at him and smiled to himself. *That's my dad*, he thought.

"Levi, I told you we were busy," Xavier said. "Why did you come here? And why are you wearing your armor?"

"Brianna and Ivy are missing," Levi said.

"What?"

Levi glanced at Viktor, who was looking away as if something in the distance occupied his attention. Levi had the sense that he was deliberately avoiding his gaze—*or was it Mr. J. Ar he was avoiding?*

"Were you over at Brianna's house earlier?" Levi asked Viktor, walking toward him.

"Me?" Viktor glanced at Levi with a befuddled expression. "I don't know what you're talking about."

"Really? That's strange," said Levi. "What were you doing just now?"

"We were just talking," said Xavier.

"About what?"

"About Ahoratos," said Evan. "Viktor was just going to show us how to get there without being called."

"Really?" asked Mr. J. Ar. He also approached Viktor, trying to get a better look at him. "I'd like to see that."

"Me too," said Levi.

"I was just joking around," said Viktor, laughing a little.

"That is nothing to joke about, son," said Mr. J. Ar in his sternest voice.

Viktor bowed his head, as if suddenly ashamed. "You're right. My bad. Sorry. Won't happen again, sir. Honest."

Viktor sounded so sincere that Mr. J. Ar relaxed a bit. He put out his hand to shake. "I don't think we've been introduced. I'm Mr. J. Ar, Levi's dad."

Viktor glanced at the outstretched hand, a smile creeping across his face. "So nice to meet you, sir."

Levi wasn't sure what exactly happened next—it all happened so fast. Viktor reached out to shake his dad's hand, but in his hand there was a sword. Levi had no time to wonder where the sword had come from. Viktor swung the sword at Mr. J. Ar, who managed to leap away in time, grabbing his Krÿs from his belt. Levi took several steps backward and pulled out his Krÿs as well, slamming it against his breastplate. He felt the hilt ignite, the blade extending to its full length. Both he and his dad aimed their swords at Viktor, who began to circle them slowly, still smiling in a cruel way, his eyes gleaming yellow. *Just like that wolf*, Levi thought.

"Go get your armor—in my car!" Mr. J. Ar shouted to Xavier and Evan, who jumped up from the dock and ran to the front of the house where Mr. J. Ar's SUV was parked. Viktor let them go, as if he didn't care at all. His whole attention was focused on Levi and Mr. J. Ar.

"So, you really want to do this?" Viktor said, his voice almost a whisper, yet filled with venom. "You know how good I am at basketball? Well, I'm twice as good at this."

"There's two of us," Levi said.

"It wouldn't matter if there were ten of you."

Levi felt his heart race; he struggled to keep his breathing even, to remember his training. Viktor was bad, all right. But if he wasn't a Prince Warrior, what *was* he?

"Who would have thought the little skateboarder would be the one doing the fighting," Viktor taunted. "I saw that mark on your finger. The mark of Skot'os. No matter how hard you try, you will never get rid of that."

"Your words aren't going to bother me," said Levi. "I wear the helmet, remember?"

"Oh, right, the helmet. Do you really think that is going to protect you? How often do you think about that scar? Hmmm?"

"Who *are* you?" Levi asked, the blood racing to his face so he could feel the pulse of it in his temples. *Stay cool.*

"I could tell you, but then I'd have to kill you. Oh, what the heck, maybe I'll just kill you anyway." Viktor lunged forward quick as a cat, thrusting into Levi's middle. Levi parried the move and knocked Viktor's sword away, at the same time swinging upward for a jab at Viktor's arm. Viktor leapt backward to avoid the blow and reset his stance, circling and smiling as before.

Block and then counterattack. Everything he learned in the hours of training seemed embedded in Levi's helmet, so he could act without having to think.

"Steady," said his dad in a low voice. Mr. J. Ar had moved behind him, although his sword was still at the ready, prepared to back up Levi if necessary.

Viktor lunged again, this time with a cut across Levi's neck. Levi ducked and counter-swung, a back-handed slash at Viktor's ribs. But once again Viktor danced away in time.

"Nice one!" Viktor said. "You're doing so well." He feigned a thrust once, then twice, making Levi jump and wince. Then he lunged forward, his sword aimed at Levi's heart. Levi parried it, sliding down Viktor's blade and pushing him away. Levi felt buoyed by his success, although he sensed Viktor had not used anywhere near his full strength yet.

"My, my, you *have* been practicing, I see," Viktor said, circling. "For what? A week? Do you know how long *I've* been doing this?"

Levi was sick of listening to Viktor taunt him. He attacked first this time, slashing across Viktor's neck. Viktor seemed surprised by this; he barely managed to duck in time. But he countered with a wicked smash on Levi's blade, nearly knocking it out of his hands. Levi stumbled forward to recover; Viktor saw his chance and raised his sword over his head for a downward cut on the back of Levi's neck. But Mr. J. Ar intervened, his sword slicing into Viktor's arm. Viktor recoiled and grabbed his wounded arm; he was shocked to see blood pouring out between his fingers. Levi stared at the blood—it didn't look red. It was sort of dark gray—

Viktor turned on Mr. J. Ar, baring his teeth. A growl rose from somewhere deep in his throat. He sounded like a . . . wolf. Levi felt a shiver.

Viktor began to fight like he was holding ten swords instead of one, slashing and thrusting with such fury that Levi and Mr. J. Ar could barely keep up. All they could do was fend off Viktor's vicious attack with blocks and parries. But Viktor's wounded arm was still bleeding gray blood, if that *was* blood, and sweat was pouring down his face. He was getting weaker. Finally, Levi took a chance, lunged forward and slashed low, aiming for Viktor's leg. He felt his sword connect; Viktor growled even louder as a thin line of dark gray blood spread from his pant leg. He lashed out, but his aim was off; Levi slapped away his sword and then kicked out his leg to push Viktor backward, toward the portal.

"This . . . body . . . too . . . constricting—" Viktor stammered, although Levi could not hear the last word clearly. Viktor whirled around and leapt through the portal, which closed up after him and disappeared.

CHAPTER 23

A New Plan

That boy and his father!" Ponéros raged around the throne room, scattering the snakes and making the Forgers who stood on either side of the massive throne quiver. Ponéros tore off the Viktor skin and cast it to the floor. There was a large rip in one arm and one leg. "Something must be done about them. About all of them! Where is the Weaver?"

"Here, Master." Chief Weaver shuffled forward and stood before his master, shaking all over, his domed head bent low in supplication.

"Fix this!" Ponéros shrieked, kicking the ruined Viktor skin with his massive boot.

"You mean—you will return? To earth?" the Weaver asked.

"I am not finished," Ponéros replied. "These children are harder to get rid of than I expected. I hold two of them, but that is not enough. We must have them all. Locked up. Forever."

"Yes, Master," said the Weaver, shuffling toward the Viktor skin discarded on the floor.

"I can only hope," Ponéros said in a softer voice, "that Santos does not fail us. He must continue to follow his desire and open the pods. Once that is done, all will be as it should be." Ponéros sank into his throne. The figures of the throne began to moan, as if his mere presence caused them unceasing pain.

"Antannyn! Come!"

A great door opened at the far end of the room, and a huge creature emerged: glowing red eyes, sleek, shining scales studded with thorns, bony wings folded over its ridged back. It crept forward on clawlike legs, its talons scraping along the polished metal floor. The snakes slithered to the corners of the room to keep from being trampled.

"Antannyn! There you are, my lovely. Come to me."

The black dragon hastened to the throne and lowered its massive head, as if it wished to nestle in Ponéros's lap. It opened its mouth and let out a terrible, strangled sound, half-cry and half-moan.

"Antannyn." Ponéros almost cooed now. "My poor old friend. Are you feeling any better?"

Antannyn's head rocked slightly. It moaned again.

"Good. I will need you soon. Once the pods are open, all will be in place. They will not escape us this time."

Antannyn made a purring noise, which came out more like a death rattle.

Suddenly a great light pierced the darkness of the throne room. A transparent figure appeared, hovering before Ponéros and his dragon, his purple robe flowing about him as if he were underwater. All the creatures in the room shrank back from the terrible light, screeching in pain. The Chief Weaver, who had retrieved the Viktor skin and was about to skulk away with it, let out a bloodcurdling shriek and fell down as if dead.

Ponéros bellowed, rising up to his full height, although he could not bear being so near the light. "Ruwach! How dare you show yourself in my throne room!"

"I give you fair warning," Ruwach said, his voice like thunder and lightning all at the same time. "If you continue to attack the Prince Warriors, those that belong to the Source, you will know more torment than you ever have before."

"Ha. You are so sure of your children? Your Prince Warriors? They still do not know who I am—who Viktor truly is. They are young. Weak. Their weakness is my strength."

Ruwach was unmoved. "Wrong. Their weakness is *my* strength."

Ponéros's answering roar was so thunderous that the figures on the throne began to wail and shake. Antannyn suddenly rose up, baring its needle sharp teeth. It advanced upon Ruwach with a hungry growl, but Ruwach simply lifted up one long arm, the sleeve falling away, exposing his radiantly glowing hand.

Antannyn yelped and fell backward as if hit with a cannonball, its jaws snapping shut. It whimpered softly.

Ponéros screamed in fury. "Get out! Get! Out!"

But Ruwach was already gone, the light with him. Ponéros slumped in his throne, weakened greatly by the light. The Chief Weaver lifted his head from the floor then pulled himself to his knees. Ponéros caught sight of him and lurched forward.

"Go!" Ponéros's voice was now more of a wheeze. "Fix the skin. Make it better than before. Stronger. I must—regain my strength. You!" His massive arm lashed out, grabbed the nearest Forger, and pulled him close.

"Go and tell the Builders. I want my new fortress completed! Now!"

He released the Forger so forcefully it stumbled backward and nearly fell. Then it marched quickly out of the throne room.

"There, there." Ponéros petted his dragon, who still whimpered in pain. "You will have your chance for vengeance. Knowing those children, they will come looking for their friends soon." A snarl invaded his fading voice. "We will be ready."

CHAPTER 24

Lost and Found

Xavier and Evan, wearing their armor, had seen most of the sword fight. Once Viktor disappeared through the portal, they rushed toward Levi and his dad, who were doubled over with their hands on their knees, trying to catch their breath.

"Man, that was epic!" Evan exclaimed. "You totally kicked his b—"

"Evan!" said Xavier. He turned to Levi. "Levi, I'm sorry. You were right about Viktor. I never thought—"

"It's okay," Levi said. "I'm just glad we got here in time."

"Ponéros must have tricked Viktor into working for him," said Evan. "Just like he did with Rook. Then sent him here to mess with us."

"Yeah, I guess so." Levi realized that his sword had shrunk back to the Krÿs. It was like it instinctively knew the danger had passed and it was no longer needed. His father's had done the same thing. Was this another of the Krÿs's secrets? He wanted to ask his dad, but now was not the time. They had a bigger problem to deal with. "We need to find Brianna and Ivy," he said.

"Right," said Mr. J. Ar, stowing his Krÿs in his belt. "We'll drive over to Brianna's house—"

"They aren't there," Levi said. "They're in Skot'os. I think."

All three Warriors whirled around to stare at him.

"Skot'os? How do you know that?" said Mr. J. Ar.

Levi wanted to tell them, but Ruwach had told him not to speak of it to the others yet. "I just—know. They're in a prison. Well, Ivy is anyway."

"But didn't we destroy the prison when we destroyed the Fortress?" said Evan.

"He must have another one," said Levi. The prison he'd seen hadn't looked exactly like the one from which they'd rescued Rook.

"Maybe he built a new fortress," Evan mused. "I remember Ruwach telling me that Ponéros could do that."

"We need to go to Ahoratos," Levi said.

"But there's no Crest anywhere," said Xavier, looking around.

"I'll take you there," said Mr. J. Ar. "If you're sure . . ."

"I'm sure," said Levi.

Mr. J. Ar sighed. He turned to Xavier and Evan. "Go get your swords," he said. "Make sure you have your seeds too. And—better tell your mom that you'll be late for dinner."

Xavier and Evan nodded and dashed into the house. While they waited, Levi and Mr. J. Ar went to sit on the edge of the dock so they could rest up and talk through what was happening.

"So Viktor tricked the girls into going to Ahoratos the same way he was trying to trick Evan and Xavier. Why didn't he try to trap Manuel too?"

"Hmmm, good question," said Mr. J. Ar. "Why don't you call him and see what happened."

Levi pulled out his phone and called Manuel. "Hey," he said when Manuel answered, "let me ask you something. Did Viktor talk to you about going back to Ahoratos on your own?"

"No," said Manuel, his voice drawn out a bit because he was thinking. "He just wanted my book."

"Your book?"

"Yes. He said it had mistakes in it and he could fix it. I almost gave it to him, but I decided not to. Then the storm came right after, and my book went missing."

"Yeah," said Levi, thinking. "That's pretty strange."

"It's funny though—what Viktor said was almost exactly the same thing my father had told me about his book. That it was full of errors and—a fairy tale."

"Really . . . uh, hold on, Manuel." Levi put the phone down and told his dad what he had said. Mr. J. Ar took the phone.

"Manuel? This is Mr. J. Ar. Listen. I want you to keep trying to talk to your father about not opening that pod. Do whatever you have to do to convince him. Don't give up, Manuel. Okay?"

"He's not listening to me, Mr. J. Ar. But . . . I'll try."

"Good man. Where is your dad now?"

"He just came home. He's very happy because the agents have found a drill and are getting ready to transport it to the high-school site. He is just waiting for it to get there."

"Okay. Go with him, Manuel. Stay with him. We will come to help as soon as we can."

"Okay, sir—where are you going?"

"We need to go and find Brianna and Ivy. We'll be . . . off the grid for a while."

"Ah. I understand."

Mr. J. Ar put down the phone.

"Hope he can do it," Levi said. "If those pods open, we're gonna have big problems—"

"Levi."

Levi turned to his dad.

"How did you know about Ivy being in a prison?"

Levi took a breath, trying to collect his thoughts. Ruwach had told him not to tell the other kids. Did that mean he could tell his dad? He hoped so.

"Dad, all I know is that Ruwach gave me . . . a gift. Because I chose not to open my locked room, he said I would be able to see things—that other people don't normally see."

Mr. J. Ar gazed at his son, his expression softening. "I'd always hoped that *I* would get another chance to acquire that gift . . . but to know that you chose well and that Ruwach gave it to you . . . I'm very proud of you, son."

"I'm not so sure this gift is all that great," Levi said. "It's making me see things I don't really want to see."

Mr. J. Ar nodded, putting an arm around Levi. "I understand. Sometimes gifts can feel like burdens. But only at first. You'll learn to appreciate it, in time."

Xavier and Evan came running out of the house with their Krÿsen stuck in their belts.

"We're ready," said Evan, hands on his hips like a superhero. Xavier rolled his eyes.

"Okay," said Mr. J. Ar, getting up stiffly. "Gather around that tree stump."

The boys followed Mr. J. Ar to the tree stump. Levi could tell Xavier and Evan were quietly excited about this, as he was. They had long wondered how it was they could get to Ahoratos without being called. Viktor must have known that and used it as a lure to trap them. Just as he'd used that fake scroll to make Brianna think he was a real Prince Warrior. Viktor seemed to know way too much about all of them; he knew things they had done and all about their desires and their interests. He even knew about their weaknesses. If Viktor knew these things, that meant Ponéros knew them too.

Mr. J. Ar took out his Krÿs and held it out with both hands, hilt up. He bent and knelt stiffly on one knee. The boys mimicked his posture, bending to one knee and holding out their small knives.

"Close your eyes," Mr. J. Ar commanded. "Bow your heads."

They did.

Instantly they felt a heat under their fingers—the Crest on the hilt of each Krÿs began to pulse with an inner light. Although the boys could not see what was happening, the Crests lifted off the Krÿsen and floated toward each other, bonding together into one large Crest that hovered above their heads.

"Open your eyes," said Mr. J. Ar softly.

The Crest. There it was, floating above them. "Grab on!" They reached out for the Crest and grabbed hold. They felt a rush, as if the ground underneath them had dropped away and they were falling at the speed of light.

The next thing they knew, they were standing on the bank of a large lake in Ahoratos. It looked almost like the pond in the Blakes' backyard, except that the water reflected the gold of the sky. And above them, nestled in a huge white cloud, was the shining castle.

"The castle!" said Levi, staring up in amazement.

"Cool," said Evan. "Maybe we'll get some ice cream before we have to go rescue the girls."

"Easy there, Evan," said Mr. J. Ar. "We have to find the Water first and get to the Cave, remember? Anyone see the Water?"

The boys looked around. The water before them was not *the* Water. There was no Crest on it. The lake stretched as far as they could see. Beyond it lay nothing but more clouds and sky.

"Maybe it's down farther," said Xavier.

"But we better hurry," said Mr. J. Ar. "Who knows what may be tracking us."

They began to trot along the beach, which wound around the large lake until it abruptly ended at a rocky outcropping. The sound of rushing water rose up from below. Xavier climbed up the rocks to have a look and sighed.

It was a waterfall. With the Crest of Ahoratos floating serenely on the surface of the foaming Water below.

"Why does it have to be a waterfall?" Xavier asked no one in particular. He turned to the others. "We're jumping. Into a waterfall." They climbed up and looked for themselves.

"After you," said Evan.

Xavier took a breath, secured his Krÿs in his belt, and leapt off the rock into the Water below. Evan did a cannonball. Levi glanced at his dad, who nodded at him and grinned. Levi shrugged, backstepped once, and jumped as far out as he could, bicycling his legs in the air until he hit the Water. He heard a splash, but after that there was no sound, a sensation of falling but not of wetness. It ended almost as quickly as it began.

———

"Welcome back, Warriors," said Ruwach.

They were all in their Warrior clothes and armor. Levi breathed a sigh of relief. They'd made it through the waterfall without being killed. He knew they would, but still that moment of actually doing it, jumping in, was always a bit nerve-wracking.

"No sweat," Evan said, striking his superhero pose again. "So that's all you have to do to get here on your own? Just kneel and hold out the Krÿs and close your eyes? Cool!"

"That is not all, Prince Evan. The posture of the body must match the posture of the heart."

"The posture? Of the heart?" Evan cocked his head to one side.

"Humility is always the hardest lesson for a Prince Warrior to learn," said Ruwach. "The power of the Source only resides in those who are humble of heart." Ruwach's hood seemed to be focused on Evan, who quickly dropped his superhero pose and smiled meekly.

"Ru, the girls are in trouble," Levi said. "Does the enemy have them?"

"He has Ivy. But not Brianna. She is still free. For the moment."

Levi felt somewhat relieved. "That's why I couldn't see her. Where are they?"

"They are in the enemy's fortress."

"So he rebuilt it?" said Evan. "The fortress we destroyed with the Olethron?"

"Yes. He builds new strongholds all the time."

"Is Viktor there too?" Xavier asked.

Ruwach offered only a nod. Levi sensed there was a lot Ruwach was not telling them.

"So we have to find this new fortress and bust the girls out of prison without getting pulverized by Forgers?" Evan asked, warming to the idea of another adventure.

"You must also retrieve the books," said Ruwach. "The books that contain the swords."

"I thought Viktor just took Manuel's book," said Levi.

"He also took Brianna's and Ivy's. And he has one other as well."

"Seems like we could use a little more help here," said Xavier, his voice laced with uncertainty. "Can't you send for Rook? And Finn?"

"You have everything you need," said Ruwach. Then he stretched out one long arm, summoning The Book. The golden object came in from one of the far tunnels, speeding toward them then stopping suddenly and floating gently on its pedestal. The pages began to flip, the musical notes they produced dancing in the air. When the pages stopped, letters floated up and rearranged themselves until an instruction appeared:

Your enemy is under your feet.

"That's helpful," said Xavier, shaking his head.

Ruwach pulled the words from the air and flung them into the orbs on each of their breastplates. They churned around in the glowing orbs a moment before dissolving.

"Okay, so, how are we going to get to the fortress? Last time we had to cross a bridge that wasn't there and all that stuff," said Evan.

"Follow the Sparks to the Cave entrance. Your transportation is awaiting you."

CHAPTER 25

Under Foot

S parks led the Prince Warriors to the entrance of the Cave, which the boys had never seen before. The Water had always brought them to the Centrum, right smack-dab in the center of the Cave.

"I never knew there was a way out of the Cave," Evan said. He raced ahead as soon as he saw daylight at the end of the tunnel. He peered out into the bright sunlight and gave a yelp of delight at what he saw.

"Tannyn!" he shouted, throwing his arms around the big green dragon's neck. "How did you . . . what did . . . where have you . . . ?" He tried to get the words out, but he was too excited. "You're okay!"

"Gorp." Tannyn sounded like he had a severe sore throat. An ugly scar on his neck and several more at the base of his tail where the thorns had pierced him told the story. But he opened his mouth in a wide Tannyn-smile and drooled happily. Xavier, Levi, and Mr. J. Ar came up to greet him as well, patting his head as if he were a big dog.

"Can't tell you how glad we are to see you," said Xavier.

"Yeah. Wait till we tell the girls," said Levi. Then he frowned a little, wondering if he would ever see them again. The journey they were about to embark upon would not be easy or safe.

As Evan climbed up on Tannyn's back, Xavier began to ask a string of questions. "How do we know if the girls are in the fortress? What if they are somewhere else? How are we going to find them? And what about the books—how can we get to them without Ponéros or Viktor knowing we're there? Assuming that's where Viktor went—"

"All these questions," said Mr. J. Ar. "Don't you trust Ruwach anymore? Or your armor? Or the instruction from The Book?"

"Of course I do. I mean, I'm not sure. So much has happened. I thought Viktor was a good guy, you know? I actually *liked* him. I wanted to *be* like him. How could I be so wrong?"

"What do you know about the enemy you face?" asked Mr. J. Ar.

"That he's a liar. A deceiver."

"Right. And what do you know about Ruwach? And the Source?"

"That they are true and right," Xavier said slowly, thinking over the words as he spoke. "But if Viktor was working for the enemy and he could fool me, then how will I ever know who I can trust and who I can't?"

Mr. J. Ar shook his head. "I can't tell you that. But I know someone who can. Why don't you ask him?"

"Is that what you do?"

"Every single time." Mr. J. Ar smiled.

"C'mon, guys!" Evan shouted, kicking his legs against Tannyn's scaly back. "Let's go already!" Tannyn echoed his enthusiasm with a garbled squawk.

"Oh, sure," Xavier said in a melancholy mumble. "Let's go fly into enemy territory and fight some Forgers and a creepy kid. Sounds like fun." He climbed up onto the dragon's back and sat in front of Evan between two spikes. Levi went up next, then Mr. J. Ar, who sat in front of him.

"I'm worried," Levi said to his dad. "About Bean— what if . . . what if . . ."

"Let's not go there," said Mr. J. Ar. "If I know Brianna, she's smart enough to evade the bad guys until we can find her."

"And Ivy? How are we going to get her out?"

"What was the message you brought to Rook when you freed him from prison?"

"Once freed, always free."

Mr. J. Ar nodded. "Do you believe it?"

"I guess so. Yes."

Mr. J. Ar nodded. "Then let's go get them."

Tannyn took that as his cue to take off but not before he opened his mouth and let out a blast of fire.

"Keep your arms and legs inside the dragon at all times!" shouted Evan as he laughed at his own joke.

Tannyn spread his enormous wings and launched straight up into the gold-swept sky.

They traveled swiftly, Tannyn gliding on updrafts and dodging skypods, until the sky changed to a splotchy red/black and the ground beneath them disappeared into a sea of dark mist. Strange, angular formations jutted from the mist now and then, making Levi think of bones in an animal graveyard. He looked left and right, fearful of seeing one of those deadly black dragons tracking them, or a swarm of Ents about to attack. But the sky, other than the skypods, was empty. Levi wondered about this. He wondered if Ponéros *wanted* them to come; if this apparent peacefulness wasn't a lure into his trap, just like Viktor had been.

Tannyn suddenly ducked his head and began to swoop lower. Levi looked over the side and saw the jagged outline of a new fortress breaking through the thick fog. It looked different from the old fortress, which had appeared more like a twisted maze of steel girders. This one seemed to be made of sharpened gray stone, with tall pointy towers reaching through the clouds.

"I see it!" Levi called out. The others looked to where he pointed.

Then Levi noticed they were headed dangerously close to the big, ugly skypod that hovered directly above the new fortress.

"Hey, Dad," Levi said, tapping his father's shoulder. "Where's he going? He's gonna crash into that skypod—"

Just then Tannyn flattened his wings and went into a full dive. Levi scrambled to grab onto the spike with both hands.

"Whoa!" cried Evan.

"I think we're landing!" yelled Mr. J. Ar.

Levi braced himself for one of Tannyn's usually bumpy landings. But at the last second Tannyn pulled up, dropping his tail and reversing his wings. He landed almost gently—for him—on the top of the big, ugly skypod.

"Wait, why did we land here?" Xavier asked. "The fortress is below."

"Maybe we'll have to rappel our way to the fortress," said Evan, sounding eager to try it.

"No way," said Levi.

The sky overhead was nearly black, making it hard to see very far beyond the glow of their breastplates. Levi could make out rocky plateaus and deep craters—like the surface of the moon. He was overcome with a sense of utter desolation and stifled a wave of fear. This was about the loneliest place he had ever encountered.

Tannyn folded his wings and settled down on his belly. He bent his neck around and looked expectantly at his passengers, as if to say: "Well? What are you waiting for?" Except it came out as a soft, raspy, "Gorp."

Mr. J. Ar slid from the dragon's back. The boys followed. They stood together on the skypod, looking around.

"There's nothing here," said Xavier in a whisper. "We need to get to the fortress."

"Tannyn brought us here," said Mr. J. Ar. "He knows Skot'os better than any of us. He was a slave here once, remember?"

"So you're saying that we have to go through this skypod to get there?" asked Levi. "But it's huge. It's at least five times as big as any of the other ones."

"I still think rappelling is our best bet," said Evan. "Or maybe a zip line?"

"There's no zip line to the fortress from here," said Xavier. He walked around the harsh "floor" of the skypod, thinking. He stopped, looking down at the ground. At his boots. Then he recalled the instruction.

The enemy is under your feet.

What had that meant? It sounded quite ridiculous.

Under your feet.

Xavier thought about that phrase over and over. Then all at once the answer struck him like a bolt of lightning.

"Under our feet!" he exclaimed, stomping on the skypod surface. "The enemy is here! In the skypod! Under our feet."

"You mean Ponéros is *in* this skypod?" asked Evan. "Right now? And the girls too?"

"Then the prison is here," said Levi. "Maybe Ponéros moved it here when the original fortress was destroyed."

"He was probably scared we'd destroy the next one too, right?" Evan said, puffing out his chest a little.

"But how do we get inside?" asked Xavier. "Do you see a door anywhere?"

"There must be a way in," said Mr. J. Ar. He gazed around. "That mound there." He pointed. "There are several of them. They all look the same. Why don't you go take a look?"

The three boys scrambled up the mound and stood on the flat top.

"Don't see a door," said Xavier.

"Hold on," said Levi. He stomped hard in the center of the mound, as if he were stomping on a spider. Immediately the surface dropped away, revealing a metal spiral staircase that glowed faintly green in the darkness below.

"Whoa," said Evan.

"How did you know?" said Xavier.

"Saw it in a movie once," said Levi with a grin.

"Good work," said Mr. J. Ar. He turned to Tannyn, who looked as though he'd fallen asleep. "Better go now, old friend. Stay close and keep an eye out for us. We are likely to be in a hurry when we come back."

Tannyn raised his head and nodded enthusiastically, crouched down and then jumped straight up, fumbling a bit before getting his wings in working order. The boys watched him disappear behind one of the more ordinary skypods strewn about the sky.

"*If* we come back," Xavier murmured.

"So, who wants to go first?" asked Evan, looking around at the others.

"I will," said Xavier with a sigh. He stepped down on the first step of the staircase. Levi followed him, wincing at the ghoulish green glow of the steps. It reminded him of the green light bulbs that had dangled from the ceiling of the prison in the fortress when they had gone to rescue Rook. There was something very unnatural and unsettling about the color. The staircase had no railing, nothing to hang onto. All around them was utter darkness. *If I fell off,* Levi thought, *how far would I fall? Forever?*

The staircase wound around in an unending spiral, until Levi became dizzy. He tried to concentrate on the dim outline of Xavier's back, glowing in the light of his own breastplate.

"This is making me dizzy," Evan said.

"Take it slow," said Mr. J. Ar, who went last.

The space around them seemed to get smaller as they descended; the giant echoes of their boots diminishing the farther down they went. *Like going down a funnel,* Levi thought. He kept a tight hold of his sword with his free hand, fearing with every step to see an angry dragon or evil Ent appear. But there was nothing to see except eerie, endless darkness.

Finally, a bluish light appeared below them, a welcome change from that awful green. An opening. A doorway. Levi felt hopeful that this descent would soon end. Xavier stepped down from the last step and entered the glowing portal.

Levi followed, then stopped in his tracks, completely baffled.

For the room they had entered looked *exactly* like the Cave.

Waves of stalactites, glowing blue from within, dripped from the ceiling, while more glowing stalagmites formed small mountain ranges all around the perimeter. Darkened tunnels led off in various directions.

"The Cave? How did we get back here?" Levi asked.

"I'm confused," said Xavier.

"Look again," said Mr. J. Ar, coming into the room behind Evan. "Do you see anything unusual?"

"No Sparks." Evan was the first to notice this.

"And no Ruwach," said Levi.

"But look, there's The Book," said Xavier. He pointed to where The Book lay open on a fancy pedestal in the center of the cave.

"That can't be the *real* Book," Levi said. He went over to check.

"Don't touch it," said Mr. J. Ar. "It could be a trap. Nearly everything here is."

"Why does it look like the Cave?" Evan asked.

"Ponéros is a great imitator," said Mr. J. Ar. "And since he covets what belongs to the Source, naturally he will try to imitate it."

"So Ponéros is here? Somewhere?" Evan asked, a new chill in his voice, as if this adventure had suddenly taken a much darker turn than he realized.

"Yes," said Mr. J. Ar. "But it is not our mission to seek him out. We're here only for Brianna and Ivy, and the books."

"Let's hope he's taking a nap or something," said Evan.

"So which way to the prison?" Xavier asked, looking around at each of the tunnels. They all looked the same, just as they did in the real Cave.

"And where could Brianna be, if she's hiding?" asked Levi.

Just then one of the tunnels lit up with purple lights.

"There!" said Evan. He started to march toward the tunnel. Mr. J. Ar grabbed him and pulled him back.

"Forgetting something?"

"The breastplate!" Xavier said. He pointed to Evan's armor, which was blinking rapidly.

"Another trap?" asked Evan.

Mr. J. Ar nodded.

"The breastplate says to go that way," said Xavier, pointing to a different tunnel that was still in darkness. The others faced that direction; their breastplates stopped blinking, shining a steady light.

"Right," said Mr. J. Ar. "Get your swords ready."

The three boys pulled their Krÿsen from their belts and pressed them to their breastplates, extending their swords.

"Okay," said Xavier. "Let's go."

CHAPTER 26

Footsteps

Brianna crouched against a wall, hugging her knees to her chest. She was so tired she could barely move. She'd been running for so long, trying to stay ahead of the Forger on her trail, that she no longer had any idea where she was or how to get back to Ivy again. The hallways all looked exactly the same. Whenever she turned a corner, there it was again, the fake Hall of Armor, but when she called out for Ivy she heard no response. If she stopped to rest, the dreadful footsteps of the Forger began to echo through the tunnel, so that she had to get up and run again. How long could she go on like this? She had no armor, no weapons. She felt lost and helpless and very weary.

Don't cry. She said that over and over to herself, even though crying was all she wanted to do. *Viktor.* He'd been working for the enemy all the time. Now she was stuck in this horrible place, and her friend was locked behind one of these doors, probably being turned to metal.

If only I could go back, she thought. To the moment before Viktor rode up on the bike, to when she and Ivy had been playing with Star on the front lawn and everything had been peaceful . . .

The footsteps reverberated through the hallway, jarring her back to the present. She jumped up, her heart racing, and started to run again. Her lungs ached, and her legs were shaking. But the footsteps got louder, ever nearer. Then Brianna tripped and fell forward, sprawling on the floor. She let out a gasp of pain but lay still. There was no point in running anymore.

"Bean!"

Brianna raised her head. She blinked. Levi stood before her, his eyes wide as if he couldn't believe she was really there.

"Levi?" She looked at him suspiciously. Hadn't a Forger made itself look exactly like Levi once, in order to trap him in a dome? How was she to know this was the real Levi?

"It's me, honest!" said Levi. "Who else would call you Bean?"

Xavier and Evan appeared on either side of him, followed by Mr. J. Ar. All of them. Brianna let out a gasp of relief, jumped to her feet, and threw her arms around Levi. Then she hugged Mr. J. Ar and Xavier, who stiffened as if taken off guard. Evan backed away, holding up his hand to ward her off.

"Uh-uh," he said. "No hugging."

"Oh, right. Sorry," Brianna said, wiping away a stray tear from her eye. She smiled despite her still hammering heart. "I can't tell you how glad I am to see you guys. How did you find me?"

"The armor led us to you," said Levi.

"But what about the Forger?"

"Forger?"

Just then a roar like a jet engine rose up behind them. They whirled to see a Forger towering over them, its giant metal hand reaching for Xavier. Mr. J. Ar had his sword out in an instant, slashing at the Forger's arm, knocking it away. It roared again, grabbing Mr. J. Ar by the neck with its other arm.

"Dad!" Levi yelled. He swung his sword and struck the arm that held his dad. The Forger shook Mr. J. Ar like a rag doll and then dropped him, its arm going haywire. Xavier stepped in and thrust his sword into the Forger's central orb. Sparks flew from its chest as it wheeled backward and slammed against the tunnel wall. It toppled over and was still, the glowing red of its eyes sputtering and going dark.

Levi dropped to his knees by his father. "Dad? Can you hear me?" He shook his father's shoulders. Mr. J. Ar grunted. His neck where the Forger had grabbed him had turned to metal. He could hardly move his jaw at all, making it difficult to understand his words.

"O . . . O . . ." Mr. J. Ar waved his arm toward the tunnel.

"He's saying go," said Xavier.

"We aren't leaving you here," said Levi. "Can you walk?"

Mr. J. Ar blinked in reply. The boys helped him to his feet.

"Which way is Ivy?" Levi asked Brianna.

"I don't know, I got totally lost, and that Forger was chasing me," said Brianna. "We were in the Hall of Armor. . . ."

"The Hall of Armor?" said Xavier.

"Not the real one. Viktor told us—anyway, the doors were open. Ivy went in, and it just closed, and she was trapped. . . ."

"Okay," said Levi. "We need to get back there." He stood up and checked his armor. "This way."

They started down the tunnel in the direction Levi had pointed. Evan gave one last look at the damaged Forger before following.

"That should teach you not to mess with the Prince Warriors!" he said.

———

They moved quickly; all was silent except for the sound of their boots echoing through the hallways and Mr. J. Ar's labored breathing. The metal on his neck had started to expand around his jaw. Levi wondered now how much time they had before it spread to the rest of him. They needed to get him to Ruwach as soon as possible.

They ran down hallway after hallway, checking the breastplate and changing course often. The hallways all looked the same, endless rows of armor and locked doors. Their progress slowed as Mr. J. Ar had more trouble breathing, until finally he collapsed against one of the doors, unable to go on.

"You guys go ahead," said Levi. "We'll stay here. My dad needs to—"

He was interrupted by a faint but furious female voice coming from the other side of the door on which Mr. J. Ar slumped.

"Let me out of here, you slime-ball!"

It was unmistakably Ivy.

CHAPTER 27

Doors

Brianna was thrilled to hear Ivy's passionate, courageous, outraged voice. It meant she was still okay
enough to be mad.

"Let me out, Viktor, you slimy maggot!" Ivy bellowed
again. "Let me out, you rotten piece of—pond scum!"

"Pond scum?" asked Evan, one eyebrow raised.

"She must be running out of things to call him," said
Levi. "Ivy!" he yelled through the door.

"She can't hear you," Brianna said. "I tried it before."

"Okay—let's get my dad away from the door first."
Levi and Xavier shifted Mr. J. Ar to the other side of the
hallway. Brianna sat down on the floor next to him.

Levi gripped his sword in both hands and brought
it over his head, like he had seen Rook and his dad do,
holding it out flat so the tip of the blade was aimed at
the door. He looked at Xavier and Evan, who did the
same thing. "I sure hope she's not standing right in
front of the door," Levi said. "Or this might hurt. One
. . . two . . . three!"

The three of them thrust their swords into the door.
There was a sharp, hissing sound, and the door began
to flash and sputter, like a television blinking on and
off. Then it disappeared altogether, replaced by the
greenish metal bars of a prison cell.

Ivy stood in the center of the cell, her hands over her mouth, her eyes so big they looked as though they might fall out of her head.

"Levi? Xavier? Evan? Is that really you?" she exclaimed.

"It's us," said Levi.

"Ivy!" said Brianna, running to the metal bars. "Can you hear me?"

Ivy nodded and started to cry, although she was laughing at the same time. "I am really glad to see you guys."

There was no door in the cell, but the swords sliced through the bars like hot knives through butter. Soon there was a big enough hole for Ivy to step through. She and Brianna hugged, both of them crying. Evan stepped behind Xavier to avoid any possibility of getting caught in the hugging crossfire.

"Thanks, guys," she said as she broke away from Brianna. "Thanks for coming after me. I thought I'd be in there forever. . . . Mr. J. Ar!" Ivy saw Mr. J. Ar slumped on the floor, the metal creeping up his neck.

"Forger," said Brianna.

"Yeah, we need to hurry," said Levi. "We still have to find your Prince Warrior books."

"Our books? They're here too?"

"Yeah. Viktor stole them after he trapped you. And Manuel's too."

Levi helped his dad to his feet. Mr. J. Ar waved his hand, indicating he was all right, although his breathing was still labored.

"This way," said Xavier. He led the others down the fake Hall of Armor, past rows of doors. Suddenly Xavier stopped and turned toward a door that looked completely different from the others. It was white, with a sleek, crystal knocker and sharply angled handle. It looked like a door to some modern type of mansion. His breastplate beamed steadily upon it.

"I think this is the one," he said. He reached for the handle and pushed. The door swung open gently, leading to a hallway wholly different from the prison cells that surrounded it. It was lined with high shelves containing boxes of all shapes and sizes, some as small as jewelry boxes and others big enough to hold refrigerators. Xavier stepped through the doorway and peered down the hall, which seemed to go on for a very long way, disappearing into total darkness.

He examined the boxes—some were made of cardboard, some of wood, and some were silver and gold. Names were engraved in the boxes or written on the sides in a fancy script.

"Who are all these people?" said Evan, stepping up beside Xavier to look at the names on the boxes. He opened a lid; a terrible odor poured out of the box, making him gag. "Something died in there," he said, coughing.

"Everything here is dead," said Levi. His eyes had begun to water. He was seeing something the others couldn't. But this time, there was no stinging sensation. He was getting used to the gift. "This is where Ponéros keeps all the stuff he's stolen from people. Everything. Even their hopes and dreams."

"And their Prince Warrior books?" said Brianna.

"Yeah," said Levi. He felt something cold run down his spine, a strange feeling that he was being watched. His eyes traveled upward. Rows of green bulbs dangled from the ceiling, casting a ghastly glow over the long hallway. But there was something else up there too—thousands and thousands of tiny red dots.

"Ents," Levi whispered. The others looked up as well. They could not see the jagged metal wings of the Ents, only the glow of thousands of eyes watching them.

Levi turned to Brianna and Ivy. "Stay here with my dad," he said in a soft voice. "We'll find the books. Dad, you might need your shield."

Mr. J. Ar blinked once to let Levi know he understood. He leaned against the door frame, breathing in short gasps.

Levi turned to Xavier and Evan, tilting his head toward the hallway. He put a finger to his lips. They began to walk down the rows of boxes, reading the labels as they went. Levi could feel the Ents tracking their every move.

When they had gone so far down the hallway that they could no longer see Mr. J. Ar or the girls, Evan stopped in his tracks and made a low noise in his throat. He pointed to a row of boxes. Levi and Xavier drew up next to him. There they saw a box with Brianna's name and one with Ivy's and Manuel's. But their names were also on boxes: Xavier, Evan, and Levi. And Finn. And Rook. All of their friends too. Ponéros had boxes for each of them.

The kids' boxes looked fairly new, but others looked old, the edges cracked and worn, as if they'd been there a long time and opened more than once.

"What do you think is in them?" Xavier asked, staring at the box with his name on it.

"I don't want to know," said Evan.

"Aren't you a little curious?" said Xavier.

Evan thought about it, pulled down his box, and opened the lid. He let out a breath of relief. "It's empty," he said. "And I hope it stays empty. I don't want Ponéros getting any of my stuff."

Xavier pulled down his box and opened it.

"What's in it?" said Evan, jumping up to see.

"Nothing," said Xavier. He sounded relieved.

Levi's box was empty too. "Guess he keeps the boxes in case he ever does steal something."

He put his box away and reached for Brianna's box. He took a deep breath and opened it.

The book was there. He lifted it out, checking to see if there was anything else in the box. He saw something scattered at the bottom—dust? Ashes? He wasn't sure. He quickly closed the lid. Then he opened Ivy's and Manuel's and pulled out the books, handing one to each of the other boys. They had to stow their swords, which had retracted to the small Krÿs size, in order to carry the books.

"Got 'em," said Levi. "Let's go."

"Wait. Ruwach said there was another one here," said Xavier. He glanced at all the boxes, his eyes resting on the one that was labeled "Aarón Santos." This box was much larger than the others and very worn, as if it had been used often. It was heavy too. Xavier carefully lifted the lid and looked inside. Reaching in among a lot of stuff he couldn't identify, he pulled out a very dusty book. He cleared off the cover; the Crest of Ahoratos glowed faintly.

"Manuel's dad's book?" asked Evan.

"The real one, I think," said Xavier.

"Cool. Let's get out of here," said Levi. He and Evan each carried one book, and Xavier had two. The Ents still loomed overhead, very quiet, their laser eyes trained on the boys. Levi held the book under one arm and reached into his pocket with the other hand, fingering his seed-shield. He figured the shield would be more useful against Ents than the sword, and since he only had one hand free, he had to choose. He pulled it out and showed it to Xavier and Evan, silently telling them to do the same. Xavier balanced the books in one hand and took out his seed-shield. Evan did the same. Levi turned to head back to the entrance, where his father waited with the girls.

But something stood in his way. Something very large and made of metal.

The Forger raised its huge fist to grab him; Levi, with no time to think, ducked and scooted under its outstretched arm. Then with his boot he kicked the Forger as hard as he could in the back of its massive leg. He expected it to hurt, but his boot seemed to have hardened around the toe so he barely felt anything at all. The Forger pitched forward at the blow, right into Xavier and Evan, who quickly flattened themselves against the shelves. Evan managed to slip past the Forger as it made a grab for Xavier, who thrust out his shield, blocking the huge metal fist.

"Xavi! Come on!" Evan coaxed. Xavier darted past the Forger, which spun around and roared, the sound like a bomb exploding in their ears. Thankfully, Levi and Evan had deployed their shields, which muffled the terrible noise.

But the Forger's roar seemed to signal the Ents on the ceiling; they descended in a flurry of clanging metal wings and flying darts.

"Let's get out of here!" Levi shouted. The three boys turned and ran. The Ents continued to bombard them with darts, despite the fact they bounced off the shields harmlessly.

Levi found it increasingly difficult to hold the book and keep the shield deployed as he ran. The hallway seemed far longer than it was before. He could see no sign of his father or the girls ahead. Maybe they were gone, maybe they had been captured by Forgers and taken off to the prison. His father was so weak, and the girls didn't have armor—

He felt his helmet warm, tightening around his head. The thoughts that ran through his mind were instantly replaced by louder, stronger thoughts: *You have everything you need.* Levi felt those words shiver down his arm, strengthening his grip on the shield and the book.

Then another Forger stepped out from the wall of shelves, blocking their path, its huge red eyes pulsing, its arms outstretched.

Levi skidded to a stop, causing Xavier and Evan to pile into him. Levi thrust his shield toward the Forger and pushed with all his might. *Resist. Resist.* Evan joined his shield with Levi's. Xavier turned his shield toward the Ents, which pressed in from the other side, forming a nearly solid wall.

"Now what?" cried Evan. "We can't carry these books and fight at the same time!"

"Dad!" Levi cried out. "Can you hear me?"

There was no answer beyond the shrieking of the Ents. Levi pushed against the Forger, who moved back an inch or two, but no more.

"We have to leave the books," Xavier said.

"No, we can't. We need them!" said Levi.

"We won't get out otherwise!" said Xavier. He threw the books he was carrying on the ground and fumbled for his Krÿs.

Suddenly the Forger in front of them doubled over and collapsed sideways, knocking boxes from the shelves. Levi saw a sword come down on its neck, nearly slicing its head off.

"Dad?" Levi yelled, wondering if it was indeed his father coming to get him. The figure was tall, broad-shouldered, his face still in shadow. But as he drew nearer, Levi saw exactly who it was.

CHAPTER 28

A Narrow Escape

Finn!" Levi shouted.

"Come on!" said Finn, pulling his sword from the Forger's metal neck. Xavier hurriedly picked up the books as the three boys climbed over the huge Forger lying amid the toppled boxes. The Ents pursued them, screeching in rage and shooting darts as they ran all the way back to the doorway.

Levi was relieved to see his father slumped on the floor with his fist thrust out, his shield covering the girls. Brianna and Ivy huddled together with their hands over their ears to shut out the horrific screeching of the Ents.

When Mr. J. Ar saw the boys coming, he pushed himself to his feet, the girls helping him. Finn whirled around and raised up his shield to join Levi and Evan.

"Take the books!" Xavier shouted, handing his books to Brianna. Ivy took the other two.

"Go on out with my dad," ordered Levi. "Get back to where we first came in. We'll meet you there!" The four boys turned their shields fully on the Ents, their combined strength sending shock waves through the swarming mass. They backed away slowly, slipping through the doorway one at a time. Finn went last, slamming the door hard and leaning against it.

"Go on," said Finn. "I'll hold them." The door puckered and splintered as the Ents continued to bombard it from the other side.

"The door can't hold them for long," said Xavier. He put his shield away. "We need to run—"

Suddenly Finn jumped away from the door, shaking his hands as if he'd been burned.

"It's hot," he said. As the boys watched, the door began to glow very brightly.

"It's on fire?" asked Evan.

Levi stared at the door, his eyes straining, watering. *Seeing.* "It's Ru," he whispered.

"I don't think those Ents are going to be getting out of there for a while."

The four of them, guided by their breastplates, raced back to the fake Cave and the spiral staircase. Brianna and Ivy were already there, holding up Mr. J. Ar, who seemed unable to stand alone now. The books were piled on the floor.

"He's not doing too well," said Brianna, her voice laced with worry.

"I'll take care of him," said Levi. "You guys take the books." The two girls and Xavier and Evan each picked up a book and started climbing the spiral staircase. Finn was still looking around, checking the various tunnels for any sign of Forgers.

Levi looked at his dad. The metal had advanced up one side of his face. Levi suspected it now covered his chest as well.

"You're gonna make it," he whispered. "You have to."

Mr. J. Ar blinked. Levi took his father's arms and put them on his shoulders. "Lean on me." Levi took a step on the staircase. "Hold onto my shoulders. Don't let go." He heard his dad's foot fall heavily on the first step, felt him leaning on his shoulders as he pulled himself up. Levi flexed his muscles against the added weight, breathing deeply. "One step at a time," he said. "You coming, Finn?"

"Right behind you," said Finn.

It was a slow, agonizing process, getting up all those stairs. Levi took two or three steps and then stopped, listening to his father wheezing, struggling for breath. *One step at a time,* he said to himself over and over. Sometimes he said it out loud.

"I've got your back," Finn said from time to time. Levi felt relief and gratitude knowing Finn was there to keep his dad from falling.

Finally, Levi sensed a dim light overhead and looked up to see the other kids peering at them from the top of the mound, whispering encouragements. A few more steps and they were out. Levi turned to help his dad crawl out of the hole. Mr. J. Ar collapsed on top of the mound, breathing in short, loud gasps, as if each breath were cut off before it could finish. Finn came up last, still on guard for any attack. Levi watched him a moment, impressed with his skill. He thought Finn could probably handle most anything thrown at him now.

"Thanks for coming," he said to Finn. "Did Ru send you?"

Finn nodded humbly. "He said I was ready."

"Yes, you sure are," Levi responded with a smile.

The sky had become very dark, heavy with black clouds. Levi stayed with Mr. J. Ar as the others descended the mound.

"Where is he?" Evan whispered anxiously.

"Where's who?" said Brianna.

"Tannyn! He's supposed to pick us up."

"Tannyn! You mean he's alive?" Brianna exclaimed. Ivy gasped in delight.

"Oh, yeah," said Evan. "I forgot to tell you that."

Brianna exploded in a huge grin she could barely contain. Tannyn was alive!

They waited awhile longer, but still Tannyn didn't show.

"Maybe he ran into one of those black dragons again," said Evan. "Maybe he's dead for real now."

"Don't say that," said Brianna. "He can't be. . . ."

And then the skypod under their feet began to rumble, like the beginnings of an earthquake. The kids looked at each other with similar expressions of concern: *what now?* One of the mounds near them shuddered, and a Forger burst forth as if it had been shot from a cannon. The kids stared in horror as the Forger landed in front of them, its round red eyes focused on the kids. More mounds shot out more Forgers on all sides. They began to move, forming a circle around the Prince Warriors, who raised their shields and banded together under the protection of the sparkling dome. But the Forgers closed in, forming one huge, impenetrable wall of metal around them.

"Tannyn!" Evan cried. "Come *on* already!"

And then, in the nick of time, he did.

A green, potbellied shape erupted from the thick bank of clouds, zooming toward them.

"'Bout time you showed up!" Evan shouted.

Tannyn spread his wings and landed with a thud in the middle of the circling Forgers. He opened his mouth and shot a stream of blue fire in a wide circle around the kids, forcing the Forgers backward. Some of them began to melt, their arms fusing together.

"Mount up!" shouted Xavier. The kids quickly scrambled onto Tannyn's back, taking advantage of his fire breath to keep the Forgers at bay. Finn and Levi helped Mr. J. Ar to his feet and half-guided, half-carried him aboard, stepping up Tannyn's ridged neck and setting him carefully between two spikes.

"I got you, Dad." Levi sat behind his father, took off his belt, and wrapped it around the both of them, securing them together.

Finn grabbed a spike in front of Mr. J. Ar. He gave Tannyn a pat on his neck. "All set." Then to the others: "Hang on!"

Tannyn spread his enormous wings, let out another blast of fire on the Forgers, and shot straight upward.

As he did, two more shapes burst from the clouds above, spiky tails whipping around to release a barrage of deadly thorns.

"Dragons!" Brianna screamed. Finn, who was not holding a book, launched his shield, covering the rest of them. Tannyn spat out more balls of fire, some of them intercepting the thorns, others forcing the dragons to veer away temporarily. But they always returned.

Tannyn swooped low then soared straight up, above the clouds, the black dragons on his tail. He took cover behind a skypod, which was soon embedded with more dragon thorns. He dipped and swayed in and out of clouds, weaving left and right, up and down. He somehow managed to keep just ahead of his pursuers and avoid the deadly thorns. The humans on board could do nothing but hang on. Tannyn flew so fast that the kids felt their cheeks ripple, their eyes blur with tears. All the while, Levi held onto his dad with one hand and the spike with the other, saying over and over, "I've got you! Hang on!"

A thorn grazed Tannyn's wing, causing him to wobble sideways dangerously; the kids felt their legs dangle in nothingness until Tannyn could right himself again. The wing flopped around, broken, and Tannyn began to lose altitude quickly. But he kept flying, pumping the broken wing twice as hard to keep himself in the air.

The black dragons surrounded him, one on each side, and flipped up their tails to shoot more thorns. Tannyn let out a blast of fire, folded up his wings and dropped straight down; the two dragons shot their thorns into each other. Both fell from the sky like stones, disappearing into the darkness below.

Tannyn spread his wings, leveling off and banking sharply at the last moment to avoid slamming into the side of a mountain. The kids gasped, hanging on for dear life. Tannyn let out a trumpeting "Gorp!" as he flew into the golden sky over Ahoratos.

"Good dragon," whispered Levi.

CHAPTER 29

Healing

Tannyn crash-landed in a flurry of wings at the entrance to the Cave. Ruwach was already there, accompanied by a battalion of Sparks that surrounded Mr. J. Ar, lifted him as if he weighed nothing at all, and carried him inside. Levi followed quickly.

Evan, Finn, and Xavier slid down the side of Tannyn's belly. Evan ran to give him a pat on the nose. "You saved us again, big guy," he whispered.

Another troop of Sparks hovered over Tannyn's broken wing, warming and comforting him. Tannyn made a noise that sounded a little like a purr, his eyes fluttering. Ruwach reached out a glowing hand to the wing; soon it was encased in light, the broken bones reknitting, new skin forming over the hole created by the thorn.

When the wing was mended, Ruwach turned swiftly without speaking and disappeared into the Cave.

"Come on, Van," said Xavier. Evan gave Tannyn's nose one more hug (he made an exception to his "no-hugging" rule when it came to Tannyn) and followed Xavier, Finn, and Ruwach inside.

Levi knelt by his father on the floor of the Cave. Mr. J. Ar was barely breathing at all now. Sparks hovered all around them both, bathing them in a balmy, soothing light. Ruwach drew near and pressed his brilliantly glowing hand on the metal encasing Mr. J. Ar's neck.

The metal soon turned red, then white, liquefying. It melted off Mr. J. Ar's neck, head, and chest, turning to dust that scattered and disappeared. His own rich, dark brown skin looked normal again. He took a full, deep breath—his chest expanding as if it had just been set free from the most brutal of cages.

"Dad," Levi whispered, relieved. He bent down and hugged his father. "I love you, Dad."

"I love you too, son," said Mr. J. Ar, his voice groggy and strained, but strong.

"Thank you," Levi said to Ruwach, his eyes wet with tears. "Thank you."

"You are welcome, Prince Levi," said Ruwach softly.

Mr. J. Ar sat up and touched his son's face, wiping away the tears. Then he put his hand on his own throat. "Feels a lot better," he said. "It was like slowly choking to death."

Ruwach's hood nodded. "What about that one?" He pointed to a small, metal scar on Mr. J. Ar's elbow. "You have had that one for many years. Why have you not asked me to heal it?"

Mr. J. Ar bowed his head. "I did not think it could be . . . healed."

"You do not have, because you do not ask."

Mr. J. Ar looked at his elbow then at Ruwach. His voice was softer than it had ever been. "Will you take this away?"

Immediately, Ruwach touched the scar with his glowing hand; it, too, melted away, disappearing as if it had never been.

Mr. J. Ar raised his arm so he could see his unblemished elbow with his own eyes. He seemed unable to speak.

"Can you heal me too?" Levi asked suddenly. He stepped toward Ruwach, holding out his finger. The metal tip was all that was left of his ordeal with the Forger that had nearly turned his whole body into metal. A reminder of his disobedience. Levi lowered his gaze, still feeling the sting of that reminder.

"Yes, I will." Ruwach touched the tip of Levi's finger with his own. The metal softened, became liquid, and then turned to dust. Levi drew his finger to his face and stared at it, feeling another tear trickle down his cheek. Healed. Made whole. And all he had to do was ask.

Ruwach's hood turned toward Brianna and Ivy. "I am glad to see you are both returned safely."

Ivy looked at the floor. "I can't believe we were so stupid to believe what Viktor told us."

"He told us what we wanted to hear," said Brianna.

"Viktor was just so—dazzling," Ivy said. "I always thought I would recognize an agent of the enemy when I saw him. Guess I was wrong."

"Hey, I thought he was pretty cool too," said Evan. "Turns out he was working for the enemy all along. That kid is *nasty*."

Xavier laughed. "You can say that again."

"Levi was the only one who seemed to know he was up to no good," said Brianna, her gaze going to him. "And we thought you were the one who was wrong. I'm so sorry, Levi."

"Me too," said Ivy. "I'm sorry I said I thought you were jealous of him. I hope you can forgive me."

Levi nodded, looking a little embarrassed. "Yeah, no problem."

There was an awkward silence, broken by Evan.

"We got the books anyway," he said proudly. "Including Mr. Santos's book. But it looked as though it had been there a long time."

Ruwach's hood nodded once. "Yes, very long. Aarón Santos had begun to question the stories in the book long, long ago. They did not make sense to him, according to his own logical thought processes. So, he made changes, small at first, but significant. The enemy took full advantage, casting further doubt on the stories of the Prince Warrior."

"So how did a true version of the book end up in that warehouse in Skot'os?" Xavier asked.

"The enemy always seeks to displace the authentic books and then encourage the forging of counterfeits so that the swords cannot be infused with the power of the Source."

"So, we need to get this one back to him, don't we?" asked Brianna.

Ruwach nodded. "Correct, Princess Brianna. You must return immediately. While you have been on mission here, Ponéros has been very active on earth."

"The pods," said Xavier in a low voice.

"They're open?" said Levi. "Already?"

"Manuel needs you. And his father does too. Go."

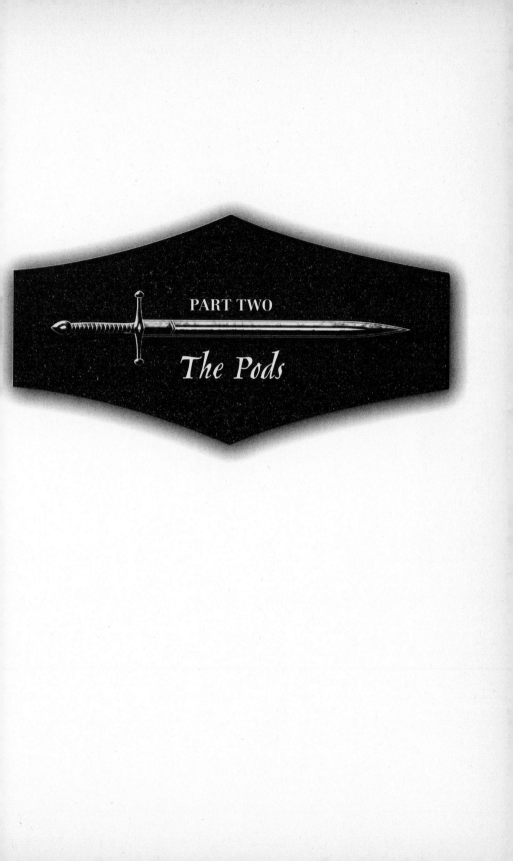

PART TWO

The Pods

CHAPTER 30

The Unleashing

Manuel got out of his father's car, staring in aston-
ishment at the hordes of people who had gathered at the skypod site. Workers in hard hats were
directing a huge piece of machinery toward the pod.
No one was wearing hazmat suits anymore; apparently the pod had been declared safe enough for close
contact. A growing crowd of spectators, kept a good
distance away by yellow tape manned by policemen,
pointed and took selfies with their phones.

Reporters were stationed at intervals behind the
spectators, talking animatedly into television cameras
and interviewing officials on the site. It was like this
was the most exciting event to ever take place in the
town of Cedar Creek. Manuel wasn't sure whether or
not it was, but it was the most dangerous. Of that, he
was sure.

Manuel focused on the machine. It was a heavy
hoist, truck-mounted drill rig, used to break through
the densest rock known to exist. His father had told
him they had been exceedingly lucky because the drill
was found at a local quarry and could be moved fairly
quickly. That was why this particular pod had been
chosen to be opened first. It was all happening much
too fast.

"Papá," Manuel said as his father got out of the car and started walking toward the drill rig. "Please, don't do this. You mustn't open the pod. You know what will happen!"

"Manuel, for the last time, stop interfering. This is science, not . . . fairy tales."

"Ahoratos is not a fairy tale, and you know it! And those pods are full of Ents. They will destroy everything!"

"Since when are you so imaginative about these things? Don't you love to investigate? Didn't you try to break open that seed that belonged to your mother?"

"Yes," Manuel said, wondering dimly how his father knew about that. "But that was different. I didn't know what the seed contained. But I do know what this pod contains!"

"And now, the world will know. And I will be the one to show them." Mr. Santos grinned in anticipation.

"I have already been asked to contribute an article to *Earth Works* magazine!"

"Papá, please, I am begging you!"

"Manuel, you insisted on coming with me to witness this momentous event, and you promised to stay out of the way. Do not break your promise to me."

"At least tell everyone to leave. All these people. Make an announcement, tell them they should go home."

"There is no danger, Manuel. The officials have kept the public at a safe distance, and we have conducted thorough tests. No traces of radioactivity or biohazards. Now for the last time, I am telling you to stay out of the way. Do not interfere anymore."

Mr. Santos turned from Manuel and ducked under the yellow tape, showing a badge so that the policeman would let him through. Manuel pushed through the crowd and ran up to the yellow tape, trying to see what was happening. The operator was maneuvering the drill into position, raising the giant arm so the drill bit was pressed against the side of the pod. Manuel thought he could feel the pod tremble, as if the Ents inside were ignited by their imminent emancipation. Soon, this place would be crawling with them—literally.

Manuel realized to his horror that he didn't have his armor. He'd forgotten to get it before he left; he'd been so preoccupied with his father and the drill. He did have his seed in his pocket, however, as he never went anywhere without it.

He moved away from the press of people and reporters, wondering what to do. He had an impulse to go up to one of the reporters, take the microphone, and warn everyone watching of the danger they were about to face. Then he imagined his father's anger if he did such a thing. So, he did the only thing he could think to do in this moment. He lifted his eyes upward toward the heavens and whispered: "Ruwach. Please. Help me."

"Hey, kid," said a voice behind him. Manuel whirled to see Rook driving up in the Creekside Landscaping truck. He jumped out and walked over. He was wearing his armor, which shimmered in the slanting sun, transparent, like a hologram. "I see your dad found a drill. That was quick."

"Yes," said Manuel. He glanced up at the sky and smiled. *Thanks, Ru.* Then he turned back to Rook. "I've tried to stop him. He won't listen to me."

Rook nodded. "Soon as I heard about it on the news I figured we were about to have an epidemic on our hands." Together they stared at the pod. It seemed like a dead thing, but they both knew better. "Where are the others?"

"In Ahoratos," Manuel said. "Brianna and Ivy were kidnapped by Viktor."

"Who's Viktor?"

"He's the new student from school. Only he isn't a student. We thought he was a Prince Warrior, but now it seems he was working for the enemy. He took my book with my sword. I can only hope they make it back in time."

"Oh, man," said Rook. "Have you looked around? Maybe they're already here somewhere."

"I haven't seen them." Manuel scanned the crowd, searching for his friends. His eyes fell upon someone he knew. He almost groaned.

"It's Miss Stanton!" he said, pointing to the girl in the ponytail, holding a Starbucks cup and taking a selfie with the pod in the background. "What is *she* doing here?"

"Gawking, like everyone else," said Rook.

As if she'd heard her name spoken aloud, Mary Stanton caught sight of Manuel and Rook and waved. She rushed over to them.

"Oh, hey guys," she said. "I was driving home and saw this going on. Kind of cool, huh?"

"No, it isn't," said Manuel.

"You probably should get going," said Rook. "It could get dangerous."

"Really?" Mary's eyes got big. "How dangerous?"

"Like turn you into a metal cyborg dangerous," said Manuel under his breath.

"What did you say, Manuel?"

"Oh, nothing. But I do think it would be a good idea if you went home. And locked your doors. And made sure your windows were closed. You know, just as a precaution."

"Why? Is it true there are aliens in that thing?" she asked in a conspiratorial tone. "Like they said on the news?"

"It's certainly possible," said Manuel.

They were interrupted by the sound of the drill revving up. The rod spun rapidly as the huge drill bit began boring into the pod.

"Look at that!" Mary exclaimed.

"Do you have your shield on you?" Manuel whispered to Rook.

"Sure."

"Good. I think you're going to need it."

Manuel watched, holding his breath, as the drill bored into the pod. At first it seemed to make no indentation at all, then all of the sudden it broke through, sending up a torrent of debris, pebbles, small stones, and flaky dust. A gasp fluttered through the crowd, and then it grew hushed. Waiting. The drill continued to go deeper into the pod. The operator increased power, making the rod spin faster.

Manuel braced himself, whispering: "Ruwach. Help. Ruwach. Help." And then, because it's what he always did when he was scared out of his mind, he started counting in his head: *One, two, three, four, five . . .*

The drill suddenly stopped, as if it were stuck. The operator tried again and again to get it started but had no luck. The men in hard hats on the ground waved their arms frantically. The operator shrugged his shoulders.

The crowd began to babble about this new development.

"What's going on?" asked Mary.

"Probably broke the bit," murmured Manuel. He felt a small sliver of hope—perhaps the drill hadn't gotten in far enough to release any Ents. Perhaps they were safe after all.

"Look!" Rook pointed as a thin ribbon of white smoke drifted out of the hole the drill had made in the pod.

"Is it Ents?" said Manuel, pushing up his glasses to see better.

"I don't think so," said Rook. "Looks like smoke."

Manuel stared at the smoke. Feathery plumes drifted from the hole in the pod, encircling each other, weaving in and out. The smoke reminded Manuel of the Mountain of Rhema, the breath of the Source. But there was no way that the breath of the Source could be coming out of a skypod from Skot'os.

"It's kind of pretty," said Mary.

The operator of the drill, giving up on starting it again, reversed the truck and began extracting the rod. More plumes of white smoke burst from the hole, swirling around the pod in delicate waves.

"That's very strange," said Manuel. "No Ents."

"No what?" said Mary.

The white smoke drifted over the heads of the workers and policemen, splintering into several separate strands that danced and wove around each other in twisting, curling ribbons. Murmurs swept the crowd, excited and a bit apprehensive as to what this smoke could be. Yet the swirling bands of smoke were so beautiful and tantalizing that no one tried to run away. In fact, they were moving toward the smoke, breaking through the yellow tape, overrunning the cops.

"They're so beautiful!" Mary exclaimed. One misty ribbon unfurled before her, and she moved toward it.

"No, don't touch it—" Manuel cautioned, but Mary ignored him. It was like she didn't even hear him. "Stop her, Rook!"

Rook grabbed Mary's arm and pulled her back. He spun her around to face them and Manuel saw, to his horror, that Mary's eyes had turned almost completely white.

"The smoke! It's infecting her somehow!" he exclaimed. "Miss Stanton! Close your eyes!"

Rook raised his seed in his fist, deploying his shield around the three of them. As soon as the shield covered Mary, she blinked rapidly, the blue of her eyes returning.

"What are you doing?" she said to Rook, as if annoyed that he'd woken her from a lovely dream.

"Look!" said Manuel, pointing to a man who had reached out to touch a strand of the mist. His eyes were already pure white. His mouth opened and the mist slid down his throat.

The man became very still, as if frozen. He spasmed slightly, looking as though he were about to throw up. Spidery cracks appeared underneath the skin of his face, until it looked as though all the blood vessels had turned gray and were about to burst out of him. The veins of gray ran down his neck and to his chest, spreading to the tips of his fingers. Around the middle of his chest, a large plate of gray metal appeared, absorbing the fabric of his shirt. He began to move mechanically, as if he no longer had control of himself. Not a man at all anymore. A machine.

"What's happening?" asked Rook in a low voice. "Seems like something has gotten inside of his body."

"Like metal," Manuel whispered, realizing what was happening. "The mist, it turns them to metal—but on the *inside*."

"We should get out of here," said Rook.

Manuel saw a man in a hard hat holding a megaphone. He too was moving toward one of the misty plumes. Manuel ran over to the man, grabbed his megaphone, and began shouting into it.

"Don't look at the mist! Don't touch it! Go home! As fast you can! I repeat—don't look at the mist!" He shouted over and over, causing some people to obey, shaking their heads and turning away. "Run! Run as fast as you can!"

The newly transformed metal-people swiveled and began marching toward Manuel, their white eyes glaring. Manuel dropped the megaphone and ran back to Rook.

"You're right. We should go. Now!"

Rook nodded, pointing to the truck. "Get in. Mary, you too." He started to lead her to the truck, opening the passenger door for her.

"What's happening!" cried Mary. "What are those—?"

"Just get in! Let's go, Manuel!"

"But wait! My dad!" cried Manuel. "I have to go and get him!"

"Hurry!" said Rook.

Manuel deployed his seed-shield and dodged through the crowd in search of his father. As he went he shouted to those around him: "Don't look at it! Don't touch it!" He doubted if any of them would listen. They were moving closer and closer to the pod, their arms up in the air, reaching toward the smoke.

Manuel saw his father lying on the ground next to the drill rig. All the workers had either abandoned it or turned into metal zombies. But Mr. Santos did not seem to be infected. Manuel raced over to his dad, covering him with his shield and turning him over. He was bleeding from a large gash in his forehead.

"Papá? Are you okay?" Mr. Santos looked at him, blinking. His glasses lay beside him, crushed.

"Debris from the drill—hit me. Glasses . . . broke. I couldn't see. Someone ran into me, knocked me down. I don't remember what happened next—"

Manuel was grateful that his father's glasses had broken. It meant he didn't see the ribbons of smoke that everyone else had seen. "Get up! Can you walk? You need to come with me! But keep your head down. Look at the ground. Don't look up."

Mr. Santos stood up slowly, and Manuel led him back to the truck, keeping his shield raised. The crowd had begun to panic as more and more people were infected, the liquid metal running into their veins, hardening their hearts. He made it back to the truck and opened the passenger door, pushing his dad onto the seat next to a frightened and bewildered Mary. Manuel squeezed in as well, slamming the door just as one of the metallized people began pounding on the window, cracking the glass.

"Let's go!" Manuel said. Rook stepped on the gas and peeled away from the scene. More of the transformed ones chased after them, several catching hold of the back of the truck, causing it to fishtail. Rook spun the wheel in a hard one-eighty to dislodge them, then shifted into low gear and slammed the gas pedal to the floor. The truck took off in a spray of gravel, jumped a curb, and shimmied onto the main road.

Mr. Santos looked back through the rear window at the awful creatures still trying to chase after them. "Some sort of gas . . . causes hallucinations, perhaps—"

"They are not hallucinations, Papá," said Manuel. "They are very real."

CHAPTER 31

The Plague

Rook drove to the Rec. It was the only place he knew they would be safe for the moment. He tried to think of what they should do, but Mary wouldn't stop asking questions.

"What's going on? What was that smoke? Is it alien? Did we just witness an alien invasion? Is this like that movie? Do you think they're friendly? I need to post this picture I took. Look! Where did those zombie people come from? Maybe it was just a stunt, like for a TV show. Is that what it was?"

Rook didn't answer. Manuel stared out the window. His father's head lay on his shoulder. He quietly moaned in pain.

Rook pulled into the front loop of the Rec, parking as close to the door as he could. He dashed out to open the front door as Manuel and Mary helped Mr. Santos inside. Rook immediately began checking that all the windows and doors were closed tightly and the shades were drawn. Mary stood in the middle of the room, still asking questions that no one would answer.

Manuel led his father to a chair and sat him down. "Miss Stanton, I need a towel," he called out. Mary quickly brought him a towel from the supply closet. Manuel held it to his father's forehead, but the blood kept coming. Soon the towel was soaked through. He pressed the towel harder to stop the bleeding.

"My glasses . . ."

"They're broken, Papá."

Mr. Santos's eyes fluttered open and closed. "What have I done?" he whispered.

"I'm not certain, but we must try and stop it somehow."

"Is there anything I can do?" Mary asked.

"Yes," said Manuel, looking up at Mary. "You can text Mr. J. Ar and ask him to come here as soon as he's back from—wherever he is. It's an emergency. He may be out of service, but text him anyway. Tell him the pod is opened. And also, can you call Brianna's, Ivy's, and Xavier and Evan's families and tell them they should stay inside with their windows and doors closed and locked, and not leave their houses under any circumstances? And if they see anything that looks like white smoke or mist they should not look at it at all? Post that on the rec center website as well, and on every other social media outlet you can. It's very important. Call 911 and tell them to put out a bulletin: do not look at or touch the mist. Got it?"

"Uh . . . okay . . ." said Mary, still confused.

"And I need a computer."

"I think there's a laptop in the office."

Mary went to get the laptop. Rook came over to sit by Manuel.

"How's he doing?" Rook asked.

"Still bleeding pretty badly. I think he needs stitches."

Mary returned with the laptop and set it before Manuel. "Can I get you anything else?"

Manuel shook his head. "Just make those calls."

"Got it!" Mary exclaimed, and went into the office. She picked up her phone and sent a text message to Mr. J. Ar.

Manuel says come to Rec. Big problems. Pod opened. Hurry!

A few seconds later a message came on her screen: *Message delivery failed.*

———————

"Can you hold this a minute?" Manuel asked Rook, who nodded and took over pressing the towel to Mr. Santos's head. Manuel opened the laptop and began typing, stopping every few seconds to stare at the screen.

"Do you think the effects of the smoke can be reversed?" Rook asked.

"I don't know. Have you ever seen anything like this before?"

Rook shook his head. "I thought there were Ents in those pods too."

"Yes, I'm wondering if the Ents inside the pods decay over time and form the mist. Or perhaps they were transformed by the enemy. In any case, the smoke infuses humans with some sort of metal substance."

"The weird thing," said Rook, "is that the humans seem to *want* to be infected."

"Yes, that is peculiar." Manuel typed some more into the laptop. "I just hope the others make it back in time. We're going to need all the help we can get."

———

Mr. J. Ar and the kids found themselves in the Blakes' backyard again, kneeling in the circle around the stump, just as they had been before they left. For a moment it seemed as though no time had passed, except that Brianna, Ivy, and Finn were with them. And they had the books.

"Good to be home," said Brianna. "I mean, back on earth anyway."

Mr. J. Ar's phone chirped. He pulled it from his pocket and looked at the screen. "It's from Mary."

"Miss Stanton?" said Ivy, puzzled. "What does she want?"

Mr. J. Ar read the text and frowned. "We need to go. It's happening. The pod is open."

———

Mr. J. Ar drove to the Rec like he was competing in a NASCAR race. Rook's truck was parked in the loop, right near the door. Mr. J. Ar screeched to a stop behind him, and everyone bailed out, running toward the building.

Evan got there first, but the door was locked. Through the glass he could see Manuel sitting at a laptop, typing furiously. Rook was hunched over his shoulder, staring at the screen. Manuel's father was sitting next to him, a towel on his head. And Miss Stanton—Miss Stanton?— was talking on her phone as she glanced over Manuel's shoulder.

Evan banged on the door and shouted. "Let us in!" The other kids joined in. Manuel looked up and pointed. Then Miss Stanton came running to open the door.

"Hurry!" she said, letting them all in. "Shut it tight. Make sure it's locked!"

"Thank goodness you're back!" said Manuel as the rest of the kids gathered around him.

"What's up?" said Levi. "What happened?"

"Pods opening. All over the place. The others weren't even drilled! They just opened on their own, as soon as the first one—"

"That was their permission," said Mr. J. Ar, his face very grim.

"What do you mean, permission?" said Brianna.

"Agents of Ponéros need permission to operate in this world. They couldn't come out of the pods until they were . . ." His voice trailed off while he searched for the right word. The Prince Warriors leaned forward, awaiting his final thought. "Invited." Mr. J. Ar let out a heavy sigh and shook his head. Then he glanced at Mr. Santos, who looked bloody and dazed. "Mr. Santos?"

"I'm fine," rasped Aarón Santos with a weak wave.

"The mist enters people through their mouths and turns them into metal," said Manuel, "on the *inside*. It seems to form a coating over their hearts as well. It's like the metal gloms onto the human parts—"

"Gloms?" said Evan, his ears perking up at the mention of this new, strange word. "We should call them Glommers!"

"Glommers," said Levi, nodding. "Not bad."

"What about our families?" said Brianna. "Are they okay?"

"Oh, I called them all, told them to stay indoors and sit tight," said Mary, looking eager to show she was helping too. "They'll be safe, right? So long as they stay inside?"

"For a while," said Manuel. "But very few buildings are truly airtight. This mist might be able to get into cracks in the foundation. It's insidious."

"In-what-eous?" said Evan.

"Sneaky," Manuel said. "It attracts people, so they actually want to be infected—"

"I did this," said Mr. Santos suddenly. Everyone looked at him. His eyes were still closed; he spoke in a halting whisper. "I did this. I unleashed this plague. I am responsible for this. Manuel tried to stop me. I should have listened to him."

Manuel got up from the computer. "Papá, we will stop this."

"Who?"

"Us."

"You?" said Mr. Santos. "Children?"

"We are Prince Warriors." Manuel spoke softly, but with deep conviction. Mr. Santos's eyes opened, as if he were seeing his son for the very first time, even without having his glasses. He nodded slowly.

"Here's your book, Manuel," Xavier said, handing him the book they'd retrieved from Skot'os.

"Mr. Santos, we have yours too," said Evan. He placed the book before Mr. Santos like a precious treasure. "Your true book."

Mr. Santos reached out and felt for the book, running a hand over the cover, as if trying to be sure it was real. He let out a ragged breath. "I remember now—as a boy. This book. I loved it then. But I lost sight of it. Forgot it. And then, when my Rosa—your mamá—" He couldn't finish.

Manuel put a hand on his shoulder. "Mamá died. But she is not lost. She left me this," he indicated the book Xavier had given him, "so I would know what her legacy was, what my destiny is. She wanted you to remember it too." He paused. "Papá, were you there? In Ahoratos? Did you get your armor?"

Mr. Santos nodded very slowly, as if remembering something for the first time. "Yes. Yes, I was. I did. But it was so long ago. It is long gone now."

"No, it isn't. Once you get your armor, you can't lose it. I learned that myself, when I flushed my seed down the toilet."

"You did what?"

"But I got it back."

"Me too!" said Evan.

"And I threw away my boots, but I got them back too," said Levi. "And Rook—Rook was in prison in Skot'os! He looked almost as bad as those people walking around out there. But we rescued him, and Ruwach set him free!"

"It's true," said Rook.

"Me too," said Finn.

"And I rejected the helmet, but I still got it back," said Brianna.

"And I made a huge mistake and walked into a prison, but these guys got me out," said Ivy.

Mr. Santos raised his head, straining to look at them. "I . . . see . . ." He fell forward, on top of the book, as if he had fainted. "Papá!" Manuel exclaimed, rushing to him.

"He needs to go to the hospital," said Mr. J. Ar. "Let me take him."

"But Dad! We need you," said Levi.

Mr. J. Ar smiled at his son, putting a hand on his shoulder. "You got this," he said. "All of you. Make me proud. Make Ruwach proud." He helped Mr. Santos to his feet, looping an arm over his shoulder.

"Take my truck," said Rook. "I think I can fit all of them in your SUV."

"Good point." Mr. J. Ar pulled the key out of his pocket and handed it to Rook, who handed him the truck keys. "Keep an eye on them." Rook nodded. He followed them to the door and raised his shield so they could get to the truck in safety.

Levi went to the window and watched his father pull away from the curb. A lump formed in his throat.

"Okay," said Rook when he came back in, glancing at Levi with a small smile. "Get your swords charged up and your armor on. We need to prep for battle."

CHAPTER 32

Preparation

Mary watched in wonder as the children she had known as rec center kids busied themselves doing bizarre things like putting little knives into strange, colorful books and running in and out of the supply closet. They were very intent and focused, as if preparing themselves for some important mission. They hardly looked like children at all now.

She glanced at Rook and Finn, who were standing guard at the windows on either side of the main doors, apparently on the lookout for Glommers.

Glommers, she thought. Metal running in people's veins? Hardening their hearts? What was going on here?

She saw Manuel return to the laptop to check something. She went to him and sat down beside him, clearing her throat. "Can you please explain to me what is going on? What are you all doing?"

Manuel glanced at her, his eyes shifting nervously. "It's kind of a long story," he said.

"Has there been an invasion? Like from outer space?"

"More like *inner* space."

"Huh?"

"There is a world—unseen but very real, more real than this world. We've been there."

"You've been—to this other world?"

"Yes, it's actually the real world. We go there to fight the enemy. We are Prince Warriors. Finn and Rook too."

"Really?" Mary blinked, looking over at Rook. "The lawn-mower guy?"

Manuel nodded.

"Oh." Mary's mouth formed a small O. "That's sort of . . . cool." She stood up and wandered over to Rook. "Hi!" Rook glanced at her. She stumbled around for something to say. "Can I get you anything? Snacks? We have—graham crackers and juice boxes. . . ." She winced a little, realizing how lame that sounded.

"No thanks," said Rook. "I'm good."

"I'll take some," said Finn, but Mary didn't seem to hear him.

"Okay. If you change your mind . . . and by the way, thank you."

"For what?"

"For—rescuing me. From the pod-smoke thing. It was very gallant." She pronounced the word gal-LANT and laughed a little.

"No problem," said Rook.

Brianna and Ivy came out of the supply closet in their armor just in time to see the end of Mary's exchange with Rook. They looked at each other and grinned. Clearly, Mary was a tad smitten.

The Prince Warriors gathered around Manuel as he announced the latest news.

"Four pods open, four white mist clouds, there's no telling how many people are already infected. Emergency services have told everyone to stay inside to avoid the cloud's toxicity, but people are still being drawn to it. Fire crews are out trying to douse it. Of course that's not working. The mist has already spread to half the town. It won't be long before the entire town and surrounding areas are also covered. Without protection, I suspect at least 20 percent of the total population will become infected within a few hours. In a day or two, it will be higher than 50 percent."

Everyone was quiet after this gloomy assessment.

"So," said Xavier, "we have to stop this soon, before it has time to spread."

"How do we do that?" asked Ivy.

"We're the ones Ponéros is after," said Levi. "We're standing in his way. He can't move freely if we're around. So we need to draw the Glommers . . . *to* us. Then maybe they'll leave everyone else alone."

"I suggest getting to the highest point we can," said Manuel. "That is also good military strategy. Occupy the high ground. It's more defensible. Plus the Glommers will be able to find us more easily."

"Cedar Point," said Levi. "It's the highest point in town."

"Perfect."

"Hold on, guys," said Mary. "There are like—" she counted quickly, "eight of you. And like *hundreds* of them. You need more help!"

Evan grinned. "We have everything we need," he said. And then added: "Except snacks. We could really use some snacks."

―――――

While Mary passed out graham crackers, chip bags, and juice boxes, Xavier called his mom. She sounded worried.

"Xavier! Where are you? Is Evan with you?"

"I'm at the Rec. Yes, Evan's here. We're fine. Are you okay? Is dad there? Are you staying inside?"

"Yes, yes, Mary called us. We had a very strange conversation. Are you with Mr. J. Ar now?"

"No. He had to take Mr. Santos to the hospital. But Mom, we're okay. Make sure to stay inside and keep all the doors and windows closed. And if you see any-thing—like a cloud or a mist—don't look at it. Go into the basement until they sound the all clear. Okay?"

"Xavier, I want you and your brother to come home. I don't like any of this—it isn't safe—"

"Mom, we're Prince Warriors. You know that, right?"

"Yes . . ."

"So let us do what we have to do. What we were meant to do."

There was a long pause on the line. Then his moth-er's shaking voice: "Okay, Xavier. I love you."

"Love you too, Mom." He handed the phone to Evan.

"Hey, Mom!" Evan said, his mouth full of crackers. "We're going to fight Glommers!"

Xavier rolled his eyes.

―――――

"Grandpa Tony?" Brianna was relieved to hear his voice on the phone. "You know what's going on, right?

Take care of Nana Lily and my sisters, okay? And—is Star okay? Viktor didn't hurt her, did he?" Brianna listened a moment, then let out a sigh of relief. Star was okay. "I'm so thankful. Tell her I'll be back soon. And don't worry! I'll be fine."

Ivy called her mom. "Hey, Mom, I'm fine. I'm with my friends. Make sure to stay inside and close all the curtains and don't look outside, whatever you do. And—can you call Dad and tell him? I know you two don't talk much but—oh. Okay. No, don't leave the house. It's better to just stay in until this clears. I'll be fine, Mom. Bye."

She hung up. Brianna looked at her. "Where's your dad?"

"He doesn't live with us." Ivy hung her head, as if ashamed.

"How come you never told me that?" Brianna asked. She had always thought Ivy's life was so perfect. It had made her not like Ivy very much at first.

Ivy shrugged. "I should have; I'm sorry. I didn't want anyone to know. I don't see him much since he moved out. But I miss him. I wish the two of them would just, you know, work things out. But I'm not sure they want to."

Brianna put an arm around Ivy. "It'll be okay."

Ivy smiled at her. "Hope so."

"Let's go destroy some evil Glommers. That will make you feel better."

"Sure will."

"The police just tried to take down some Glommers in the park," Manuel called out, focused on the laptop screen. "Bullets just bounced off them. Police don't know what to do. None of their weapons have any effect on them."

"There's only one weapon that will stop them," said Rook. "Time to go. Everyone ready?"

"Can I come?" asked Mary, coming up beside Rook. "I mean, I'd like to help." Rook shook his head.

"Maybe you can stay here and—keep tabs on things?" He made eye contact with Manuel, who got the message and nodded eagerly.

"Oh, yes, Miss Stanton, we could really use your help in . . . monitoring the advance of the Glommers and . . . reporting back to us. You'd be like . . . our central command."

"Okay," Mary said, brightening. "I can do that."

"And Mary," said Rook, "don't let anyone in. If you see any mist coming into the building, go down to the storm cellar."

"Got it."

"Once we get to the Point, you shouldn't have to worry. The enemy's forces will be focused on us."

Mary swallowed. "You and a bunch of kids?"

"Don't worry," said Rook with a solemn expression. "We won't be alone."

CHAPTER 33

Cedar Point

T hey're coming."

Finn turned from the window and spoke to the kids gathered around Manuel.

Xavier went to see for himself. Zombie-like Glommers were in the street, marching toward the rec center like a platoon of tin soldiers.

"Okay," said Rook with a sigh. "Let's go. Mary, lock this door after us. Then go to the office and close the blinds."

"Uh, okay." Mary gave Rook another smile. "Good luck," she said. "Or—whatever you guys need."

"We can beat them," said Ivy. "Those dudes can't move too fast with all that metal weighing them down."

"Not yet anyway," said Manuel, his voice trembling slightly.

"Get in the car as fast as you can. Don't stop to look at them," said Rook. "On three: one, two, three."

They burst through the doors and dashed for the car. The Glommers caught sight of them and immediately changed course, picking up their pace. They began to cry out in loud, groaning voices that shivered in the air.

"They're moving faster than I thought," said Ivy as she leapt into the car, followed by Brianna and Evan. They climbed into the third row, while Xavier, Evan, and Manuel got in the middle row. Finn sat in the passenger seat. Rook slammed his door shut and started the engine. He had to pass right by the Glommers as he sped out onto the main road. One of them stood in his path, its arms raised, bellowing loudly. Rook floored it, but swerved at the last second, leaving skid marks on the road as he sped away.

The kids stared back at the weird beings standing in the road with their white eyes and humanlike appendages laced in metallic webbing. It was stunning how quickly and thoroughly the mist had infected these people.

As the Prince Warriors drove through the town, more and more of the Glommers joined in chasing them, forming up in ranks behind the car and marching in lockstep.

"Can you drive any faster?" asked Levi.

"We need them to follow us," said Xavier. "The more that come after us, the fewer around to cause problems for unprotected people. We need to gather them all at the Point."

Rook finally arrived at the bottom of Cedar Hill, where the paved road became a dirt track, meant for four-wheelers and mountain bikers. He shifted into low gear and charged up the hill, his back wheels spinning out on the rutted road. He expertly navigated the narrow track, weaving around the thick growth of mountain cedars that gave the town its name. The car bounced over tree roots and deep ruts while Rook warned his passengers to keep their seat belts fastened.

"This is like riding Tannyn," Evan remarked under his breath.

"Let's hope the landing is a little better," said Ivy.

They soon drove out of the woods as the hill steepened, becoming more rocky with fewer trees. Rook drove in a zig-zag pattern, straining the SUV engine to the limit.

"I might be getting sick," said Brianna, covering her mouth.

"Don't throw up in my dad's car!" said Levi.

Rook sped to the top of the hill and shut off the engine. A sign posted in front of them read:

The kids piled out and began to survey the hilltop. It was possible to see the entire town from this hill, including all the damage being done by the Glommers and the mist that continued to waft through the air. It was no longer in curling plumes; the mist had spread out like a blanket over part of the town, looking no more harmless than a low-lying fog.

"It's everywhere," breathed Manuel.

Levi noticed an official-looking historical marker: "Site of the Battle of Cedar Point, 1835, where a small band of rebels held off invaders for forty-five hours while waiting for reinforcements."

Guess we aren't the first ones to try and hold this hill, he thought to himself. *Forty-five hours.* Almost two days. Of . . . resistance. They were going to face a similar battle today: resisting the enemy in order to win the day. Would it take two days? Or longer?

You have everything you need.

"Levi!" Rook called. Levi went to join the others who had gathered together, checking to make sure their weapons and armor were ready. Now that it was becoming real, they were all growing visibly nervous.

"We could really use an instruction from The Book right about now," said Manuel. But no new instructions spun out of their breastplates or lit up their phones.

"Resist the enemy, and he will flee," said Finn. "That was the one I got—when I was fighting those Forgers on the cliff that day you guys showed up."

"That's a good one," said Evan thoughtfully.

"Be strong and courageous," said Ivy. *"Don't fear and don't be discouraged.* Mr. J. Ar always quotes that one."

"We aren't fighting flesh and blood, but the powers of darkness in the unseen world," said Brianna.

"Perfect, Bean," said Levi.

"Guys, go for the heart, or where the heart should be, same as the Forgers," Rook said. "It's going to be pretty hard, but if you can pierce it, you might be able to disable them."

"Yes, that area seems to act as a nerve center," said Manuel.

"But they still sort of look like people," said Brianna under her breath. "We're not going to really kill them, are we?"

"You won't kill their human parts, only the inhuman ones," said Rook. "That's what the sword does."

The kids nodded as they stood together at the top of the hill. They took out their Krÿsen and raised their swords.

A noise rose up from below them, the sound of rustling leaves and breaking limbs. The kids looked down to see the trees at the bottom of the hill trembling and collapsing.

"They're coming," said Rook.

A few minutes later the Glommers came into view. They barreled up the hill, mowing down trees and anything else that got in their way. There were so many—maybe a thousand or more now. The mist settled upon them, as if binding them together in a single purpose.

Suddenly heavy, ominous storm clouds rolled in over the army of Glommers, casting them in a deep shadow. Yet the sun still shone down on the Warriors on the hill, striking their armor so that it blazed like a beacon to those with eyes to see.

A bone-chilling shriek sounded overhead as a dark shape broke through the clouds, spreading long, spiny wings.

"The black dragon!" Evan was breathless, pointing.

"Antannyn," said Levi, his voice quavering.

"What's an Ant-a-nin?" asked Ivy.

"The biggest of the black dragons. The one that almost killed Tannyn."

"How did it get here?" asked Brianna.

"Must be another portal," said Manuel. "Possibly due to the pods being opened."

Despite their fear they stood straight and silent, holding their swords up high so that the blades gleamed with an inner fire.

CHAPTER 34

Resistance

Levi glanced up at the huge black dragon circling overhead, the white mist creeping over the town, the Glommers marching up the hill. As the enemy presence loomed larger and larger, Levi felt smaller and smaller. He glanced around at their paltry force. Only eight of them. How could he and his friends stand against so much evil?

You have everything you need.

He felt his helmet heat up, replacing the doubts in his mind with the truth he already knew.

The Glommers looked like an oceanic tide of half-metal humanoids engulfing the hill. Suddenly, Levi felt his eyes begin to ache as if he were very tired. Tears blurred his vision. He closed his eyes and waited. He had learned to recognize the signs. He was going to see something the others couldn't.

When he opened his eyes again, he saw them.

Lights. A shower of tiny white lights falling all around him, like early snow. Levi knew instantly what they were: Sparks—the twinkling puffs of light from the Cave. He looked at the others, but he could tell by their expressions that they couldn't see what he was seeing.

The Sparks grew brighter, more radiant than any lights Levi had ever seen. Lights so bright it made everything else—even the white mist from the pods—seem dull and sad.

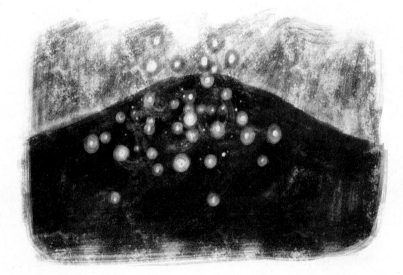

The Sparks encircled the Prince Warriors like a hedge, a barrier. And then Levi saw that the lights were growing larger, each miniscule glimmer blooming, exploding like fireworks, shooting out tendrils of light. The brilliant shafts wove themselves into shimmering figures as tall as buildings, beautiful and noble. Levi could make out the familiar shapes of breastplates over flowing robes, shields, and swords. . . .

Warriors!

Levi gasped, nearly falling over backward in amazement. They were so big, so beautiful! Illuminated by the ethereal light he had only ever seen in Ahoratos. He felt his arm shaking with the thrill of what he saw. He wished they all could see it. He wished they could experience the burst of hope and courage these Warriors had awakened in him.

"They're here!" he whispered, for his voice seemed locked in his throat. He tried again. "It's the Sparks! They've come to help us!"

The others glanced at Levi and then at each other in confusion. They saw nothing but gathering Glommers. Their faces registered the same fear that he had felt a moment ago.

If only they could see this, Levi thought. He shut his eyes tight, whispering from the depths of his heart: *Let them see it too. Ruwach, please, let them see it. Just this once.*

And the air was suddenly filled with music, soaring chords, and thrumming drums. The Warriors were singing. Levi wondered if he was the only one who could hear it. He glanced at Brianna.

"Listen! Can you hear that?"

"Hear what?"

"Listen!"

Brianna looked out over the hill, her brow furrowing. Then she let out a small gasp of amazement and strained her neck upward.

"I hear it," she whispered.

"Now look! See them?"

Brianna looked around, confused. Then suddenly she squinted, as if blinded by the sun.

Her mouth curved into a luminous smile.

"I see them! They're so beautiful!"

"What?" asked Ivy, beside her.

"Listen!"

Ivy listened. Then her eyes opened wide as well and she started to laugh. "They're here to fight with us!"

"No," Levi said with a smile, "I think they are here to fight *for* us!"

Down the line, each of the Prince Warriors received their sight. Ruwach had opened their eyes and their ears. Levi felt joy and gratitude fill his heart as he watched his friends become energized by the sight of this supernatural army fighting for them.

Above them, the giant black dragon, Antannyn, screamed out a call to battle. The Glommers answered the call with a frightening bellow and surged up the hill. The Prince Warriors stood straight, knowing that this battle was no longer theirs alone. The Sparks went before them, disrupting the ordered lines of Glommers and cutting down whole swaths of them with their magnificent swords. "Charge!" shouted Rook above the noise of the advancing army. The Prince Warriors let out an answering cry of their own, joining their voices to the Warriors' song, and charged into the fray.

Finn felt anger rise up in his bones as he saw the Glommers charging toward them. He lunged forward and smashed his sword into one after another, sending them crashing down the hill. This was the anger that used to make him do things he didn't want to do, the anger that got him locked up in Skot'os in the first place. Now it poured out on these terrible creatures that came at him, wanting to destroy him and his new friends. *At least now,* he thought, *the anger is directed at the right enemy, the true enemy, the one that seeks to kill everything good in the world.*

Manuel stayed closed to Finn's side. He thrust out his shield to keep the Glommers away. He was certain he wouldn't be able to wield the sword in battle. This was so different from their practice sessions. Glommers were everywhere, despite the sweeping devastation reaped by the Sparks. There were always more of them to fill in the gaps.

He saw suddenly that Finn was surrounded, at least six of the Glommers attacking him at once. Rook was busy elsewhere; there was no one around to help but him. Manuel knew he should step in. But his arm was shaking so badly he couldn't hold the sword steady. . . .

Suddenly one of the Glommers flew backward, as if hit by a blast of wind. Then Manuel saw one of the tall, spectral Warriors slashing with his sword, sending another Glommer flying. Manuel felt his arm grow steadier, seeing this magnificent warrior helping Finn. He saw a Glommer grab for Finn's arm. Finn yelped in pain, arching backward. Manuel jumped forward, thrusting his sword into the Glommer's heart. Instantly it let go of Finn and whipped around wildly, like all its circuitry had gone haywire. Finn recovered his balance and thrust his sword into another attacker. He glanced at Manuel and nodded. Manuel nodded back. Then he looked up at the Warrior standing over them. The Warrior lifted his sword in salute.

Brianna and Ivy kept their backs to each other in protection as they moved down the hill, staying close to the ghostly Warriors for extra protection. They had worked out a system; whenever a Glommer came near, Brianna would go for the leg, knocking it over so that Ivy could run her sword through its heart. Their method was wickedly effective. The girls were so much smaller that the Glommers usually didn't even notice them until they felt the sting of their swords.

Xavier had paired up with Levi, the two of them slicing through Glommers one after the other until they were fewer and fewer. He paused from time to time to check on Evan, who stayed close to Rook. Evan would ram a Glommer with his shield and then thrust his sword into the metal plates in its chest when it was off-balance. He yelled a number with every Glommer he knocked down: "Fourteen! Fifteen! Sixteen!" Xavier smiled to himself remembering the times he'd heard his little brother in his bedroom counting the make-believe dragons that he was slaying. His shrimpy little brother was one big-time Warrior.

The battle was already winding down. Most of the Glommers lay in broken heaps scattered all over by Ruwach's unseen army, occasional flickers shooting from their pierced chests. The mist, too, seemed to have dissipated, retreating down the hill.

Xavier let down his shield for a moment to give his arm a rest and wiped the sweat off the side of his face. Had they really done it? Broken an entire enemy army? With the help of the Warriors—the Sparks. He wondered how he and the other kids were able to see them. They must have been there all along, from the very beginning. Watching them, protecting them, fighting for them. Ruwach had told them time and again: You have everything you need. And they did.

Suddenly he heard Rook's voice yelling behind him: "Xavier! Behind you!" He turned, feeling all the blood drain from his face as he saw the huge black dragon, Antannyn, swooping in toward him.

Xavier had no time to think. The huge dragon opened its mouth, revealing rows of jaggedly pointed teeth. Xavier thrust out his sword, which glanced off the black dragon's thorny head. It snatched the sword in its teeth and wrenched it from his hands, tossing it away.

Xavier stumbled backward, fumbling in his pocket for his seed-shield. The dragon flicked its forked tail over its head, preparing to launch a thorn.

Just then Rook appeared out of nowhere, leaping toward the black dragon, his sword held in two hands over his head. As he landed, his sword pierced the dragon's neck. Antannyn let out a strangled shriek as its tail wavered and the thorns went wide, missing Xavier entirely. But the dragon wasn't dead—its neck was too well armored. The dragon swung its massive head toward Rook, snatching him in its jaws with brutal force. Rook tried in desperation to strike at the dragon's nose with his sword, but Antannyn threw up its head and hurled him into the air. Rook's body sailed high and then fell, crashing against a boulder halfway down the hill.

"Rook!" Xavier screamed.

Rook didn't move.

Evan pointed and shouted. The others cried out in horror. They all began to run down the hill toward Rook's still form. Xavier forced his legs to move, to go to Rook and make sure he was okay, but Antannyn blocked his path.

"Poor Rook," said a familiar voice. Xavier looked up. There, sitting on the dragon's back, was Viktor. He was wearing an elaborate suit of armor but no helmet, his handsome face twisted in a sinister, cocky smile. "Shouldn't mess with the black dragons. I tried to tell Manuel. They can't be killed by the sword of a Prince Warrior. Too bad Rook didn't know that."

Xavier wanted to run at him, to wipe the smile off that mocking face. But then he realized his sword was still on the ground. He raised his shield, forcing the dragon to snap its head back in reaction to the twinkling dome of red lights.

"Do you really think that shield is going to protect you?" asked Viktor with a laugh.

"It stopped the Olethrons," Xavier said. "It sent them all the way back to Skot'os. To destroy your master's fortress."

Viktor's face changed, the amused expression disappeared. Xavier thought his eyes flared yellow. He shouted something in a language Xavier didn't understand, and Antannyn flicked its tail over Viktor's head, releasing a thorn. Xavier saw it coming and stood perfectly still, his arm thrust out before him, the seedshield sparkling all around him, although every part of him wanted to run.

Resist.

The thorn hit the shield like a jackhammer—and then bounced off. Viktor shouted the command again. Another thorn. Xavier suddenly didn't care if he shot a hundred thorns. He felt a cold rage burning inside him, overcoming his fear of the dragon. He thought of Rook, lying on the hill. Hurt. Maybe dead.

"Why don't you come down and fight me, face-to-face?" Xavier said. "One-on-one. You and me."

Viktor tilted his head, as if thinking about this. "Maybe next time." He called out another order and Antannyn spread its huge black wings, lifting its head to let out a blast of hot steam. Xavier dove to the ground, grabbed his sword, and leapt up again, hurtling himself onto the dragon's neck. The dragon shook its head, trying to throw him off, but Xavier clung to the spikes on its neck and climbed up toward Viktor. He heard Viktor laugh and shout another command. Then the dragon lurched under him. It was taking off. Into the air. Flying like a fighter jet. Xavier tumbled over, clutching its neck, barely hanging on. His seed went flying from his grasp, but he still had his sword. Viktor's now strange, hideous laughter grew louder, echoing in his ears.

The dragon banked and shot upward. Viktor raised his black sword and slashed at Xavier's hand, trying to dislodge him from the dragon's neck. Xavier managed to block the blows with his sword while clutching the dragon's neck with his other arm. Below, his friends watched in terrified silence.

Xavier threw up one leg and wrestled his body over the dragon's neck, ignoring the pain of the thorns that seared through him like a branding iron. But then the dragon dove downward and Xavier lost his grip. He felt himself falling and reached out to grab onto something, anything. By some miracle he latched onto one of the dragon's forelegs, feeling its sharp claws digging into his arm. His legs swung loosely under him as the dragon swooped upward again. *This is it, I'm done for,* he thought. His head fell back, his eyes lighting on the underside of the dragon's belly. He saw something pale, right behind the dragon's foreleg. A patch of unarmored flesh. He suddenly remembered a picture from the Prince Warrior book, a dragon lying on its side, with a sword in its belly. Its belly! Right there, that one spot. Holding on with one arm as the dragon soared higher, Xavier raised his sword and thrust it into that pale patch of flesh.

He felt no resistance—his sword sank all the way in. The dragon's whole body shuddered; it screamed and began to fall, its wings flailing, spinning like a top. Xavier hung on to the leg and shut his eyes, his breath locked in his throat as Antannyn dropped from the sky and slammed into the earth.

Somehow or other, Xavier landed on the dragon's belly rather than the hard ground. He let go and bounced off, doing all he could to keep control of his sword as he somersaulted down the hill. The dragon continued to plunge all the way to the very bottom. There it lay still, black smoke billowing off its body. Xavier, when he'd finally stopped rolling himself, struggled to his feet and looked down at the dead dragon, whose armor was now turning to dust and blowing away. The animal inside the armor, if it was an animal at all, was quite scrawny and withered, its wings like spindly sticks.

Viktor was nowhere to be seen.

CHAPTER 35

Rising and Falling

Xavier stood a long moment, staring down at the pile of dragon dust. Had he really just killed Antannyn? The most fearsome dragon in Ahoratos?

He didn't have much time to celebrate. He spun and ran up the hill, leaping over piles of mangled Glommers. He noticed as he ran that the metal veins on their bodies were disappearing. The humans were beginning to rise, gazing about in confusion.

Sirens pierced the air as police cars, fire engines, and ambulances assembled at the bottom of the hill. People cried and called to each other, trying to figure out what had happened, how they suddenly found themselves on this rocky hill. Xavier ignored them and kept running toward his friends, who were all crowded around Rook.

As soon as he got there, he knew it wasn't good. He felt his stomach bottom out.

"Rook?"

Evan looked up at his brother, his face dirty and tear-streaked. He shook his head. Xavier knelt down, looking at Rook's battered face. His eyes fluttered slightly, a smile touched his mouth.

"Cool move," Rook said in a rasping voice. "Killing . . . a . . . dragon."

"I'm sorry," Xavier said, tears filling his vision. "I wasn't paying attention—you saved me. . . ."

"No, you . . . saved . . . me. . . ." Rook's chest heaved slightly, as if he couldn't catch his breath. His eyes closed. His head fell to one side.

"Rook!" said Evan. "Wake up!" Finn slowly bent down and put his arm around Evan's shoulder. Brianna and Ivy wept together. Levi just stared, blinking hard to avoid tears.

Xavier got up and walked a few paces away, folding his arms. Why would Rook thank him? This was his fault. He'd let down his guard, he never saw Antannyn coming for him. Rook had warned him, intervened, saved his life, and now he was dead.

Policemen and paramedics hurried up the hill carrying stretchers and suitcases of equipment. People gazed at them with vague expressions and shook their heads as emergency crews asked them questions. The metal inside of the Glommers had disappeared, leaving no trace of the enemy.

"Who's this?" said a paramedic, seeing Rook on the ground.

"His name is Rook," said Xavier. "He's . . . a friend."

"What happened to him?"

"He fell."

The paramedics rushed over to Rook and took his vitals. They shook their heads, confirming what the others already knew. Rook was loaded on the stretcher as the paramedics prepared to carry him down to the ambulance.

Xavier watched with the others as they carried Rook away, too stunned and grieved to speak. Then Manuel walked up to Xavier, holding out his phone.

"I can't reach Miss Stanton," he said. "When I call, the phone rings over and over, but she doesn't pick up."

"Maybe she went home or her phone died," said Xavier. He hardly cared about Miss Stanton, about anything. He wanted to go home. To see his parents. To hope that maybe when he woke up tomorrow morning, Rook would be alive again.

"We should go back to the Rec," said Levi. "I called my dad. He's going to meet us there with Mr. Santos as soon as they're done at the hospital."

Xavier sighed. "Who's going to drive?"

"I will." Finn stepped forward.

Xavier nodded to him. One by one the kids began to climb back up the hill, their hearts heavy with Rook's death but also swelled with the knowledge that they had won the battle. They had defeated the enemy and saved a lot of people who had been infected by the mist. Their town was safe.

Manuel kept trying to reach Mary on the way back to the Rec. The others sat quietly, staring out the window as ball fields, movie theaters, pizza parlors swept by. They passed the high school and realized that the pod was gone. Vanished.

"All the pods have gone," said Levi, checking his phone. "Just disappeared."

"How are we going to tell Miss Stanton about Rook?" said Brianna, her eyes still red-rimmed from crying.

"It's all my fault," Xavier said.

"No, man," said Levi. "It's Ponéros's fault. All of it. Rook did what he wanted to do. He wanted to help defeat the enemy. And he did."

"Hard to believe it's really over," Ivy said in a soft voice.

"Yeah," Xavier answered.

Only it wasn't.

Brianna burst through the doors of the Rec, calling out, "Miss Stanton!" She saw her sitting in a chair at the middle of one of the long tables, staring into space. Something about her gaze seemed a bit strange. She didn't speak. In fact, she seemed to be crying.

"Miss Stanton, why weren't you answering . . ." Brianna said. Then the office door opened, and someone came out. Brianna froze, recognizing the confident saunter, the dark hair, the charming, insolent smile.

"'Bout time you all got here."

The others had come into the center as well; they stood staring in shock as Viktor moved toward Miss Stanton, who flinched as he came near. She seemed unable to move at all, even though there wasn't anything physically holding her. Viktor sat on the table near her, one leg bent up, the other swinging down casually. He leaned back on one arm and tossed the other arm over his knee, like he was having his picture taken.

"She's keeping my stuff warm for me," Viktor said.

Brianna saw then that Miss Stanton was not sitting on a chair at all. She was sitting on the trunk. The trunk where they kept their armor. And their books.

Brianna's gaze returned to the handsome, dark-haired boy she'd almost had a crush on.

"She let me in," Viktor said. "I didn't have to force my way in. I guess I sounded a little like Rook. I've been practicing that. Look at her. No armor. No protection. You shouldn't have left her so defenseless." He made a *tsk tsk* noise with his tongue. "I had to break the news to her that Rook was dead. She didn't take it very well. And when I told her I'd killed him, that sort of sent her over the edge." He paused as Mary broke into a fresh round of sobs. "But I like her. She's so weak and pathetic. I'm taking her back with me. In exchange for the loss of my dragon. Along with all this." He patted the trunk. "I've got all your books in here. They'll make a nice addition to my collection. I have thousands of them, you know."

"You stole them?" Brianna asked tightly.

"Some of them. Most of them were just—left behind. Abandoned. Forgotten. Like your dad's." He pointed to Manuel. "Pretty easy pickings."

"Why, you . . ." Manuel started. Finn held him back, shaking his head.

"You can't have those books," Levi said, coming to stand by Brianna. "They belong to us."

"Do they?" Viktor chuckled sarcastically.

"You can't have Miss Stanton either," said Ivy. "Let her go!"

"Make me."

Brianna pulled the Krÿs from her belt and slammed it against her chest, extending her sword. She stood like the fiercest of warriors, one foot planted in front, the other in back, as if readying herself for battle. Levi and Ivy raised their swords as well, standing shoulder to shoulder with Brianna, undaunted by Viktor's threats. Xavier stood by Levi, no longer hesitant or intimidated by Viktor, prepared for whatever needed to be done. Next to him was Manuel, his sword no longer wavering in his hand. Finn, confident and self-assured, stepped up next to Evan, who despite his small size seemed to stand tallest of all. They were ready to face the enemy, to face any battle in which they were called to fight.

"Look at you all," Viktor said with a short laugh, his eyes darting from one to the other. "All dressed up so pretty. Look at those fancy swords. But here's the truth: none of you can help your precious Miss Stanton now. You see how this goes? The unprotected ones are all *mine*."

"You're wrong," said Brianna in a clear voice. "Miss Stanton, tell him to let you go."

Mary just stared, her eyes wide, her mouth working but no sound coming out.

"Tell him, Miss Stanton. Tell him to let you go. He can't hold you. He has no power in this place. He just wants you to think he has power so you will do whatever he says. But he doesn't. He is nothing!"

"What did you call me?" said Viktor, sitting up straight.

"You call yourself Viktor. Because you think you will have victory. You are such a fool. You. Are. NOTHING!"

Viktor let out a violent shriek and lunged at her. Brianna threw her shield up against him, forcing him back.

"Tell him, Mary!" she ordered.

Mary's mouth trembled as several sounds began to spill out: "Let . . . me . . . go . . ."

"Let. Her. Go!" Brianna echoed, taking a step forward. "And give us back our books. NOW!"

Viktor lashed at Brianna, but she deflected him with her shield and then, seeing a moment's advantage, lunged her sword into his body.

Viktor bellowed in pain. He stumbled back, his eyes rolling, turning yellow. But he didn't fall. He grimaced as streaks of gray vines spread over his face and down his neck and arms.

The kids stepped backward, shocked, as Viktor began to morph into something huge and terrible. Waves of molten metal rippled over his human skin, smooth and seamless; he grew taller as more of his body became encased in metal, his arms and legs bulging with thick folds of muscle. A golden helmet grew over his head, the color matching the yellow of his eyes. His mouth opened, revealing two rows of long, sharp teeth.

"You think you can kill me?" the monster hissed, the voice like hot metal plunging into cold water. "Don't you know who I am?"

Brianna stared at the giant before her, hearing the grating, savage voice, and she knew. She *knew* . . .

"Ponéros," Brianna whispered. She glanced at Levi, who saw it also.

Viktor *was* Ponéros.

"You—" she stammered, edging backward.

The monster continued to expand until its head reached to the ceiling high overhead, twenty feet in the air. Its massive metal arms encompassed the entire room. Its shadow fell over the Prince Warriors, a shadow darker than any night they had known.

The Prince Warriors edged backward, their swords still raised although they were clearly overcome by the size of this monster, this enemy. Levi glanced at his own sword—suddenly it looked much too small. All their swords together could never overcome this darkness that loomed over them.

Then Levi felt a strange warmth at the back of his neck, like someone was resting a comforting hand upon him. His eyes blurred, invaded by a new light, a light no one in the room could see but him. Then, somehow, he understood.

And he did the unthinkable.

He lowered his sword.

Then, he reached toward Brianna and lay his hand on her sword arm, pressing it down.

"What are you . . . ?" she began.

"Lay it down," he said. Then louder, so they all could hear. "Lay it down."

"We can't surrender," Brianna whispered in his ear.

Levi didn't answer. He continued to stare straight at Ponéros, his gaze unwavering. The others saw the complete assurance on his face, and slowly they began to understand. One by one, the Prince Warriors lowered their swords and their shields, standing quietly before the gigantic beast. Ponéros's yellow eyes widened at the sight, letting out a bray of hideous laughter.

"So! You see now! I. Killed. Rook." The voice, full of boastful triumph, blistered their ears. "And. I. Will. Kill. All. Of. You."

The warriors stood frozen, their swords at their sides, dwarfed by the abominable voice and the fearsome shadow that overwhelmed their hearts. The hairs on the napes of their necks stood at attention, electrified by adrenaline. And for a split second, the eeriest of silences swept through the room.

"You. Will. Not."

The hush had been broken by a different voice that filled the room with a presence so great and majestic it made even Ponéros shrink back in terror.

Ruwach.

He was no longer small. He was enormous, brighter than the sun. He threw back his hood, and for the first time ever, the kids saw his face. A face of such exquisite beauty it was almost too much to take in. A face that seemed beyond all the goodness and rightness that could possibly exist in the universe.

And in this moment Levi knew—they all knew and understood—that what they had always needed to defeat Ponéros had been with them all along. *The Source* had given them everything. From the beginning.

In Ruwach.

The armor, the Sparks, The Book, none of it meant anything without him. *He was everything.* Indeed, they'd be triumphant in every battle—past, present, or future—because Ruwach was there to fight for them.

Ruwach raised one finger and pointed it at Ponéros. A beam of pure white fire radiated from his hand into the giant monster's iron chest. Ponéros was propelled backward. He roared as smoke billowed from his chest, the sound making the whole building tremble. The Prince Warriors were thrown to the floor as the force of Ponéros's demise swept over them. Mary shrieked and toppled off the trunk, which began to glow and rise, hovering in the air. Ponéros made a desperate grab for the trunk, but Ruwach threw out his glowing hand and cut off the monster's arm. It fell to the floor with a crash, shriveling up like a piece of paper thrown into the fire. With that, Ruwach raised up both hands, fire spilling out of his fingers in dizzying whorls, encircling Ponéros, who screamed and bellowed and thrashed about as the consuming fire burned him into nothing— empty and dark and devoid of life.

And, just like that, in the face of the one who commanded every battle, Ponéros was gone.

And all was quiet once again.

CHAPTER 36

Ambassadors

The Prince Warriors looked around the Cave in wonder as Sparks danced above their heads. They were surprised to be back so soon after all that had happened. Viktor and the Glommers were gone. Everything was peaceful again.

"Welcome, Warriors." Ruwach gave them their usual greeting. He was small again, his face hidden inside the folds of his purple cloak. "You won a great battle. You have done well."

The Prince Warriors couldn't quite recount all that had happened that day of the battle. But they knew they had contended with the enemy and, with Ruwach's presence near, had defeated him. They knew that their victory would not have been possible without Ruwach's power, a power that his unassuming form often masked.

"Is Viktor—Ponéros—gone now? For good?" asked Evan. "'Cause I really don't want to run into that guy again."

Ruwach made a noise that sounded like a sigh. "Ponéros will not give up so easily," he said.

"Then neither will we," said Brianna, stepping forward and lifting her chin. The others nodded.

"Yeah," said Evan. "But I hope we don't have another mission already, 'cause I'm still kind of beat from the last one."

Ruwach made a noise that might have been a chuckle. Then, without speaking, he spun around and sped down a tunnel. The kids followed, jogging to keep up with Ruwach's usual fast pace. They raced into the Hall of Armor but kept going, into a larger, brighter space the kids had never been before. Once there, Ruwach stopped dead. The kids, prepared this time, didn't run into each other when they came to a stop before him.

They looked around, astounded at this new room. It looked a little like a fancy museum. Beautiful displays of armor hung on the walls all around them, each one accompanied by a large golden placard.

"What is this place?" asked Evan. "A new Hall of Armor?"

"This is the Hall of Honor," said Ruwach. "I have brought you here to give you each a special gift. But first, I have something to show Manuel."

Ruwach raised a draped arm toward one of the sets of armor, set apart from the others.

A puzzled expression washed over Manuel's face. He turned and slowly walked toward the armor, leaning in to get a better look. He searched it carefully from top to bottom, wondering what Ruwach might want him to see. It was quite beautiful, the breastplate engraved with flowers—roses. Something about those roses jarred Manuel's memory, making his mind flicker with nostalgia. Then his eyes landed on the placard at the base of the armor.

The roses. Rosa. His mother.

"Mamá." Manuel's voice cracked as he ran his fingers over the metal plate in disbelief. "This is my mamá's armor?"

Ruwach nodded again. "She was one of my most gracious and brave Princess Warriors. And, more than anything, she loved you."

"Will I—ever see her again?" Manuel asked.

Ruwach's hood nodded. "Of course you will."

Manuel pinched the corners of his eyes, his chest heaving slightly at the memory of his mother. Brianna walked to him and put her arm around his shoulder. Then, one by one, all the other Prince Warriors did the same thing. It was quiet a long time.

"Thank you," Manuel said finally, his voice rising in strength. "Thank you for showing me."

Ruwach reached toward Manuel, one of his long, bright glowing fingers emerging from his sleeve. He touched Manuel's cheek, and his finger seemed to absorb the tears that lingered there, wiping them away.

"Hey, look." Xavier saw another suit of armor that looked familiar to him. He went toward it and pointed as the other Prince Warriors gathered to see. "It's Rook's."

There was Rook's armor, displayed on the wall, with his name engraved on the golden placard beneath.

Xavier turned to Ruwach, his face questioning. Ruwach moved to him and placed a hand on his shoulder.

"Do not be troubled, Prince Xavier. Rook is free. Like all the Prince and Princess Warriors who have gone before him, he dwells with the Source. And you will see him again, one day."

Xavier bent his head as a tear trickled down his cheek. "Thank you," he murmured.

Then Ruwach spread his arms wide. "I have gifts for all of you," he said. "Kneel."

The kids slowly knelt, looking from one to the other in curiosity. Then Ruwach pulled something from his sleeve—a medallion engraved with the Crest of Ahoratos, bright gold, on a golden chain.

"You are now citizens of Ahoratos," Ruwach said. "You have been granted all the rights and privileges that come with this honor."

"Yes!" cried Evan, pumping his fist. Xavier nudged him, and Evan quickly put his hands behind his back, looking remorseful. "Sorry."

Ruwach went on. "But with this privilege comes a burden: as ambassadors of Ahoratos, you will live on earth and take seriously your mission of wearing your armor and standing firm against the enemy. And you are tasked with carrying the message of the Source wherever you go."

Ruwach paused, his voice softening, becoming more personal. "Beloved, you do not have to take this medal. You do not have to declare citizenship. But how I long for you to receive all of the gifts I have planned for you, all of the abundance that only comes to those who choose to make Ahoratos their true home."

Ruwach moved toward Xavier and placed the medallion around his neck. The Crest of Ahoratos flared. Xavier swallowed hard, lifting the medallion to get a better look at it.

Ruwach went down the line, presenting a medallion to Levi, then Brianna, and the others, allowing them to make the choice to accept their citizenship. When he was done, he ordered them all to rise. Slowly they got to their feet.

"I say to you all, well done, Prince and Princess Warriors. And welcome to Ahoratos. Remember that this is your true home. Always."

The kids looked at each other and began to smile. Evan burst out laughing.

"Best. Day. Ever," he said.

Epilogue

The score was 54-52 with six seconds to go. The Bedford Timberwolves had taken the lead with a perfectly executed jump shot. The game seemed to be over. Fans in the bleachers were already celebrating, shouting *Timberwolves Rule!* over and over.

It was Xavier's first championship game as a member of the Cedar Creek Lions basketball team. They'd come into the tournament as underdogs; the Timberwolves had won the championship three years in a row, and it looked like they were going to win again. Only five minutes ago the Lions had been leading by ten points, but it had been swiftly whittled away by a late Timberwolves comeback. When Xavier saw the other team's ball swish through the net during that last play, he too thought it was over. There were no timeouts left.

He glanced to the sidelines and saw Coach Thompson give the signal for the play he called "The Squeaker," which they had practiced over and over for just this sort of situation. It was a long shot, but it was the only choice they had. Adrenaline raced through Xavier's veins. This would be his chance to clinch his position as the best long-range shooter on the team. If he made the three-pointer, he would take his team to victory. He would be the hero.

Xavier headed to the side of the court as the point guard took the ball, stepped behind the line, and passed it inbounds. Xavier jumped and grabbed the ball, whipped around, and dribbled down the court, dodging defenders who were all over him.

Five seconds.

He was three steps from the three-point line. *I can make it*, he thought as he pressed toward the basket. He could win this thing and nab the trophy for his team.

Four seconds.

But then out of his peripheral vision he saw his teammate Wilkins already positioned on the three-point line, his arms in the air. Wilkins was totally open. He had a clearer shot.

Three seconds.

Xavier swiveled to find an opening in the defense and then made the split second decision to pass the ball to Wilkins, who leapt up for the shot. The ball sailed down court and swished through the net as the buzzer sounded. The Lions had won at the buzzer, 55-54. And Wilkins had made the unforgettable final shot.

Cedar Creek fans went crazy. The stands erupted as jubilant friends and family stormed the court. Their teammates jumped on Wilkins, wrestling him to the floor in celebration.

Xavier's mom was the first on the court to give Xavier a hug, followed by a more manly embrace from his dad, and a congratulatory smack on the shoulder from Mr. J. Ar.

"I see you remember what I taught you," Mr. J. Ar said with a laugh.

"Yes, sir," said Xavier.

"You coulda taken that shot, Xavi," said Evan, his eyebrows raised. "Then you'd have won the game!"

"I thought it was very selfless," said Ivy, who came up to greet Xavier with Levi and Brianna. "Great job, Xavier."

"Yeah, stellar," said Brianna.

Xavier smiled, glancing over as Wilkins was now lifted onto the shoulders of his teammates and paraded around while they chanted his name.

"Why didn't you go for it?" Levi asked.

Xavier shrugged. "Wilkins had a better shot."

"We'll meet you outside," said Ivy. "Want to go for ice cream?"

"Sure," said Xavier. "Thanks for coming, guys."

Xavier turned as Coach Thompson came up to him and shook his hand.

"We wouldn't be here without you, Xavier," he said.

"Thanks, Coach."

The Lions had won their first championship, and it felt good. But Xavier knew the feeling would be temporary. He had battled Ents, Forgers, Glommers, and Ponéros himself, so basketball didn't seem nearly as important as it once did. And victory, true victory, had a whole new meaning.

Xavier headed to the locker room. It was practically empty, as most of the team was still on the court celebrating. *That could have been me,* he thought. Maybe he should have kept the ball and made that basket himself.

He heard a beep from inside his locker. His phone. He reached in and pulled it out. The UNSEEN app had opened, and there was a message on the screen:

Set your mind on things unseen.

He sighed to himself. A reminder from Ruwach. As good as it would feel to be lifted up on the shoulders of teammates, hearing his name chanted, it felt even better to know that what he really needed, he already had. And that who he really was an ambassador of Ahoratos on assignment from Ruwach. Nothing else mattered.

That didn't mean he couldn't have fun doing things he enjoyed. And it also didn't mean that it would always be easy. There were plenty of challenges and obstacles ahead. Those things would never entirely go away. But at least he knew, as did all the Prince Warriors, that he already had everything he needed to deal with whatever came his way.

He grabbed his gym bag and his jacket, shut the locker, and headed out the door. He saw his friends waiting for him on the sidewalk. But then he stopped, aware of a warm glow overhead, like a streetlamp, only brighter. He looked up and let out a breath.

It wasn't a streetlamp.

It was the Crest.

Turning slowly just above his head.

Acknowledgments

With extravagant gratitude to . . .

. . . **Dan Lynch**. You have been an incredible leader and partner in this project. Thank you for coming alongside of us in this vision. I will always be grateful for your investment in me, this ministry, and this work.

. . . the committed team at **B&H Publishing Group**. Michelle, Rachel, and Jana, thanks for making fiction so fun.

. . . **Gina Detwiler**. Thank you for dreaming big, thinking deep, and casting your creative vision wide enough to capture the essence of these characters and this story. You've been one of the brightest and best surprises of this season in ministry.

. . . **Tim and Tracy**. This series could never have come to fruition without your family. You are friends. True friends. Thank you.

. . . **my mother, Lois, and mother-in-law, Mary**. Thank you for living and loving well. You have cultivated children and now grandchildren who are warriors for God and His kingdom. Your example has shown me how to raise sons with integrity and character. I am indebted to you.

. . . **my brothers, Anthony and Jonathan, and brother-in-law, Von**. Thank you for shaping the lives of my sons, your nephews. They are growing into men who will love the Lord with their whole hearts, walk in wisdom, and live with strong character and moral diligence . . . because they have watched you do the same. You have been courageous models of everything real men were designed to be. Jerry and I are eternally grateful.

. . . **Jerry Shirer**. Thank you for giving me the space and freedom to flex new creative muscles. You're the best husband a gal could ever ask for.

. . . **Jackson and Jerry Jr.** You are men of integrity, character, and honesty. Warriors of the King. I'm sitting on the edge of my seat to see how He is going to empower you to make your mark on the world.

About the Authors

Priscilla Shirer is a homemade cinnamon-roll baker, Bible teacher, and best-selling author who didn't know her books (*The Resolution for Women* and *Fervent*) were on *The New York Times* Best Seller list until somebody else told her. Because who has time to check such things while raising three rapidly growing sons? When she and Jerry, her husband of sixteen years, are not busy leading Going Beyond Ministries, they spend most of their time cleaning up after and trying to satisfy the appetites of these guys. And that is what first drove Priscilla to dream up this fictional story about the very un-fictional topic of spiritual warfare—to help raise up a new generation of Prince Warriors under her roof. And under yours.

Gina Detwiler was planning to be a teacher but switched to writing so she wouldn't have to get up so early in the morning. She's written a couple of books in various genres (*Avalon* and *Hammer of God*, under the name Gina Miani) and dramas published by Lillenas and Drama Ministry, but she prefers writing (and reading) books for young people. She lives in Buffalo, New York, where it snows a lot, with her husband and three beautiful daughters. She is honored and grateful to be able to work with Priscilla on The Prince Warriors series.

Don't miss the rest of The Prince Warriors series!

The Prince Warriors

The Prince Warriors and the Unseen Invasion

Unseen:
The Prince Warriors
365 Devotional

Unseen:
The Prince Warriors App